"This is the kind of book you can't wait to get home and read every night—to meet up with characters you genuinely like in a feels-so-real place you want to be. *Almost Home* is wholeheartedly engaging and uplifting, sweet and sentimental, but also smart, witty, and brilliantly down-to-earth. Finishing this book is like hugging a good friend goodbye—you don't want to let her go."

Sara Peterson, editor in chief, *HGTV Magazine*

"A story of kindness, friendship, and healing, *Almost Home* shines. At an Alabama boardinghouse in the 1940s, characters going through troubled times find hope and help through each other."

Nancy Dorman-Hickson, coauthor of the award-winning *Diplomacy and Diamonds* and a former editor for *Progressive Farmer* and *Southern Living* magazines

"Valerie Fraser Luesse's *Almost Home* beautifully depicts that uncertain time in post–World War II America when people from all walks of life were trying to find their way in a world where nothing was the same. Each character contends with their own struggle but learns that when love, compassion, and support are offered, even strangers can turn into family."

Stephanie Patton, publisher/editor, *The Leland Progress*

"A ragtag group of strangers finds commonality and strength under one roof (literally) in Valerie Fraser Luesse's witty, wise, and moving second novel. *Almost Home* abundantly reveals how friendship and faith endure in spite of—and sometimes because of—trying times, and how the things that tear us apart can also bring us together."

Jim Baker, journalist and author of *The Empty Glass*

Books by Valerie Fraser Luesse

Missing Isaac
Almost Home

Almost Home

A NOVEL

Valerie Fraser Luesse

R
Revell
a division of Baker Publishing Group
Grand Rapids, Michigan

© 2019 by Valerie F. Luesse

Published by Revell
a division of Baker Publishing Group
PO Box 6287, Grand Rapids, MI 49516-6287
www.revellbooks.com

Printed in the United States of America

Library of Congress Cataloging-in-Publication Data
Names: Luesse, Valerie Fraser, author.
Title: Almost home : a novel / Valerie Fraser Luesse.
Description: Grand Rapids, MI : Revell, a division of Baker Publishing Group,
    [2019]
Identifiers: LCCN 2018034284 | ISBN 9780800729639 (pbk. : alk. paper)
Subjects: | GSAFD: Christian fiction.
Classification: LCC PS3612.U375 A79 2019 | DDC 813/.6—dc23
LC record available at https://lccn.loc.gov/2018034284

Scripture quotations are from the King James Version of the Bible.

19 20 21 22 23 24 25   7 6 5 4 3 2 1

For Missey

PART 1

The Arrival

April 3, 1944

Dear Violet,

    How's everything over in Georgia? I bet you thought you'd never hear from your big sister again! What with getting the lake ready to open and looking after all my boarders, I'm about half crazy. I told Si that if I don't soon get a minute to prop my feet up and catch my breath, he might as well run on down to Trimble's and pick me out a casket.

    Did I tell you they've gone to selling caskets upstairs at the mercantile? They've got big yellow name tags you can tie on the handle once you make your selection. Then you just pay at the register, and that sweet little Gilbert boy that stocks the shelves will haul your purchase to the funeral parlor on a flatbed truck. It's so much more convenient than driving all the way to Childersburg when a loved one passes, but it's a little spooky to shop for your dry goods, knowing what's overhead. And anytime you cross the river bridge, you're likely to meet a casket bound for the funeral home. How about that? Before we can cross Jordan, we've got to cross the Coosa.

    I have to tell you, sister, I've been sorely missing somebody to talk to since you and Wiley moved away to Georgia. I've got people all around me from morning till night, but now and again you just want to have a conversation with somebody that doesn't need you to fry something, iron something, or mop something up. You got anybody to talk to over in Georgia?

    Back to my boarders. Granddaddy Talmadge must be rolling over in his grave. I can hear him now: "Yankee carpetbaggers!" I'm a little ashamed of myself for renting to them, what with his Confederate uniform still hanging in the attic, but we sorely need the money. They say this Depression's near about over, but I reckon somebody forgot to tell Alabama.

My boarders seem to come and go in cycles. The ones that rented from me at the beginning of the war have all left, and I just filled up with new people. We rented the last of the upstairs rooms a couple of weeks ago, one to a perfectly horrible couple—the Clanahans from Reno, Nevada—and one to a young husband and wife from Illinois, name of Williams. I did NOT show those Reno people our old room—just put them in that drafty back bedroom and saved ours for Mr. and Mrs. Williams when they get here, which ought to be any day now. Something tells me they need it. (Little Mama's house is talking to me again!)

I'm babbling on and on about nothing, but I sat down here with a purpose, Violet. What with all the comings and goings at home, I've decided a thing or two. I think God gives us soul mates—not many but enough to get us through. And I'm not just talking about husbands and wives. I'm talking about those one or two people we meet on life's journey who see straight through all our nonsense and love us one hundred percent, no matter what. You're my soul mate, sweet sister. And I never fully appreciated that till now.

Well, I'd best go before I have to reach for that pretty handkerchief you embroidered for me. Some days I hold to it like a lifeline. Hope y'all are still coming for the Fourth. It wouldn't be a fish fry without my Violet.

Kiss the young'uns for me and give Wiley a hug.

Your loving sister,
Dolly

one

Anna Williams leaned out the truck window and let the wind blow her damp auburn hair away from her face. She remembered her grandmother's parting words: *I fear Alabama will suffocate you.* With each warm gust of wind, Anna felt a fresh wave of loneliness. The family she had left behind in Illinois seemed a million miles away right now. She had yet to see her new home but already missed the old one so much she could hardly bear it.

"Need to stop?" her husband asked without taking his eyes off the road.

"I'm alright." She took a sip of the soda he had bought her at a Texaco station just outside of Birmingham. It wasn't ice-cold anymore, but it was better than nothing. A quick glance in Jesse's direction told her nothing had changed—not yet, anyway—but she was hoping and praying.

Jesse had what radio newsmen at the front called "the thirty-yard stare"—a vacant, somber gaze. It had settled onto his face like a heavy fog and hovered there for the past year. Even though her husband wasn't a soldier—flatfeet and hardship had kept him out of the service—he was fighting a battle just the same.

Some men collapse under the weight of a failing farm, but

Jesse had stood firm—sadly, for both of them, by turning to stone. Now he had decided that the only way to revive their farm was to leave it behind, at least for a while. He was driving them away from everything and everybody they loved, but Anna was determined not to cry in front of her husband. She had to believe that somewhere deep down, he still had a heart, and she didn't want to break it by letting him know just how desolate she felt.

She looked out her window and took in the countryside. Alabama was so *green*—a thousand shades of it. Everywhere you looked were towering pines, their branches thick with needles that faded from deep olive to sage to pale chartreuse at the very tips. With the truck windows down, Anna could occasionally catch the heady fragrance of honeysuckle, which draped the fence lines and mounded so heavily in spots that it threatened to take down the barbed wire and liberate the cows. The lush pastures made a thick carpet of grass that looked like emerald velvet. You couldn't look at grass like that and smell its perfume without wondering what it would be like to stop the truck, strip off your sweaty clothes, and lie down in a bed of cool, green sweetness. That had to be a sin. And it would likely stampede the livestock.

Anna thought to herself that this Southern landscape didn't so much roll as billow, like a bedsheet fluttering on a clothesline, as the mountains and foothills of Tennessee sank into flatlands around Huntsville, only to soar up again just above Birmingham. The pickup was headed down a two-lane highway that had carried the couple straight through the Magic City—that's what the radio announcers called Birmingham, though Anna had no idea why—and now she and Jesse were getting their first glimpse of rural Shelby County, where they would be living for the next couple of years.

"Help me watch for a dirt road off to the right." Jesse was

turning off the Birmingham highway and onto a county black-top. "It's supposed to have a sign by it that says 'Talmadge Loop' or something like that."

They drove past several white clapboard churches and what Anna guessed were cotton fields. She spotted a soybean field or two—at least that much was familiar.

"There it is," she said, pointing to a crooked wooden sign nailed to a fence post.

Jesse followed what did indeed appear to be a big loop—more a half-moon of a road, really, connected to the county highway at each end. It was sprinkled with houses, some noticeably nicer than others. Anna saw a yard full of children—colored and white—playing around a tire swing in front of a rickety little house. The walls looked as if they would collapse like a line of dominoes if you so much as leaned against them.

"I thought they didn't believe in mixing down here," she said absently, though she knew Jesse wouldn't answer. Sometimes she felt as if her husband had an overwhelming need to pretend she wasn't there.

Jesse pulled into a narrow driveway that led to a stately white two-story house surrounded by oaks and pecan trees so impos-ing that they had to be a hundred years old. As she stepped out of the truck and felt a breeze, Anna did her best to fluff out her skirt and loosen her sweaty blouse, which was sticking to her like wet tissue paper.

She took in her surroundings. Weathered and in need of fresh paint, the old house still had an air of grandeur about it. Both stories had deep, L-shaped porches with scrolled ban-nisters wrapping around the front and southern side of the house. The windows were at least six feet tall and flanked by dark green shutters.

Across the road was a long, narrow building that looked a lot like a barn, except for a gigantic side porch big enough to hold a row of Adirondack chairs. Steps led from the porch into a hole almost as big as a football field. Nailed to one of the few pines left standing was a plywood sign that read, "Future Home, Lake Chandler."

"What do you make of that?" Anna asked, pointing to the sign. "How do you build a lake?"

Jesse just shrugged and motioned for her to follow him to the house. He pulled the cord on a small iron bell mounted beside the front door and waited.

Standing on the porch, Anna realized that the only thing separating inside from outside was screen wire. The front door and all the windows of the house were wide open, but there were screens nailed over all the windows and a screen door at the main entrance. Anna had heard horror stories about the mosquitoes down South and prayed she could get back home without catching yellow fever.

She could hear a distant female voice singing "Praise the Lord and Pass the Ammunition." Jesse looked agitated, shifting his weight and running his fingers through his hair again and again. He gave the cord another yank. The singing abruptly stopped, and a woman who looked to be about fifty came hurrying through the house in a fusillade of footsteps.

"Can I help you?" she said with a smile as she reached the screen door.

"Name's Williams," Jesse said. "Here for our room."

Anna knew he had never rented a room from anybody in his whole life. When they married, they were so excited about the farmhouse he had inherited from his grandparents that they spent their honeymoon there. Last night she had slept in the cab while he slept on a quilt in the truck bed. They just pulled off the road and parked till they were rested enough to keep moving.

"My land!" the woman exclaimed, opening the door and ushering them inside. "I bet y'all are burnin' up. Come on in here and cool off." She led them to a worn but elegant Victorian settee in front of tall windows in an octagonal parlor, where two rotary fans aimed manufactured breezes all over the room. "Now you two just sit there and collect yourself while I go get you some tea."

"There's no need—" Jesse tried to stop her, but she was long gone.

Soon their host returned, carrying a tarnished silver tray with two goblets made of fine etched glass. They were filled with iced tea, each with a big wedge of lemon on top. "Here you go," she said. "Are y'all hungry? Supper's not till six, but I can get you a slice o' pound cake or make you some sandwiches with the roast beef I had left over from supper last night. Would you like just a little bite o' somethin' to tide you over?"

"No," Jesse said.

"Are you sure? Because it wouldn't be a bit of trouble. I could just—"

"Ma'am, we really just want—"

"We appreciate it, we really do." Anna interrupted her husband for fear he might be outright rude. "But we had lunch on the way down."

"Well, alright then. You just let me know if you change your mind."

"We will—and thank you, really. I'm Anna. This is my husband, Jesse. Could you tell us how we might meet the owner of the house and get settled?" Anna thought it best to relieve Jesse of any need for conversation. He sat slumped on the settee, cupping the tea goblet as if he needed an anchor to cling to.

The woman, who had taken a seat opposite the two of them, looked startled. "You want to meet the—oh, honey, you just did! I mean, I'm her. You'll have to forgive my bad manners. I've been runnin' around here like a chicken with its head cut off, tryin' to get my latest boarders situated, and when y'all went to ringin' that bell, I got so flustered I plain forgot myself. I'm Mrs. Josiah Chandler, but you can call me Dolly, and you can call my husband Si—if you ever see him, that is. He's so busy workin' on the lake, I've about forgot what he looks like."

"It's nice to meet you," Anna said. She smiled at her host and took a sip of tea.

Dolly was petite, with what Anna's grandmother would call a "feminine frame." Her chestnut bob was slightly curly, with just a few streaks of gray, and that dark hair made her periwinkle eyes look all the bluer. She wore a cotton shirtwaist dress in a yellow floral print.

"I like your tea," Anna said. "I've never had any quite this sweet."

"All my boarders comment on my tea," Dolly said with a smile. "The secret is lettin' the sugar melt while it's hot and then quick-chillin' it with ice. I just hope we can keep it sweet with all this rationin'. Oh, well, that's why Si keeps bees. If we run outta sugar, we'll just switch to honey. How long have y'all been on the road?"

"Two days," Anna said.

"Mercy!" Dolly shook her head. "My back hurts just thinkin' about it."

"Is it always this hot in April?"

"Oh, no," Dolly said. "In fact, it can get downright chilly. I thought we were just havin' a little heat wave, but *Farmer's Almanac* is predictin' an early summer—it mighta done started. Believe you me, it's gonna get a lot worse before it gets any better. July and August are always scorchers. That's how come we're hurryin' to get the lake done. Si didn't come up with the idea till February, so that put us in a bind to get it done by summer. We always have a big fish fry on the Fourth o' July, and since ever'body on the loop and quite a few folks from church will come, Si figured that was as good a time as any to promote our new business. He says we're entrepreneurs. I say we're poor as Job's turkey and sellin' everything but the family silver to stay afloat!"

Anna and Dolly laughed together while Jesse stared into his tea.

"What will you charge to swim?" Anna asked.

"Fifty cents, but you only have to pay once a day, and we're plannin' to stay open till five o'clock in the evenin', so you can swim till you prune up if you want to. We'll be closed on Sunday, o' course. As long as I've got my right mind, there will be no money changin' on the Sabbath Day."

"What's that building next to the hole—next to the lake, I mean?"

"Why, that's the skatin' rink," Dolly said. "It's been open for a whole year now. Got a dance floor in there too, and Ping-Pong tables down on the far end o' the porch. The concession stand's right by the front door. It costs a quarter to skate if you bring your own, fifty cents if you need to rent a pair o' ours. Ping-Pong's a dime a game, but we don't charge folks anything to dance or sit on the front porch and visit. We figure they'll end up feedin' nickels into the jukebox or buyin' a Co-Cola if they stay long enough, and we can't see any point in bein' greedy. Ever'body needs a little enjoyment right now, don't you think?"

"Yes," Anna said. "I think you're absolutely right."

"Now listen," Dolly went on, "I know you're a long way from home and prob'ly missin' your mama already. But don't you worry. You'll make it back to Illinois. Alabama's just a little stop on your journey. And there's nice people here and good churches to go to. And if you need anybody to talk to, why, I've been told I'm a pretty good listener, so you just feel free."

"Thank you, Dolly." Anna was trying hard not to blink as her eyes began to sting. It's strange, she thought. Sometimes, when you're so sad that you're barely holding yourself together, it's the kindness of another person—a simple gesture from someone trying to bring comfort—that unleashes the tears. And she knew that Jesse, as usual, was far too preoccupied with his own frustration to notice that she too had reached a breaking point.

"If we could—if we could just get our room," he said, standing up and holding out the tea goblet.

"Why, of course," Dolly said politely as she took it from him. "I'll do whatever I can to make you comfortable. You're a guest in my home."

"About time," Jesse mumbled as she left the room. "Can't she see that we just want to get this over with?"

Anna knew he was prepared to go on and on about Dolly wasting their time and meddling in their business—and she knew she couldn't stand to listen to another word of it. But just then he turned to look at her, perched on that elegant settee, wearing the clothes she had slept in, and for once he was struck silent.

She could guess why. All these months, all this time, she had worked hard to make sure she never showed any sign of disappointment in him—not a hint of frustration, let alone anger. But what she felt now—and what she was sure he could see on her face—was an unsettling mix of fury and disgust.

For the first time since their downward spiral began, Jesse actually tried to explain himself. "Anna, all I meant was—"

"I don't care what you meant," she said without raising her voice. "What *she* meant, in case you missed it, is that she doesn't have to put up with any nonsense. You saw all those caravans coming down here. Dolly's probably got a waiting list a mile long. My father said all I have to do is make one collect phone call and he'll send me a bus ticket home."

Dolly came back into the parlor and could no doubt see that she had interrupted something. "Well then, let's get y'all

18

settled," she said. "Come on upstairs, and I'll show you where everything is."

She led them up a sweeping staircase that opened into a spacious sitting area on the second floor. Bookcases big enough for a library lined the walls. The floors were covered with tapestry rugs that looked a little threadbare. There was a settee like the one in the parlor, along with a couple of armchairs and a rocker. Between two tall windows overlooking the lake-to-be was a door that opened onto the upstairs porch. Unlike the one below, it was screened. Anna thought how lovely it would be to sit here and read a good book or embroider on a rainy afternoon. Narrow hallways led from the sitting area to what she imagined were bedrooms.

"The porch there is a nice place to pull up a rockin' chair and have your mornin' coffee or a glass o' tea on a hot summer day," Dolly said. "And it's here for ever'body, so just make yourself at home."

As Dolly walked them through the upstairs, Anna watched her straighten lampshades and make quick swipes with her hand to clear any dust that she spotted. "Now, the two bedrooms on the opposite side there—one belongs to a Mr. and Mrs. Hastings. Actually, Dr. and Dr. Hastings. They were both college professors up in Chicago, but I guess times are hard there too. Both of 'em lost their jobs, which is a cryin' shame, if you ask me. They're the nicest people—and all that knowledge just goin' to waste. He works at the plant, and she substitute teaches over at the high school from time to time. 'Course, it won't be long till school lets out for the summer, so I imagine we'll be seein' a lot more o' her."

Dolly let out a tired sigh as she pointed to the room in the back corner of the house. "That room there belongs to the Clanahans from Reno, Nevada. They're out for the afternoon. Both of 'em work the early shift at the plant, so you'll only see 'em at suppertime, and that'll be plenty. I'll confess it right now—those two try my patience and test my religion."

"Why?" Anna asked.

"They're rude in that kinda way that makes *you* feel like the one who made the misstep—like *you're* the one with no raisin'. They're gone before Si gets up, and I've been carryin' his supper to him over at the lake so he can work late. The Clanahans have been livin' in this house for two weeks, and Si's never laid eyes on 'em. He will tonight, though. We'll see what he has to say then. In the meantime, just try not to get your feelin's hurt by whatever meanness they might decide to spew."

Dolly led Anna and Jesse to two rooms at the front of the house. "Mr. Joe Dolphus has that small room right there. He lost his wife a year ago and moved here as much to get away from that empty house as to find work, I expect. He's just as kind and pleasant as he can be."

She gave them a big smile as she pointed to the other door, adorned with a wreath made of corsages. Their flowers were long gone, but the ribbon and crinoline that Anna imagined had once adorned ball gowns for dances and cotillions offered a cheery welcome from the heavy old door.

"Now, this room right here—this room is yours." Dolly opened the door to an immense bedroom. The ceiling must have been fourteen feet high. Anna loved the smell of old polished wood and the way her footsteps echoed when she walked across the floor. There was a walnut four-poster bed, a dressing table with a round mirror, a washstand, and an armoire with full-length mirrors on each of its wide double doors. A small rocking chair had been placed in front of the fireplace opposite the bed, and tall windows overlooked the lake. Best of all, the room had its own private door onto the porch. Anna wasn't sure why, but something about this grand old bedroom both excited and comforted her. For the first time in forever, she felt hopeful.

"It's beautiful, Dolly," she said. "It's just beautiful."

Her host smiled. "When me and Si first decided to take in boarders, I had a feelin' somebody was comin' who would need this room—this one in particular—so I've been savin' it. This room belonged to me and my sister when we were growin' up. If these walls go to talkin', you let me know because they've overheard a lotta our secrets. Wouldn't want 'em to start tellin' on me in front o' my comp'ny."

"I'll let you know if I hear anything you'd want to put a stop to," Anna assured her.

"You do that. Oh! I almost forgot. There's a bathroom up here, but with seven people, it can get a little crowded. We've still got our old bathhouse and outhouse in back. And you're welcome to use me and Si's downstairs bathroom, as long as the Clanahans aren't around. Far as they know, our bathroom's off-limits. I shudder to think what that man could do to a sink."

Jesse finally spoke. "Is there a key to our room? We'll want to keep it locked when we aren't here."

"There's no keys to the rooms, but there's a latch on the inside for privacy," Dolly said. "Also, you can flip down that doorstop on the bottom—won't nobody come in on you with that heavy ol' thing holdin' 'em back. And if you're worried about your valuables, that wardrobe locks, and the only key to it's right there in the keyhole."

"But how can we make sure—"

"I'm sure it will be fine," Anna said. "Thank you."

"Well, that about covers everything," Dolly said. "Breakfast is on the table at six every mornin', and whoever's here at lunchtime can fix a sandwich or somethin' outta the kitchen. Supper's at six every night. So just remember 'six' and you'll never go hungry in my house."

"We'll remember," Anna said.

"Well, I'll leave you to it then," Dolly said. "If you need any help bringin' in your things, just come and get me. I'll be in the kitchen." She suddenly clapped her hands together and laughed. "I'll bet you that's what they put on my tombstone: 'Here lies Dolly Chandler. She was in the kitchen.'"

Anna laughed with Dolly, following her down the stairs of a grand old home and out to a dusty pickup that held everything she owned.

two

By suppertime, Anna and Jesse had silently unpacked their belongings and settled into their room after he carried her rocking chair—the only piece of furniture they brought with them—upstairs for her.

Now Anna stood on the porch just outside their room, the early evening breeze lifting tendrils of her long hair away from her face. She turned to see Jesse staring at her through a big glass pane in the door to the porch. Suddenly, the door came ajar and creaked open all by itself, startling both of them.

Stepping through the opening that Dolly's house had offered, Jesse took his wife's hand. "I'm . . . I mean, it's just this place . . . and everything we've . . ."

Anna knew he was struggling to muster an apology, and ordinarily she would have come to his rescue. But right now she was far too tired, lonely, and homesick to throw out a lifeline. All she could do was stare at him.

"Guess we should go downstairs?" he said.

Anna followed him off the porch and down the grand stairway.

The two of them were the last of the boarders to reach Dolly's dining room, which was in the center of the ground floor. Even with nine people at the long, rectangular table, there was room to spare. Both the table and the elegant dining chairs looked very old—worn but refined—and an ornate crystal chandelier hung down from the high ceiling, centering the table. So spacious was this room that it didn't feel the least bit crowded, even with a china cabinet on either side of a buffet on one wall and two Victorian chaise lounges flanking a fireplace on the other. Dolly had just set the last dish on the table—a heaping platter of fried chicken—when Anna and Jesse came in.

"Ever'body, I'd like you to meet Mr. and Mrs. Williams," Dolly said. "They're from Illinois, and I know y'all will make 'em feel welcome."

Three of the four men at the table stood when Anna came into the room. The fourth only glanced up briefly at the Williamses and kept talking to a woman with bleached blonde hair sitting next to him.

"That's my husband, Si, at the head of the table," Dolly was saying.

"Pleased to meet you both," Si said, shaking Jesse's hand. "Ma'am," he said, giving Anna a polite half bow.

"How do you do," Anna said. Si Chandler was only a little taller than Dolly but much darker, no doubt from working in the sun. He had short, salt-and-pepper hair combed straight back and a neatly trimmed mustache.

"The gentleman right across from you is Mr. Joe Dolphus from Leland, Mississippi," Dolly said.

A tall, soft-spoken man with gray hair reached across the table to shake Jesse's hand. He repeated Si's polite bow to Anna and said, "Please call me Joe."

"We're Anna and Jesse," she said with a smile.

Dolly gestured toward a well-dressed couple who appeared to be in their late forties. Anna thought they looked like city people. "Now, this is Dr. Hastings and his wife—also Dr. Hastings," Dolly said. "They're joinin' us from Chicago."

"I believe we're well beyond 'Doctor' at this point," the man said. "Please just call us Harry and Evelyn." He shook Jesse's hand and said to Anna, "Very pleased to meet you," while his wife gave a little wave in the Williamses' direction.

Finally, Dolly nodded toward the couple seated to her left. "This is Mr. and Mrs. Clanahan from Reno, Nevada."

"You mind if I smoke?" the woman with the bleached blonde hair said. "If we're gonna be chatting each other up all night, I might as well light one till you finally decide to serve the food."

"You're welcome to smoke, but not at my supper table," Dolly said.

The woman rolled her eyes as everyone took their seats.

"Si, we're mighty pleased you could join us tonight," Dolly said. "Would you please offer thanks?"

Dolly's husband asked the blessing, and then the two of them began passing plates and bowls around.

"So y'all just got here today?" Si asked.

"Yes," Jesse answered. Anna desperately hoped he would help her make conversation at this table full of strangers. Even the old Jesse was never much for crowds, but he would at least come to her aid in a situation like this.

"We left home a couple of days ago and just got here this afternoon," Anna added.

"Bet you slept in whatever you drove," Mrs. Clanahan said. "Doesn't look like you got two nickels to rub together."

Anna felt her cheeks turn red-hot as Jesse stopped passing a plate of dinner rolls, suspending it in midair and clenching his other fist in his lap. She caught a glimpse of Si looking up from his place at the head of the table to give the blonde woman a cold stare.

At that moment, something very odd happened. The crystal

chandelier shimmied, making a delicate tinkling noise above the table.

"Well, if Anna and Jesse were wealthy, they'd be mighty outta place at this table," Dolly said. "None of us would be breakin' bread together if times were better for us, now would we?"

"Well said, Dolly," Harry agreed as Jesse passed the rolls on around the table.

"Tell us, Anna, where exactly are you from in Illinois?" Evelyn asked.

"Oh, it's a tiny little town—you probably never heard of it in a big city like Chicago. It's called Red Bud."

"You don't say!" Harry exclaimed. "How about that, Evelyn? We had to come all the way to Alabama for you to meet anybody from Red Bud!"

"Harry's grandmother grew up there, and as long as she lived, all we ever heard about was that little town—how Christmas was prettier there and the grass was greener there and the people were nicer there," Evelyn explained. "Having met you two, I see she was telling us the truth all those years."

Anna looked at Jesse and smiled. She was worried he would leave the table if that horrible Clanahan woman said anything else.

"So how do you plan on filling up that hole you call a lake?" Mrs. Clanahan asked Si as she propped her elbows on the table, bit into a chicken leg, and began smacking.

Si narrowed his eyes at her ever so slightly. Anna noticed that Dolly had begun fidgeting with the silver dessert spoon above her plate.

"I mean to pump it full o' water from the creek behind it," Si said.

"Oh," was all the blonde woman said as she licked her fingers, then reached across the table and grabbed another piece of chicken with her bare hand.

Again the chandelier shimmied.

"Here, let me just pass this around again," Dolly said. She got up and passed her platter of chicken—no doubt, Anna thought, getting her food out of the Clanahans' reach, lest the other guests refuse to touch it.

"I've been meaning to ask you, Joe," Harry said, "your hometown of Leland—is that in the Mississippi Delta?"

"It is indeed," Joe answered.

"Is it true that the soil is pitch-black there and the fields are flat as a tabletop?" Harry asked.

Joe nodded. "That is no exaggeration. One ol' farmer back home—fella by the name o' Patton—used to joke that he could start plowin' a row o' cotton on Monday mornin' and wouldn't have to turn around till Wednesday afternoon."

Everybody had a good laugh, except the Clanahans.

"Harry has always been fascinated with the Mississippi Delta," Evelyn said. "I believe he fancies himself a displaced Southerner."

Harry smiled at his wife. "I'm not *that* bad."

"Oh no?" she countered. "Kindly explain your music collection."

"I am a *professor* of music, Evelyn—or at least I used to be."

"Yes, but you taught Bach and Beethoven, while you listen to Leadbelly."

"Just broadening my horizons," he said with a wink at his wife. "Si and Dolly have graciously offered me access to the Victrola in their music room," Harry told Anna and Jesse. "I invite you to join me any weekend afternoon and share my record collection."

"Thank you," Anna said. "That's very kind of you."

"You mentioned a creek—to pump your lake water?" Jesse said to Si.

"That's right," Si answered. "It's called the Tanyard, and

the stretch of it that runs behind the lake is deep and cold, so pumpin' should be fairly simple. It's not very good for fishin' there—you have to walk downstream a piece to catch anything worth fryin'. You enjoy dippin' a line?"

"I do." Jesse sent the rolls on around again.

"Well, I'll tell you this much—if you love to fish, you have come to the right place. I'll show you exactly where to go. There's several great spots you can walk to from here. My personal favorite is a quiet little slough off the creek. It's real tucked away and it's on our land, so don't nobody go back there but us. You and me can go walk it tomorrow afternoon."

"Now, Si—" Dolly began.

He looked at his wife. "We're just gonna walk it, not fish it, Dolly." Turning back to Jesse, Si explained, "My wife's a Southern Baptist—they'd sooner cuss their mama than fish on Sunday."

Jesse couldn't help smiling, which made Anna downright gleeful. He was in there somewhere. She just had to believe it.

They managed to get through supper without any further insults or even conversation from the Clanahans. Anna volunteered to help Dolly clear the table and serve pie and coffee.

As everybody else praised Dolly's dessert, Mrs. Clanahan only poked at hers with her fork. "What on earth is this?" she finally said.

"Why—it's—it's a pie," Dolly said. "Made with fresh strawberries and sweet whipped cream on top—my grandmother's recipe."

Mrs. Clanahan smirked at her. "Guess I should've expected a hillbilly dessert from a hillbilly hotel."

For the third time, crystals tinkled above, so much so that one broke free of the old chandelier and landed squarely in the center of Dolly's table.

Si slowly pushed back his chair and stood up. "Mr. and Mrs.

Clanahan, I'm gonna have to ask you to get your things and leave our home."

Anna saw Dolly's mouth fly open.

"*What?*" Mrs. Clanahan exclaimed. "Are you *nuts?*"

"Get your things and leave our home," Si repeated.

Mr. Clanahan remained slouched in his chair. "We're not about to leave," he said to his wife. "We're paid up through the end of the month."

"Dolly," Si said, "please go and get their money."

Dolly hurried away from the table and returned with the Clanahans' payment, which she laid on the table in front of them.

Mr. Clanahan snarled at Si. "And what if we don't feel like leaving?"

Si spun around and walked out. When he returned to the dining room just a minute or two later, he was carrying his shotgun, which he loaded and cocked right there. Everyone else—including Mrs. Clanahan—pushed away from the table and moved to the opposite side of the room. Anna's heart, which was already racing, skipped a beat when Jesse stepped in front of her, shielding her from any stray shotgun shells.

Mr. Clanahan only sneered at Si and leaned back in his chair.

Si took aim and blew one of the legs off the chair, sending his unwanted guest tumbling backward onto the floor. Now Mr. Clanahan was scrambling to stand as he watched Si reload.

"Here now!" the man from Nevada said, backing up and holding his hands out in front of him as if to stop the next shell coming out of that barrel. "There's no call to get excited."

"I'm not excited," Si calmly said as he kept walking slowly and steadily toward the obnoxious couple, aiming the shotgun squarely at them. He backed them all the way to the stairs. "Get up those stairs and get your things," he said. "If you're not outta this house before Dolly's grandfather clock chimes again, I'm comin' up there, and this time I'll aim higher."

The Clanahans glanced at the clock and then ran all over each other hurrying upstairs to gather their belongings. Before the clock could strike again, they came racing back down with their suitcases. Dolly had retrieved their abandoned money from the dining room table and handed it to them as they fled out the front door. She led her other guests back to the table to finish their dessert, but Si and his shotgun stayed on the front porch till the troublemakers were completely out of sight.

Anna looked around the table and could see that everybody was still a little unraveled when the man of the house came back to his place to finish his pie. "This is an especially rich one, Dolly," Si said after he took a couple of bites. "I'm mighty sorry about what I did to your mama's chair, but don't you worry none. I can fix it."

"I know you can."

The boarders were quiet as everybody tried to regain their composure and finish their dessert. Finally, after a long silence, Dolly asked, "What tipped you over, Si?"

He looked up at her and said, "Nobody disrespects your fine cookin', Dolly—and I mean nobody."

Dolly shook her head and smiled. Then she looked around the table. "Would anybody care for seconds?"

"I reckon I better," Joe said quietly. "Till he runs outta shells."

The Chandlers and their guests all burst out laughing. Even Jesse had to chuckle at the wry man from Mississippi.

"No need to worry, Joe," Si said. "Ammo's mighty pricey these days. Got to use it sparingly unless I'm shootin' at somethin' I can eat, and you don't look very appetizin' to me."

"I'd be tough as an old crow," Joe said.

"Dolly would definitely have to work you into a stew," Si told him. "Gentlemen, would you be so kind as to lend me a hand out at the well house?"

Joe and Harry immediately pushed back from the table.

"We'd be honored," Harry said. Jesse looked puzzled but followed suit.

"What's wrong with your well house?" Anna asked as the men stepped outside.

"Nothin'," Dolly said with a sigh. "Except that Si keeps his homemade spirits out there."

"You make him keep it outside?" Anna asked.

"I do. I won't have any spirits in my house. Nothin' stronger than my muscadine wine, which I believe to be more like the wine in the Bible and not likely to cause intoxication—don't you think?"

"Oh, I agree," Evelyn said. "Where did you say you keep it?"

three

"Dolly, m'dear," Si called into the kitchen, where his wife was making a fresh pitcher of lemonade.

"In here, Si."

"Come with me. I've got somethin' to show you."

She followed him through the dining room and into the front hallway, where he stopped. "We're goin' into the parlor," he whispered. "But don't say nothin' while we're in there because the windows are open. I just want you to see what Anna and Jesse are doin' on the porch."

Dolly and Si walked quietly into the front parlor, where they could look out the windows and see Anna and Jesse sitting next to each other in rocking chairs. The young couple would go for minutes on end rocking in silence before one of them would make a feeble attempt at conversation and the other would struggle to reciprocate.

"Did you enjoy the message today?" Anna asked.

"I did. He's a good preacher."

Silence.

"What did you think of the music?" he asked.

"Oh, I loved it. Never heard anything quite that lively in church."

Jesse nodded. More silence.

Si motioned for Dolly to follow him back to the kitchen where they could talk.

"That was downright painful to watch," Dolly said.

"I know. What we gonna do about it?"

"I don't know what we *can* do. Those two have plumb forgot how to talk to one another."

"Mm-hmm," Si said.

"Why, they've got no idea how to *enjoy* each other anymore."

"Mm-hmm."

"And they're young! They ought to be havin' the *best* time!"

"Tell you what. Let's take 'em to the slough. We'll be away from everybody else, enjoyin' some of the prettiest spots in the county. Maybe if we can give 'em somethin' to talk *about*, we can help 'em find their way to a conversation. And them rocks in the creek's mighty slippery. He'll prob'ly need to hold her hand."

~∞~

Si, Dolly, Jesse, and Anna left their shoes on the creek bank and stepped into clear, cold water that was about a foot deep. The creek bottom was ideal—soft but firm enough so that you didn't mire up.

As they reached a shallower stretch of the creek, Si said, "Dolly, you'd best hold my hand goin' over these slippery rocks—wouldn't want you to twist your ankle or anything." Dolly took his hand and glanced over her shoulder just in time to see Jesse taking Anna's.

"This is the prettiest creek I've ever seen!" Anna exclaimed.

"It sure is a nice one, Si," Jesse agreed.

The Tanyard was a beauty, crystal-clear water seamlessly flowing from deep to shallow and back again, accommodating a lush, wooded landscape as it drifted along. The section they were wading now was far beyond the lake. Here the water was shallow and swift, flowing over flat rocks as big as coffee tables.

"Right up yonder around that bend, there's a little slough that's great for fishin'—or swimmin', dependin' on your mood," Si told Jesse over his shoulder.

As they neared the slough, Dolly winked at her husband and said, "You better not let me slip and fall in like I did last time, or I'm not fixin' you a bite o' supper."

"Better hang on to 'em, Jesse," Si said as he put his arm around Dolly and looked out over the perfectly oval pond that bowed out from the creek. "Unless you're a better cook than I am, we need to keep our ladies dry."

Jesse put his arm around Anna and helped her wade a little closer to the spot—about eight feet wide—where the creek spilled into the slough.

"Man, Si," Jesse said. "When you pick a fishing hole, you don't mess around." The water was like glass—smooth and clear—forming an idyllic pool, sunny and bright at its center with overhanging shade trees around the edges. It was about fifty yards across.

"She's somethin', ain't she?" Si said with a big smile.

Dolly, who had never once fallen into the slough, looked into the clear, gleaming water. She gazed at a reflection—Jesse with one protective arm around his wife and the other pointing to a jumping fish so that Anna wouldn't miss any of the magic this place held. And it held plenty.

four

On Dolly's front porch, Anna handed Jesse his lunch and watched him walk down the steps. Halfway to his pickup, he turned around, came back on the porch, and gave her a kiss on the cheek. "Wish me luck?"

Anna laid her hand against her face. "They're lucky to get you," she said. Then she watched him drive off to his first day on a new job and, they both hoped, to a new life.

When he was out of sight, she went back upstairs to make their bed and tidy their room. That's when it hit her: she had absolutely nothing left to do but feel homesick.

Hurrying downstairs, she found Dolly washing the breakfast dishes. "Let me dry?" Anna asked.

"Oh, heavens no!" Dolly said. "You're not payin' rent money so you can dry the dishes."

"Please, Dolly? All my life I've been getting up at five every morning to milk a cow and feed chickens and cook breakfast and wash the dishes. I've never known an idle day, and I don't think I can stand one just now."

"Alright then. Grab that dish towel over there. But after that, I want you to take a little time to wander around. This ol' loop is perfectly safe—you can consider ever'body here your neighbor.

And you can wander the creek down behind the lake. Just watch for snakes and don't go too far into the woods."

"Okay," Anna promised as she began drying and stacking the dishes. "Do you have many snakes around here?"

"In warm weather we do, but most of 'em's harmless. Just remember—the bad ones tend to have a spade-shaped head."

"I don't think I want to get close enough to a snake to judge the shape of its head."

"Ha! I see your point. Watch where you step and you'll be fine. Let's talk about somethin' more pleasant. Tell me about your family." Dolly grabbed a handful of silverware and dropped it into the soapy water. "Are they all from Illinois?"

"Just about," Anna said. "Jesse's folks and mine have lived in the same town forever—farmers on both sides."

"What do y'all raise?"

"Corn mostly—and winter wheat."

"You got any brothers and sisters?" Dolly asked.

Anna nodded and smiled. "All brothers—four of them. Mother says that if I hadn't finally come along, she would have spent her whole life washing overalls and mopping up after muddy farm boots."

Dolly nodded. "That sounds about right. Men are men and there's not a thing in the world we can do about it." She eased all the glasses and coffee cups into the soapy water.

"Dolly," Anna said, "I couldn't help noticing that right before the Clanahans left, the chandelier sort of . . ."

Dolly laughed. "I guess it's a little spooky the first time you witness it, but Little Mama—she was my grandmother—always said her house could talk. Si and all the other men in the family say it's just old walls and floors settlin'. But I believe a little part o' what we give to a place stays with it forever. Little Mama and my mother both loved this house as much as I do. I like to think that when they passed, they left some o' that love and maybe a little o' their wisdom behind. It's the two o' them I hear when this house goes to talkin'. Feels like they're reachin' down from heaven and wrappin' their arms around me."

"Would you tell me about the house—when it was built and when your family moved here—if you don't mind my asking, I mean?"

"Oh, heavens no, I don't mind!" Dolly rinsed two coffee cups and handed them to Anna. "My Granddaddy Talmadge was a sawyer from Talladega County, Alabama," she began. "He met Little Mama at a church supper right after the war—he fought at Chickamauga—and told her on the spot that he meant to marry her. Now, Little Mama's daddy was a judge, very prominent, and he told Granddaddy Talmadge that until he could build her a suitable house, he could forget any notions of matrimony."

Dolly picked up a china tureen and slipped it into the sink, swirling her dishrag inside to clean away any trace of the breakfast grits.

"Well, that was all it took," she went on. "Granddaddy Talmadge made up his mind that his sawmill would become the biggest in Alabama, and it did, even with all he had to contend with during the Reconstruction. He used the money he made from his lumber business to buy a thousand acres o' farmland here—and this ol' house, which was built sometime in the 1840s. Oh, it was in terrible shape—sat abandoned for years before he bought it from the county—but he knew he could bring it back. All the lumber he used to restore it and to build that big mule barn you can see out the window there—it was heart pine, every bit of it. He had some of his men at the mill saw all that lumber and haul it down here on huge drays pulled by mules. Once the judge saw the restored house with its double porches and pretty bannisters, he consented to the marriage."

"That's so romantic!" Anna said.

Dolly smiled. "I reckon it is. The original horse barn was still here when he bought the house—that's what Si turned into our skatin' rink. If you was to rummage around in the attic over there, which used to be a hayloft, you'd prob'ly find a bridle or a saddle, along with his spare skates and Co-Colas. A lotta the furniture in the house was also here when Granddaddy Talmadge bought the place. Little Mama thought it was so fine that she wouldn't let him get rid of any of it."

"So the original owner built the skating rink—the horse barn, I mean?" Anna asked.

"That's right."

"Do you know anything about him?"

"Now *that's* quite a story. But I haven't got the foggiest notion how much of it's true, so I oughtn' to be a-tellin' it."

"Please tell me—I love old stories."

One by one, all the serving pieces went into the dishwater as Dolly told Anna about the mysterious stranger who had built the Talmadge home place.

"Well . . . this much I *do* know is true. The house was built by a man who called himself Andrew Sinclair."

"Called himself?"

"I'll get to that in a minute. Nobody around here knew anything about him, and they'd never heard of anybody with that name. He just showed up outta nowhere, rumored to be buildin' a fine house and horse barn and puttin' a lotta money into the offerin' plate at the Presbyterian church every Sunday. Won him plenty o' friends in the congregation—particularly the ladies, who thought him a mighty handsome fella. His colorin' was very dark and there was something European to his accent, they said—just a little tinge of it. I don't have to tell you—or maybe I do—Alabama women lose their minds over anything European. Near 'bout every girl in that church set her cap for him, but it was the only one who *didn't* chase after him that caught his attention. Ain't that just like a man? By and by, Andrew Sinclair asked the minister, Reverend O'Dwyer, if he might call on his youngest daughter."

"He wanted to court the preacher's daughter?"

"Well, I can't say I blame him. Catherine O'Dwyer was a beauty. There's a portrait o' the family hangin' in the vestibule o' the Presbyterian church—you can see for yourself. And that ol' cuss of a preacher—prob'ly a sin to say that—people said he was as ambitious as a Philadelphia lawyer. Couldn't hitch his daughter to a rich man fast enough. Wasn't long after the weddin' that the Presbyterians started buildin' the grandest parsonage this little town had ever seen. It's still there—right behind the church and almost as big. Now, that much is true."

"What about the other part—the part that might be true?"

"Well, it's like this. Andrew Sinclair didn't know or care a thing about farmin', so he couldn'a been the son of a South Carolina planter, as he supposedly claimed. But what really got folks talkin' was the way he came to the rescue durin' a ferry crossin' right before he married Catherine. The whole Presbyterian congregation had boarded the Coosa River ferry for a camp meetin' in Talladega County. The water was high that spring and runnin' mighty swift. When that boat got away from the ferry captain, Sinclair took over and started shoutin' all kinda river boatin' commands to the crew. He saved the entire Presbyterian church from drownin'. But as grateful as they were, they all had to wonder—how'd he know how to handle a boat that size in a river so swift?"

"Did they ever find out?"

"That's where the speculation comes in. Some people said Sinclair married Catherine just to get a foothold in the community. Others said he was in love with her from the start. We'll never know because the two of 'em disappeared on their wedding day—and likely drowned in the Coosa River."

"That's terrible!"

"They left the house like they had stepped out for a walk or somethin'—supper table looked like it had just been set—and they were never seen or heard from again."

"Well, didn't anybody look for them?"

"For a while. But then a few weeks later, a fisherman on the river hooked the very topcoat Catherine had worn on her wedding day, and another one found a silver cuff link with the letter S engraved on it. That cuff link was in the belly of a big ol' catfish. Fagan Brumbaugh's great-granddaddy—lived just a few miles down the road—he found it when he was cleanin' his catch."

Anna had begun absently twisting the dish towel in her hands. "Well . . . but . . . that doesn't have to mean they drowned, does it?"

"No, honey, it don't. Sure looks like it, though. That's prob'ly why people still talk about the silly notion o' buried treasure."

"What treasure?"

Dolly shook her head. "Now again, this is all pure talk—and it's talk that's a hundred years old. But anyway, the very day the couple married, a Yankee bounty hunter turned up in Childersburg. Said he was runnin' down a river pirate—Louisiana man by the name o' Andre Chauvin. 'Course, once ever'body found out the Sinclairs had vanished into thin air, they didn't take long puttin' two and two together. They'd never breathe it to no Yankee bounty hunter—some lines we don't cross—but amongst themselves, the community decided Andrew Sinclair was really Andre Chauvin and that he had gotten wind o' the bounty hunter and escaped with his bride through some secret passageway in this house, one that led to the Tanyard, which would take them to the river. And because they figured a pirate like Chauvin likely had more treasure than he could carry with him on such short notice, they speculated that it's hidden somewhere in the house or maybe buried on the property."

"Do you think that's true?"

Dolly shrugged. "That's the story the old folks tell. But now looka here—me and Violet made a game outta that ol' tale when we were kids. We've rummaged through every room in this house, lookin' for secret passageways. If there ever was one, we woulda found it. I don't imagine any self-respectin' pirate, what's done risked his life many times for his loot, would go off and leave it just 'cause one li'l ol' bounty hunter was after him. If he really was a pirate, I expect he found a way to take it with him. It's prob'ly at the bottom o' the river."

"Well . . . what about Catherine's family? Did they just give up on her?"

"Nobody knows. Presbyterians keep things close to the vest. They're not like us Baptists. If we know it, we've told it."

"Gosh," Anna said.

"I'll admit this much. There's been times—like when our property taxes come due every year—when I wished like everything that we *could* find some buried treasure on this ol' place. Bless Si, he'd be perfectly happy in a two-room cabin on a few acres, but he knows I just couldn't bear to lose Little Mama's house, so he works hard to keep it for me. We're hopin' it'll get a little easier with the lake and the rink both bringin' in money, along with our boarders." Dolly picked up a few stray plates and lowered them into the sink. "But enough about the cobwebs in my pocketbook. What about you, Miss Anna? Tell me all about your mama and daddy."

Anna shrugged. "Not much to tell, really. Both of them grew up on farms and never wanted to be anyplace else. Mother never meets a stranger. My father doesn't talk much, but he's just this strong presence, you know? You feel like nothing bad can happen to you when he's around."

Dolly nodded. "I know exactly what you mean." She handed Anna the last of the plates and started on the biscuit pan and cast-iron skillets.

"My mother loves needlework," Anna continued. "She has a big quilting frame that she puts up outside when the weather's warm. I brought three of her quilts with me—just to remind me of home—but I doubt I'll ever put them on the bed down here." She felt that old familiar sadness as she realized that almost nothing from her old life had a place in her new one.

"Now, don't be so sure," Dolly said. "It might not snow this winter, but it'll dip way down, 'specially at night, and you might need all three o' your mama's pretty quilts. In the meantime, tell you what—I'll have Si go up into the attic and bring down Little Mama's old quilt rack. That way you can make a pretty display for your mother's needlework, even when you don't need it on the bed. How 'bout that?"

Anna was smiling, but she could feel the tears welling. All she could do was nod as she stacked the dry pots and pans. "Can I put these away for you?"

"No, honey." Dolly dried her hands. "I like to oil my cast iron before I put it up. Some cooks don't even wash theirs because they say it flavors the food better that way, but I like a clean skillet."

There was a brief silence in the kitchen before Anna said, "He wasn't always like this—Jesse, I mean."

"I guessed as much."

"Losing everything . . . it's just been so—so hard on him."

"And I'll bet he's got no idea how hard he's been on you?"

Anna shook her head as the tears began to flow.

Dolly hugged her and held her tight. "They never do, honey. They never do."

five

Anna stood for a moment under the sprawling oak at a front corner of Dolly's yard, looking to the left and the right. Which way to go? She decided to head left and explore the stretch of road that she and Jesse hadn't driven. It was flanked with trees here and there, offering a little merciful shade.

Dolly had loaned her a wide-brimmed straw hat to shield her face, and she was wearing the coolest thing she owned—a loose, sleeveless white cotton blouse and a full skirt made of feather-light, green-and-white gingham.

On the porch of a pretty little house not too far up the road, Anna spotted an old woman sitting in a rocking chair. The woman beckoned to Anna, who hesitated before walking up the short driveway and standing at the foot of the steps. "Hello," she said. "My name is Anna." She noticed that the woman's eyes were very pale—cloudy even—and they were staring straight ahead, never looking at her.

The old woman smiled. "Good morning, Anna. I'm pleased to make your acquaintance. My name is Lillian."

Anna stepped onto the porch and sat down in the rocker next to her. Small and frail, the woman had her shoulder-length silver hair neatly pinned back on each side. She wore a blue cotton dress and navy bedroom slippers.

"Hello, Lillian."

"You're smiling," Lillian answered.

"How did you—I mean—"

Lillian threw her head back and laughed. "Don't worry, dear. I know I'm blind. It has been so for a long time now. But the Almighty gives us what we need to get by. I can hear things other people can't—like footsteps on that dirt road and the sound of a smile. You are from the Midwest."

"Yes! How can you tell?"

"Voices say all kinds of things. How long have you been here?"

"Since Saturday. We moved into a room at Dolly's house—Dolly and Si Chandler. Do you know them?"

"Of course! Everybody on this loop knows everybody else. It has been so for all eternity. I bought my little house from them."

"Do you live here by yourself?"

"Yes. This loop has been a comfort. I like having people around me. What about you? What brings you here?"

"Work. My husband—his name's Jesse—he came down to work for the Army."

Lillian nodded. "There's more to your story, I believe. And I divine it to be a sad one. But I'll not trouble you with the telling. I cannot abide meddlers and never intend to be one. However, I will say this. I believe there is happiness in store for you and your Jesse."

"I sure hope you're right. My mother used to say that I was the only one of her children who inherited my father's patience. But it's being tested."

"Persevere, Anna, persevere. All will be well."

"Can you tell I'm smiling now?"

"Yes! And you keep on."

"I guess I'd better get going. Is there anything I can do for you?"

"As a matter of fact, yes," Lillian said. "See the Mason jar on the table between us?"

"Yes."

"There's the most wonderful honeysuckle vine growing along the hedgerow of that house up there by the highway. They've always let me clip whatever I wanted, but now I can't get up there. I love the scent of honeysuckle in the spring and summer. Would you mind snapping off a few pieces of it and putting them in water for me when you come back by? There's a pump around back."

"I'd be happy to. Anything else?"

"Just come back and see me again."

"I promise."

She and Lillian said their goodbyes, and Anna made her way to the hedgerow at the house by the highway. What she saw in the side yard stopped her in her tracks. Seven girls—some about Anna's age, some younger—were seated on quilts in front of a big cedar tree on the open lawn. They were wearing long, powder-yellow formal dresses, each girl holding a single large, white bloom. A tall, lanky young man with a big camera was taking their picture. The girls kept giggling and teasing him.

"Hurry up, Dougie, or we'll all be memaws before you take the picture!"

"Do you move this slow when you're rabbit huntin', Doug? No wonder you're so skinny!"

The young man took several pictures before the girls got up and took turns hugging him and kissing him on the cheek. "Thanks, Dougie! We owe you a big pitcher of lemonade." They looked like something out of a picture show, and Anna was so fascinated by them that she forgot they could see her too—standing stock-still in the middle of the road, brazenly staring.

"Hey, look!"

One of the girls had spotted her, and now they were all holding up their dresses and running toward her. Every one of them was barefoot. Though she was tempted to run herself, Anna knew that would make her look even more foolish than she already did. Before she had time to think about it, the girls had swarmed her and were peppering her with questions.

"What's your name?"

"Did you just move here? I bet you're from some big city up north."

"Are you stayin' at Dolly's? We're all kin."

"You wanna come to the wedding?"

"Are you from New York City?"

"Mercy, let the poor girl breathe!" said a svelte brunette wearing pearl earrings. "I'm Alyce. And that's June, Jo-Jo, Peggy, Margaret, Helen, and Kathleen. Here, have a magnolia—our way of sayin' welcome." She handed Anna the white bloom she was holding.

"Thank you," Anna said with a smile. "My name's Anna—Anna Williams. My husband and I just moved here from Illinois."

"*Husband*," Jo-Jo repeated, and all the girls erupted into giggles. "None of us has made it down the aisle yet," she said, "but Alyce, Peggy, and Kathleen are engaged."

"Are y'all stayin' with Si and Dolly?" Alyce asked.

"Yes," Anna said. "I've never seen a house like that."

"Our mothers and Dolly are first cousins," Alyce explained.

"One o' these days, I'm gonna put on a weddin' dress and walk down that big staircase with my veil flowin' behind me and get married in Dolly's front parlor," Jo-Jo said.

"I feel like an idiot, staring the way I was," Anna confessed.

"You Illinois girls don't put on bridesmaids' dresses and run around the yard barefoot?" Margaret asked with a grin.

Anna laughed. "No, we don't."

"We're all gonna be in a wedding next Saturday, so we de-cided to try on our dresses together and ask Doug—he's another cousin—to take our picture," Alyce told Anna. "You wanna come with us to the wedding? They're havin' cake and punch in the fellowship hall afterward—should be a lotta fun."

"Thank you—really—but I don't know anybody yet, and I'd feel a little out of place. I sure appreciate the invitation, though. It was nice to meet all of you."

"You too!" Alyce said. "Come visit anytime. Kathleen and Margaret and me, we're sisters and we live here. The rest o' the girls live on around the loop, past Si and Dolly's."

"Thank you again," Anna said. "Have fun at the wedding."

A stern-looking older woman came onto the porch and called to the girls, "You all better get in here before you get grass stains all over those dresses!"

"Gotta run," Jo-Jo said. "See you soon!"

Just like that, the seven girls disappeared in a swirl of yel-low chiffon.

"Oh, wait!" Anna called. "You mind if I—"

She was too late—none of them heard her. But they didn't strike her as the type of family who would deny an old woman sweet flowers that she could smell, even if she couldn't see them.

Snapping the vines till she had a small bouquet, Anna thought about the bridesmaids in their yellow chiffon. Being the solitary outsider in such a tight circle of girls made her feel lonely. This was one of those times when she wished she were more like her mother. Presented with a spontaneous wedding invitation, Anna's mother would've gone in a heartbeat—and had a grand time. But Anna took after her father. She would much rather have one close friend than twenty casual acquain-tances, and she tended to move slowly in forging those bonds. With just one trusted friend—or Jesse—at her side, she could handle most anything, but she had never been any good on her own.

That's one of many things she loved about marriage—being a partner and having one. Ever since she and Jesse were teenagers, she had gone anywhere with him because she loved him dearly and trusted him completely. But their hard times, specifically the way he had handled their troubles, made her doubt the union she had believed in for so long and desperately needed right now. She was hoping that this strange place might somehow bring back the familiar—that old sense of togetherness she had always cherished. It didn't make much sense, but that was her hope.

By the time Anna returned to the little cottage, Lillian had gone back inside. Likely the late morning heat was too much for her. Anna took the Mason jar around back and hand-pumped some water into it. The honeysuckle looked pretty in the old jar. She tucked Alyce's magnolia bloom into the sweet vines to make Lillian an extra fragrant bouquet. She could see that the backyard was too shady for grass and wondered why someone so old and frail didn't prefer to sit back here where it was cool. But then she realized that the front porch brought Lillian visitors and company. She liked "having people around"—wasn't that what she had said?

Anna placed the bouquet on Lillian's porch and went on her way.

Back at Dolly's, she stepped across the road to the lake. Already she was mimicking the Chandlers, calling a giant hole "the lake" when it had yet to see a drop of water. Stepping onto the deep porch, which ran all the way down one side of the skating rink, she looked out and imagined a glassy pool. From here she could see several high platforms, with ladders running down their sides, rising up from the lakebed—for sunbathers, no doubt. At the opposite end of the lake was a soaring platform and ladder at least ten feet above what would eventually be the surface of the water. A long boardwalk with benches and a couple of rope swings ran between the lake and a small gravel parking lot alongside the road. Music drifted out the windows of the skating rink.

"Well, Miss Anna, what do you think?"

She turned to see Si smiling at her. "I've never seen anything like it. What's that?" She pointed to the high tower at the opposite end of the lake.

"I predict that'll be the big draw. See, I'm gonna run me a trolley line from the top of that tower to that telephone pole right yonder at the corner of the skatin' rink." He pointed to a tall pole at the far edge of the porch.

"You mean people will climb that big tower and swing down?"

"Yep. And when they get to the middle o' the lake, they can drop off into the water. Won't that be fun?"

Anna frowned. "What if somebody chickens out and doesn't let go?"

"I thought o' that. Dolly rigged me up a first-aid kit that I keep behind the counter inside. Prob'ly need to add more bandages to it. Come on in and I'll show you the rink."

Glenn Miller was playing on the jukebox, but the skating rink was empty. "Soon as school lets out, the skatin' rink'll fill up," Si explained. "Lotta the younger kids live close enough to walk. The teenagers all come on the weekends with their dates, but I 'magine the lake'll bring 'em here all week long."

"Well, I can't wait to see it."

Si glanced out the door, which he had left standing open. "Come on out here. There's somebody I expect you'd like to meet."

Following him onto the porch, Anna saw someone about her age walking toward them. She was carrying a tall, flat book of some sort.

"Hey, Si," she said.

"Hey yourself, Miss Daisy. Daisy Dupree, meet Anna Williams—just moved down here from Illinois with her husband, Jesse."

Anna and Daisy exchanged hellos.

"I thought you ladies oughta meet on accounta you've both got green eyes, which I find a rarity. I figure you must be soul sisters—two green-eyed ladies from far-flung places landin' right here on this loop together. You headed for the creek, Daisy?"

"Like always."

"Mind takin' Anna with you? She'd prob'ly like somebody younger than me to talk to."

"Wanna come?" she asked Anna.

"Sure." Anna followed her across the porch. Daisy was pretty. She had high cheekbones and ivory skin, and her caramel-brown hair was cut short, with fringy wisps around her face. She was wearing a short-sleeved cotton blouse with little flowers around the cuffs, and overalls rolled up above her ankles.

"Hope you're not wearin' your good shoes," Daisy said to Anna as they stepped off the porch and began making their way down a narrow trail to the creek.

"I don't have any," Anna said.

Daisy stopped and turned to face her. "That bother you?" She looked genuinely concerned.

Anna thought it over. "It's not the things themselves I miss. It's just that, when I'm reminded of all the things I'm doing without, it makes me realize how much everything has changed—and that's what makes me sad."

Daisy nodded slowly. "I follow that." She turned and led Anna a little farther down the trail to a quiet spot just out of sight of the lake. They sat down on a mossy carpet, with the shady canopy above so thick that Anna could catch only little glimpses of blue sky through all the green. Right here the creek was deep and cold, bubbling and sighing as it cascaded over rocks.

"You can't wade here because it's too deep," Daisy explained, "but I just wanted to stop long enough to try and catch those wild lilies over yonder before they fade away. Then we can walk on to the shallows if you like." She took an eraser and a small piece of charcoal out of her front pocket and opened what Anna now saw was a sketchbook.

"Are you an artist?"

"I 'magine there's plenty o' people would disagree. But I like to paint and draw."

"Where did you learn how?" Anna asked as Daisy began sketching the lilies. But then she caught herself. "I should keep quiet while you're working."

"That's okay," Daisy said, keeping her eyes on the lilies. "I can talk and draw at the same time. Besides, I'd rather have comp'ny than a finished drawin' today."

"Why's that?"

Daisy stopped sketching for a moment and turned to Anna. "Because exactly fourteen months ago . . . I got the telegram."

As Anna's hand flew to her mouth, Daisy resumed her drawing.

"Daisy, please forgive me. I'm so sorry I asked. I had no idea."

Daisy reached over and laid a hand on Anna's arm. "Don't feel bad. I think I kinda wanted you to ask. Sorry I blurted it out like that. Charlie was a tail gunner. I'm mighty proud of him . . ." She shook her head and changed the subject. "Why don't you tell me your story?" she said, sketching mirror images of the flowers she was studying.

Anna sighed. "It's not a very happy one just now."

"Lemme guess—farm girl."

Anna nodded. "Jesse's been struggling to save our farm for

several years now, but we had to auction off everything except our house and barn and most of our land. He didn't qualify for the draft—flatfeet—so we moved down here to be near the Army plants. Jesse got a job at the one in Childersburg. He's hoping he can make enough money to get us going again when the war's over."

"If you don't mind my sayin', there's an awful lotta Jesse in what was supposed to be *your* story." Daisy added shadows to her drawing, which made the leaves on the lilies look touchable. She stopped to examine her work, then looked at Anna. "That how it's always been?"

Anna shook her head. "No. We used to talk about everything and do everything together. But ever since our farm fell apart . . . I don't know, it's like he thinks it's all his fault, and he has to fix it by himself. Until he can do that, I guess he plans to pretend I'm not there."

"There's a ring on his finger that says he's got no right to do that."

"What do you mean?"

"I mean hard times ain't a bit rougher on a man than a woman. Men just wanna feel like they're carryin' this big burden all alone and protectin' you from everything. But they're not. They're just makin' it harder on you by makin' you feel lonely and useless. Charlie tried that nonsense on me right before he enlisted."

"What did you do?"

Daisy smiled. "I took some o' the money I had tucked back for an emergency and bought a bus ticket to Biloxi, down on the coast. Then I packed me a small suitcase. After supper one night, I went and got my suitcase outta the bedroom and asked Charlie if he would mind givin' me a ride to the bus stop in town. You shoulda seen the look on his face! He turned snow-white."

"What did he say?"

"Well, he went to stutterin' and stammerin' and wantin' to know why on earth I needed to go to the bus stop. I showed him my ticket—which I knew I could cash in—and told him I was goin' to Biloxi. And then I told him I already had me a job at the shipyards in Pascagoula. That was a big fat lie, but I was too fed up to worry about the particulars. 'Why on earth?' he wanted to know. That's when I looked him in the eye and said, 'Charlie Dupree, if you keep refusin' to share your trials with me and makin' me live alone for all intents and purposes, I can think o' lots prettier places to do that than here on this Mississippi cotton farm. I'm gonna go live by the Gulf o' Mexico. And you can just stay here and follow through with whatever plans you're makin' because they don't seem to include me. Now hurry up—my bus leaves in an hour.' Then I marched out the door with my suitcase."

"What did he do?"

"He came stumblin' outta the house and got in the truck. Drove me all the way to the bus stop in town. I have to say, I was gettin' a little nervous because I only had ten dollars to my name if he let me go. But just as I was reachin' into the back of the truck to get my suitcase, he stopped me and said, 'If I tell you how bad it is and how ashamed I am, will you stay with me?' And I said, 'I believe that's why they call it marriage.' We took a drive together and ended up at the Delta Deluxe—that's a burger joint back home. While we had cheeseburgers and Co-Colas, he told me we were fixin' to lose everything if he didn't enlist. He knew he'd be drafted sooner or later and wanted my blessin' to sign up so he might start the money flowin' and have some say in where he ended up."

"And did you—give him your blessing, I mean?"

Daisy slowly nodded. "I told him I'd rather lose everything we had than lose him, and if he was doin' this because he thought I couldn't live without that ol' farm, he was crazy. But I wouldn't stand in his way if enlistin' was what he really wanted." She was quiet for a moment before she said, "What if I *had* stood in his way? What if I'd pitched a hissy fit and screamed and cried and begged him not to go? Maybe then he'd still be alive."

"What-ifs are big sticks with which we smite ourselves," Anna quoted. "That's what my mother says."

"Oh yeah? What else does Mama say?"

"That all we can do is the best we can do, and all we can see is what's in front of us. So there's no point in looking back and judging ourselves based on things we know now but didn't know then. You were doing the best you knew how to do for Charlie at the time. You were helping him do something you thought was really important to him. That's nothing to be sorry about."

Daisy smiled, but then, in an instant, she burst into tears. Anna put her arms around her new friend and did the best thing she knew to do at the time. She let Daisy cry.

CHAPTER

six

After a few weeks at Dolly's, Anna had settled into the morning routine. She had just filled one platter with hot biscuits and another with smoky bacon and now was peeking into the dining room, watching Jesse and Si deep in conversation. Her husband mimicked the motion of casting a line, and she knew the two men were onto their favorite subject: fishing.

"Honey, are we ready with the biscuits and bacon?" Dolly had a coffeepot in one hand and a big bowl of scrambled eggs in the other. Evelyn was coming behind her with a tureen of grits.

"Ready for the table," Anna answered.

The women paraded into the dining room and delivered breakfast. Once Si offered thanks, the usual morning chatter began.

"I thought maybe we could go for a drive or something today," Anna said to Jesse as the others talked about the latest news of the war. "Dolly said there's a good restaurant right on the river in Childersburg—might be fun?"

Jesse moved his food around with his fork, looking down at his plate, and Anna knew he was about to deliver bad news.

"What's the matter?"

"Well . . . it's just that I promised Si I'd help him paint the boardwalk over at the lake today."

"But *why*? You're so busy during the week—I just thought since it's Saturday . . . Never mind."

"Anna—"

Jesse was interrupted by Dolly, who was making a round with the coffeepot. "Can I fill your cup, honey?"

"Thanks, Dolly."

"Now, Jesse, if you all had plans today, don't you let my ol' boardwalk get in the way," Si said. "I can manage just fine."

"No, it's okay," Jesse said. "I can help—this morning, I mean. But I'd like to save the afternoon for Anna."

"Well, alrighty then."

Anna gave him a smile. Back before all their troubles started, he couldn't steal enough time with her. When she would drive his lunch to the fields, he would beg her to stay "just for a little while and keep me company." She knew what that meant. It's a wonder that corn ever got harvested. Now there always seemed to be a wall between them. But with the women of the loop giving her courage, she was hoping to take it down, one stubborn stone at a time if necessary. She would just have to be patient a little longer.

Anna had walked Jesse to the lake after breakfast and thought she might find Daisy on the creek bank. But she wasn't there. A morning breeze was stirring the oaks and the pines overhead, their peaceful sighs blending with the gurgle and splash of creek water over flat rocks. She tossed two oak leaves into the water and watched them float away, enjoying the peaceful pleasure of seeing them ride the creek together. But then the current suddenly pulled them apart, and Anna could feel it drawing her down too. Maybe a visit with Lillian would cheer her up.

As she reached her friend's porch, Lillian beckoned to her. "Good morning, Anna."

"Good morning," Anna said, taking a seat on the porch. "It's a beautiful day!"

"Yes, I know—I can feel it. The sun is especially bright, the sky a glorious blue, I imagine."

"That's exactly right."

"And how is your Jesse faring?"

"Better—a little better each day."

"And I divine Miss Anna is happier because of it?"

"She's trying. How about you? How are you doing?"

"Fine, just fine. Old Southern women don't change much. We just rock slower and slower till we don't rock anymore."

"Well, I'm glad to see you're still rocking."

Lillian laughed. "Ha! Me too!"

They sat quietly together until Lillian said, "What is it you came to tell me, Anna?"

Anna thought for a moment before she answered. "Have you ever tossed leaves into a creek and watched them float downstream—before you lost your sight, I mean?"

Lillian smiled and nodded. "I can recall such a vision."

"I was on the creek before I came here, just looking for something to occupy my mind, I guess. I dropped two oak leaves in the water to see where they would go. At first they stayed together—they were side by side when they rode a tiny little waterfall between two rocks—but then the current pulled them apart and they went their separate ways. Why couldn't they just glide down the Tanyard together?"

"Leaves are at the mercy of the current, Anna, but you and Jesse are not. You can choose whether to float wherever it takes you or swim against it. And you can choose whether to travel together or let the rocks divide you. That's a decision you must make together. Otherwise you could land on opposite sides of the river."

"I don't know what to do, Lillian."

Her friend handed her a handkerchief from her pocket. "Sometimes we must take a look back before we can see the way forward."

"What do you mean?"

"What is your fondest memory of your time with Jesse—the one that rises above all the others?"

Anna blotted her eyes with Lillian's handkerchief and smiled. "It happened at a little country store when we were teenagers. We hadn't gone on our first date yet, but we were 'noticing each other,' as my grandmother says. I had walked to the store to sell eggs, and Jesse was at the gas pump, filling his father's pickup. He smiled and waved at me. I smiled and waved back. When I came out of the store, he was still there, waiting for me—for *me*. You can't imagine how many times I had sat in the stands at school, watching him play baseball or football, wondering what it would be like if he actually talked to me. Jesse had pulled the truck under a shade tree and lowered the tailgate. He wanted to know if I'd like to sit for a little while and have a Coke with him. We talked so long that Mother sent one of my brothers to see what had become of me."

"And why does that day with Jesse stand out?"

Anna watched a butterfly flutter around a flowerpot on Lillian's porch. "I guess it's because . . . that was the beginning. It was the first time we really talked, the first time we were alone together, with no one else around to come between us. And it was the first time I knew what it was like to have somebody look at me as if he could see me all the way through. I remember thinking, 'So this is what it would be like to be part of somebody, to belong to somebody and have them belong to me.'"

"Perhaps you need to remind Jesse of that day."

"What good would that do?"

Lillian smiled. "When we are lost, it can be quite helpful to retrace our steps."

"Can you tell I'm smiling?"

"Ha!" Lillian clapped her hands together. "Good! I would much rather hear smiles than tears."

"Let's talk about something besides me and my troubles. Can I ask you about a story Dolly told me when I first came here—about a man named Andrew Sinclair?"

"Ah yes—Andre Chauvin, the river pirate."

Anna gasped. "You mean you believe the story?"

"Don't you?"

"I want to."

"Well, by all means, do."

"Can you tell me what you know—if you don't mind, I mean?"

"Of course. Let me think just a minute and see what I might recollect." Lillian's eyes narrowed, staring straight ahead as she rocked back and forth. At last she said, "My mother and father knew the Chauvins—before they married, I mean."

"They did?"

"Yes. I remember Mama always said she found it hard to believe that one so handsome as Andre could ever have been a river rogue. And Papa would answer, 'Dear woman, that's likely what made him so good at it.'" Lillian smiled at the memory.

"So they were friends, then—your parents and the Chauvins?"

Lillian thought for a moment and nodded. "My father grew up in Louisiana."

"I guess that's what he had in common with Andre?"

Lillian's eyes narrowed again, as if she were trying to picture her father and the pirate together. "Yes. Louisiana—and the great joy Papa took from being on water. Creek, river, lake, or pond—he loved them all. I guess he missed the bayous of his childhood. My mother grew up here."

"So she would've known Catherine from church maybe?"

Lillian thought about it and again nodded. "That sounds right."

"Did your mother tell you anything about Catherine? Anything you wouldn't mind telling me? I know it was a long time ago, but is there anything else you can remember?"

Lillian looked straight ahead and silently rocked back and forth.

"Dolly said Catherine's father arranged the marriage?"

Lillian's expression changed, and Anna feared she had somehow offended her friend. "I'm sorry, Lillian. Did I say something wrong?"

Lillian's face softened as she closed her eyes and shook her head. "No, dear Anna. 'Tisn't you that stirs my anger. 'Tis what could have befallen young Catherine had Andre Chauvin been cut from a mean cloth."

"I don't understand."

"Her father, the good reverend, effectively sold his own daughter to a river pirate. That greedy old rascal was the worst sort of clergyman, my mother always said—drawn to the power of the cloth but wholly lacking in the compassion. The pirate wanted a wife; the minister wanted a fine new pastorium and traded his own daughter for the money to build it, without even bothering to find out who exactly was purchasing his own flesh and blood. That happened before I was born, but Papa never could speak of that preacher without swearing. He could not abide hypocrisy."

"How could Catherine's father do that—make her marry somebody she barely knew just so he could live in a big house? How old was she?" Anna had no idea why her heart broke for a young bride who had been dead for years.

"You feel it, don't you? Her fear, her sense of betrayal? Poor girl wasn't even twenty yet."

Anna nodded, forgetting that Lillian couldn't see her.

"Only a woman understands. The reverend had visions of overflowing coffers, and he didn't care at all what Catherine might have to endure. He planned to use her to keep the money coming in. Her mother was just as bad. But they both miscalculated."

"How?"

Lillian smiled. "They misjudged Andre and underestimated Catherine. The two of them never set foot in her father's church again or gave him another red cent, and good for them! But, of course, they both disappeared."

"Well . . . what about servants? Rich people living in a house that big—they must've had servants who knew what happened to them."

"Only one, a Creole cook and housekeeper. She lived in that little shotgun house right out yonder at the edge of that cotton field." Lillian pointed in the general direction of an unpainted house she could not see, barely visible to Anna from the overgrown hedgerow at the far edge of the field. "The Creole woman appeared in Alabama with Andre and disappeared when he and Catherine did. I can't help but wonder if there might be some small piece of their story in that little shack. But I'm far too blind and feeble to get there. You might have a look, though."

"Do you think Andre and Catherine escaped through a secret passageway in Dolly's house?"

Lillian smiled and shook her head. "Who can say after all these years? I don't know that they would've needed one. A pirate would've made it his business to know the waterways around here, and Andre could've easily followed the Tanyard through the woods to the Coosa River. All he would've needed was a boat and a map tucked away somewhere beyond the slough, where the creek deepens on its way to the river, and he and Catherine could slip off into the night. I doubt there's any passageway."

"Do you believe they drowned once they got to the river?"

"I do not."

"What makes you so sure?"

Lillian frowned. "I cannot say. But I know it in my bones."

Anna sighed. "It's just so . . ."

"Romantic?" Lillian finished for her.

"Yes!"

"I thought so too when I was your age. But now, we must remember Andre's wicked past. All of his riches were stolen."

"Yes, but maybe he had a reason for doing what he did. Or maybe Catherine changed him."

Lillian smiled. "Perhaps."

"I've taken too much of your time. Can I do anything for you?"

"No, my dear. Sunny days speed by. Enjoy them every one. Be on your journey, and fare thee well."

Anna returned to Dolly's just in time to see her sprinting across the front yard, carrying a picnic basket.

"Anna—thank goodness!" Dolly called to her. "Could you carry Si and Jesse their lunch for me? I know they must be starvin' to death, as early as they got goin', but I've got two pies about ready to come outta the oven. They'll get burnt to a crisp if I don't keep an eye on 'em."

"Happy to."

"Thank you, honey." Dolly handed Anna the basket and hurried back to the house.

Anna delivered lunch to Si and Jesse, who had painted their way almost all the way down the boardwalk, and then reported back to Dolly, who asked if she would mind gathering some vegetables for supper. Now she was making her way down a long row of green beans, stopping occasionally to listen to the doves and the mockingbirds.

"That you in there, Anna?" She looked up to see Daisy standing at the end of her row. She was wearing her overalls and a straw hat.

"Hey!" Anna waved to her.

"Want some comp'ny?"

"Sure!"

Daisy laid her sketchpad on the grass, picked up a garden basket, and joined Anna in the green beans. "My land!" she said as she started picking. "How many rows did they plant?"

"I counted six."

"They must really like these things."

The two of them silently filled their baskets for a few seconds before Anna said, "It sure feels good to *do* something— something to help, I mean."

"We still talkin' about pole beans?"

Anna smiled and shook her head. "Not exactly."

"Jesse wouldn't let you help with the farm?"

"When it was going strong, sure. But after everything started coming apart, he blamed himself so much that I guess he thought he had to be the one to fix it."

"Stubborn breed, those husbands."

"Hey, I don't think I ever asked you why you came here to start with. Did Charlie get a job at the Army plant before he enlisted?"

"No, *I* got a job there *after* he enlisted. No way could I sit in that empty farmhouse all day wonderin' what was happenin' to him over there. But by the time I made up my mind to get a job, the shipyards down on the coast weren't hirin'. So when I heard about jobs in Alabama, I packed that same suitcase I threatened Charlie with and drove myself here. I worked at the plant up until—well, up until I got that telegram."

"Don't you want to go home to Mississippi? I mean, what about your farm?"

Daisy stopped picking and turned to face Anna. "I guess now's as good a time as any to tell you what kinda person you're associatin' with. Every mornin' when I wake up and every night before I go to bed, I look up at the sky and ask Charlie to please forgive me for what I did."

"What do you mean?"

"I sold it. I sold our farm."

"But why?"

"The thought o' goin' back there all by myself and knowin' that he died tryin' to save a piece o' land . . . I couldn't stand it. I just couldn't. Every time I looked at those fields, I'd be thinkin' that Charlie gave his life for 'em—and I let him do it. I *let* him, Anna. So when the bank called and made one last offer, I took it. That's the worst thing I've ever done in my life. Charlie was brave enough to die for our farm, and I wasn't even brave enough to live on it."

"I never thought about it before," Anna said. "Would I want our farm if Jesse weren't there with me? I don't think I could stand the sight of it. And if Charlie was anywhere near as stubborn as every man I know, nothing you said or did would've stopped him from going. Even if you could've talked him out of enlisting, he would've been drafted like all the other boys. It's not your fault he died, Daisy."

"Sure feels like it."

"Well, it's not."

Both of them returned to filling their baskets.

"Even without your farm, don't you want to go back to Mississippi?" Anna asked after they had been quiet for a little while. She couldn't fathom staying in Alabama without Jesse. She knew she would be on the first bus back to Illinois if she should ever find herself in Daisy's situation, God forbid.

Daisy shook her head. "My folks are the type that believe once you're outta the nest, you don't fly back. Besides, there's way too much Charlie there. Our old church, our old friends—just the thought o' facin' all that stuff makes me feel sick to my stomach. His family didn't take too kindly to me sellin' the farm. It's easier on ever'body—his folks and mine—if I'm not around. I guess I'm sorta hidin' out. Plus I like Miss Ella. Her house is a lot smaller than Si and Dolly's, so I'm her only boarder. We both like tendin' to our own knittin' and don't get on each other's nerves."

Anna shooed away a dragonfly that was fluttering around her basket. "Dolly said you've got four brothers, just like me."

"Yeah," Daisy said. "But yours don't seem to have affected you the same way mine did, what with you pickin' beans in a skirt."

Anna smiled. "Not much for dresses?"

"I used to like dressin' up for Charlie. Just don't have the desire anymore. I'd feel like I was disrespectin' him if I got all gussied up when he ain't here to see it."

Reaching the end of their row, Daisy and Anna set down their overflowing baskets, grabbed two empty ones, and waded into the tall squash plants.

"Did your brothers get called up?" Anna asked.

"Just the one closest to me. His name's Mack. I write to him every week. The others were too old for the draft. Did yours have to go?"

"All but George, the oldest," Anna said. "I haven't written the others as much since we moved down here, and I feel awful about it. I need to get my letters going again."

"Well, I'm sure they understand you're dealin' with a lot yourself."

"You really think so?"

Again, Daisy stopped picking and looked at Anna. "You

mind if I make a little observation? You're mighty hard on yourself. You can't fix everything for everybody. You can't be the one that makes *all* the clouds go away."

Anna thought it over. "You know, you're the first person who ever said that to me. Most of the time, whatever I do for my parents or Jesse . . . it just never seems to be enough."

"That notion comin' from you or them?"

"I'm not sure. I don't think it comes from Jesse. He's happy with whatever I want to do—at least he used to be. I have no idea what he thinks now."

"Anna, you gotta take this bull by the horns. I know it's hard. But you two can't keep goin' on like a coupla strangers. Just get him off to yourself, take a deep breath, and out with it, girl! Tell him you're done with this nonsense. You're his wife and you mean to have a husband again. Just give it to him straight. Men can't decipher hints and moods, so you gotta put what you're feelin' in a cast-iron skillet and hit 'em over the head with it."

Anna giggled. "Will you come with me when I do it—maybe help me lift the skillet?"

"Gladly. It's time to fish or cut bait, sister."

"Guess I need to be bold like Catherine."

"Who's that?"

"A girl who lived here a long time ago. Has anybody around here told you the story of Catherine O'Dwyer and Andre Chauvin?"

Daisy looked puzzled. "Andre Chauvin—you mean the river pirate? What's he got to do with this place?"

Now Anna was confused. "If you don't know about him from here, where do you know him from?"

"Everybody in the Delta grew up hearin' about the pirates on the Mississippi River. Me and Mack used to climb all over Daddy's bass boat, pretendin' we were shipmates on Stack

Island—that's where a lot of 'em hid out. Andre Chauvin had his own hideout, a place called Rockaway Cave. He was the one that drove our history teachers crazy."

"How come?"

"They wanted us to believe that all pirates were wicked thieves and murderers, but we all thought Chauvin was a hero, no matter what the teachers said. They even made us pray about it a few times."

"Why did the kids think he was a hero?"

Daisy paused to swat at a mosquito on her arm and then rearranged the squash in her basket to make room for a few more. "There was no record of him actually killin' anybody. He *threatened* to kill people all the time, but he always managed to talk 'em into givin' up their cargo before he had to do anything drastic. And he never took anything from poor people like fishermen and farmers—robbed mostly the timber barons that swindled a lotta Delta people outta their land. And then at Christmastime, money would just turn up on those poor families' doorsteps. That's why all the boat captains on the Mississippi called Chauvin the River Robin."

"Well, there's a chance your River Robin built Dolly's house," Anna said.

"Are you kiddin' me?"

While they topped off their baskets, Anna relayed the story of Chauvin and Catherine.

"Well, I'll be danged," Daisy said. "First rainy day, you and me might need to do a little snoopin' in Dolly's attic."

"You read my mind. Remember I told you about Lillian, the lady I like to visit around the loop?"

"Yeah."

"Well, her parents knew the Chauvins. She says their only servant was a Creole woman who lived in that little shotgun house at the far edge of the cotton field across from her house.

The woman disappeared with Andre and Catherine. Lillian says we might find something at her place."

"I'm game," Daisy said.

Anna blotted her damp forehead with the back of her hand. "Let's go inside and get something cool to drink."

The two of them carried their heaping baskets to Dolly's kitchen, talking all the way about a shotgun house and hidden treasure and a pirate's beautiful young bride.

∽◦◦◦∾

"Well, hello, Daisy!" Dolly said. "What a nice surprise!"

"Hey, Dolly. I spotted Anna in your garden on my way to the creek."

"Would you all like some fresh lemonade?"

"Just pour it over my head," Daisy said. "It's hot as blue blazes out there."

"I think I'll have some with you." Dolly took a pitcher from the icebox and poured everybody a glass as they all sat down around the kitchen table.

"How's Ella's rheumatism?" Dolly asked.

"About the same," Daisy said. "She still does pretty much what she wants to except in damp weather. Never feels good when it's rainy."

"I reckon not."

Evelyn came into the kitchen. "Do I hear the civilized conversation of women?"

"Well, I don't know how civilized we are, but we're conversin' alright," Dolly said. "Have a seat and I'll get you some lemonade."

"No, no—I can wait on myself." Evelyn poured herself some lemonade and joined the group.

"Evelyn, I don't think you've met Daisy—she lives just around the loop," Dolly said.

"Pleased to meet you, Daisy."

"Same here."

"And what is our topic?" Evelyn asked.

"We hadn't rightly settled on one," Dolly answered.

"Well, allow me to take the lead," Evelyn said. "Men are crazy."

All the women laughed.

Dolly picked up a copy of the *Progressive Farmer* Si had left on the table and fanned herself. "Honey, you'll need to come up with somethin' newsier than that to hold our attention."

"Honestly, Harry can come up with more schemes that involve things for *me* to do. The latest is a nursery. He says I would need to run the greenhouse—which neither of us knows a thing about—and he would be 'in sales.' It is unclear to me whom our customers might be, as everyone out here grows everything from seed and has absolutely no need for a nursery."

"What on earth put that notion into his head?" Dolly asked.

"He saw an ad for a greenhouse in a magazine." Evelyn rolled her eyes and took a sip of her lemonade. "I guess I shouldn't be so hard on him. He spent his whole life studying, teaching, and playing music, and now he's making ammunition in a factory. He's just hoping to find a way back to our old life, I suppose."

Anna held the cold glass of lemonade against her cheek, still rosy from the sun. "It's the same with Jesse. He's trying so hard to get us back to where we were before. But I'm not sure that's possible. Everything's changing so fast."

"Tell me about it," Daisy said.

The table got suddenly quiet as Anna and Dolly tried to figure out what to say, while Evelyn was completely in the dark.

Daisy looked around the table. "Come on, ladies. You're makin' me feel like a bulldog in a beauty parlor." Then she turned to Evelyn and said matter-of-factly, "My husband got killed in the war."

"Oh!" Evelyn exclaimed. "Well, I am just an idiot. Please forgive me, Daisy."

"Nothin' to forgive. If Charlie was here, he'd be drivin' me as batty as your husbands drive you. Y'all have got to promise not to treat me different or I'm not gonna swill lemonade with you anymore."

Evelyn offered Daisy her hand. "On behalf of the group, I accept your terms." The two shook on it.

"Give us a progress report on the lake, Dolly," Evelyn said.

"I can help there," Anna chimed in. "Two really sweaty men are almost through painting the boardwalk."

"Mercy." Dolly shook her head. "Si says that as soon as they finish that, he'll start fillin' the lake. I can't imagine it—a lake where there didn't used to be one. Will people come to a lake just because we put one there? Then again, it's already hotter than usual, and here it is just April. I don't know what we'll do if nobody comes—and I don't know what we'll do if *ever'body* comes. I hope we can go on and make all the money for our tax bill this summer so I don't have to worry about it all the way through Christmas. We cut it mighty close last year."

"I have every confidence that your new enterprise will be a success," Evelyn assured her.

"Why, thank you, Evelyn. Still, how's Si gonna run a lake and a skatin' rink without any help, and how am I gonna run a boardin'house and help him over there?"

"We'll pitch in," Anna said.

Daisy and Evelyn nodded in agreement.

Evelyn dramatically lifted her lemonade glass. "I propose a toast—to the ladies of the lake!"

"To the ladies of the lake!" The others laughed, clinked their glasses, and saluted the sisterhood that Dolly's house had conjured.

seven

Anna closed her book and set it down in the glider. She had found a copy of *Gone with the Wind* on the bookshelves upstairs and brought it to a quiet spot underneath a pecan tree in Dolly's backyard. Jesse had promised her the afternoon once he finished helping Si with the boardwalk, but she wasn't counting on it. That had become her habit—hoping but not expecting—because it was easier than being disappointed again and again.

She closed her eyes and felt the warm sunlight seeping through the canopy above. Si was predicting a thunderstorm tonight, but right now the sun was shining, occasionally dimmed by a cloud drift. A cool, steady breeze was blowing, rustling the leaves overhead. They seemed to be whispering to each other, telling secrets from their undulating branches.

"Is this seat taken?"

When she opened her eyes, Jesse was standing there, all cleaned up and smiling down at her. "Be my guest," she said.

He sat next to her and rested his arm on the back of the glider behind her.

"I thought you might have to go back to the boardwalk," Anna said.

"When I found out I had a date this afternoon, I made sure we finished this morning."

"Did you ask my father if you could call on me?"

"I did. He turned me down, so we'll have to sneak around."

"Where exactly are we sneaking to?"

Jesse pointed to the far end of the lake. "I spotted a trail through the woods the other day—might be fun to see where it goes. Maybe we could slip off to that restaurant of yours for supper?"

Anna smiled as Jesse took her by the hand and helped her out of the glider, then led her to a wooded path at the far end of the lake, opposite from Daisy's usual spot. It was much wider than the footpaths around the Tanyard.

"This looks like people have driven on it," she said.

"I know. That's what I noticed about it. Made me wonder what anybody would be driving *to*, way back in here."

They crossed a small wooden bridge over the creek and kept following the path, deeper and deeper into the woods, taking their time and walking in silence. Anna suddenly got a mental picture of Daisy and Lillian shaking their heads at her.

"Do you remember," she worked up the courage to ask, "the very first time we were alone together, when we bumped into each other at the general store and talked on the tailgate of your truck?"

Jesse smiled. "You were wearing a white blouse and pink-checked shorts, and your hair was in a ponytail."

"You had on dungarees and a light blue shirt with the sleeves rolled up."

"Here's something you don't know," Jesse confessed. "We didn't really bump into each other."

"What?"

"I found out when you delivered eggs, and then I made sure my father's pickup was low on gas that day."

Anna stopped and turned to him. "Are you *serious*?"

"I was too scared to ask you for a date and too embarrassed to try talking to you in front of everybody at school or church. Had to do a little scheming."

She shook her head. "I thought my heart was going to jump right out of my throat when I came out of that store and found you waiting for me."

"I thought mine would beat itself to death before you finally came back outside."

"I would've sat there on that tailgate and talked to you all day and all night if Mother hadn't sent for me. I remember you told me you were saving up to buy some cows."

"And you said I'd have them in no time. I had no idea why, but it was like you believed in me back then—something about the way you looked at me."

"I still look at you like that, Jesse. And I never stopped believing in you. You just stopped believing in yourself."

He gave her a sad smile and kissed her on the forehead. "I know."

Hand in hand, they walked on into the woods, until Anna said, "Do you remember that spring dance—the first one I was ever allowed to go to—when the band started playing—"

"The 'Missouri Waltz,'" Jesse said. "Just as you stepped inside the town hall in that lilac-colored dress with the floaty skirt. My brothers told me that if I didn't go ask you to dance after I'd been mooning over you for a month, they'd take me to the woodshed and tan my hide. So I worked up my courage as quick as I could. Probably stepped all over you with my two left feet."

"No, you didn't. But I wouldn't have cared if you did."

Again, they were quiet before Jesse said, "Do you miss home—having one of our own, I mean?"

"Sometimes. Mostly I miss all the time we had together when it was just the two of us on the farm. But we couldn't have found a better place to stay than Dolly's. They treat us like family. As long as we're together, that's all that matters."

Jesse took a deep breath and let out a long sigh. "I failed you, Anna. And you're the last person on earth I'd ever want to let down. For the life of me, I don't know why I couldn't figure out a way to get us through."

She stopped walking and turned to face him. "Don't you see, Jesse? You didn't fail me, or our farm. We just got swallowed up. Look around you. Harry's got all kinds of college degrees, but he couldn't figure out a way to stay in Chicago. Joe's got as much horse sense as anybody I've ever met, but he's right here under the same roof with us. Even Dolly—she grew up in such a fine house, but now she has to rent it out to strangers. You couldn't find a way through because there wasn't one."

Jesse had misty eyes when he kissed her hand then looked away. Anna knew he needed a happier topic. "I wonder what Snowflake's doing right about now?"

"Probably ruling your mother's porch the same way she ruled ours," Jesse said with a smile.

Snowflake was a gorgeous white long-haired cat with brilliant blue eyes. She had mysteriously appeared, healthy and well fed, on Jesse and Anna's porch the day after their wedding and refused to leave. No one ever came looking for her. Anna had always seen the cat as a kind of guardian angel and a sign of good things to come.

"Remember how she hopped up in your grandmother's porch rocker and settled in like she was ready to receive callers?" Anna asked. "The first time I saw her, I felt like the luckiest girl in the world. I got to be your wife and live in your grandparents' house, and then on top of all that, we had this beautiful cat to watch over us."

Jesse put his arms around her. "Anna, you've always been so easy to please. And you deserve so much more."

She was about to answer when something startled a covey of quail in the trees. The flapping of wings in flight caught Jesse and Anna's attention, and they looked up to see that they were standing in a clearing dotted with headstones.

Anna gasped. "Oh my gosh, Jesse."

They walked together to the center of the graveyard and stopped before a tall obelisk of a monument. Anna ran her hand over the lettering. "Wyatt Gunter Talmadge. This must be Dolly's grandfather."

Jesse stepped a few feet to the side and read the names on a simple, unadorned headstone. "This one's Dolly and Si's. Anna, come over here—you need to see this."

He was pointing to a very small marker less than a foot tall. It had a marble lamb on top and a marble vase holding a fresh magnolia blossom and honeysuckle at its base.

Anna knelt on the ground and gently ran her fingers over the lamb. "Samuel Josiah Chandler. Born April 12, 1922. Died October 1, 1927. Oh no, Jesse."

He knelt beside her and held her as she cried for Dolly and Si and a precious child that would never grow up.

eight

Sunday morning had the women of Dolly's house scrambling all over the kitchen. The Baptist church was having guest singers in the morning worship service, with dinner on the grounds after, so Dolly had to serve breakfast to her boarders and get her covered dishes ready at the same time.

"If it wasn't for y'all, I'd have to throw myself in the Coosa River!" Dolly called to Anna and Evelyn, who were clearing the breakfast buffet they had set up earlier to speed the morning meal. Dolly hastily wrapped plates and platters as well as she could, given that tinfoil was so hard to come by these days. Luckily, she had several tureens with lids, and Si had secured those with elaborately tied fishing line.

Harry, Evelyn, and Joe were Methodists, while Jesse and Anna were Presbyterians, but they had come to feel like family in Dolly's house, so they all went to the Baptist church together.

"Si, I'm ready for you," Dolly called from the kitchen.

Si led Joe and Jesse into the kitchen to help load all of Dolly's food into the trunk of their car. "Let's hope the old Ford holds together with all this extra weight," Si said.

"You tryin' to tell me I'm gonna be walkin'?" Joe asked with a grin.

"Naw, Joe, we'll strap you to the hood if it comes to that."

Anna hurried out to hand Si one more casserole dish before he closed the trunk. She looked up just in time to see Daisy stepping off the far end of the porch at the skating rink and disappearing into the woods.

Dolly sighed. "She still won't go to church?"

Anna shook her head. "Not just yet. She says it makes her cry to even think about hearing all the old hymns Charlie loved, so she'll just have to do her praying in the woods for now. I feel bad going off and leaving her all alone every Sunday."

"She's where she needs to be right now, honey. And she understands that you're where you need to be." Dolly smiled and nodded toward the truck, where Anna was happy to see Jesse waiting for her.

For months and months before they came to Alabama, he had been climbing into the driver's seat and staring straight ahead till she got herself in. But this place was changing him. Now he waited for her the way he used to.

He walked around the truck with her and opened her door. After he climbed in, he didn't start the engine right away but instead turned to look at her, as if he were about to say something.

"What is it, Jesse?"

He tilted his head a little to the side, the way he always did when he was working out a problem. "I'm not sure. But I think I can figure it out if you can bear with me just a little longer?"

"I can manage that," she said with a smile.

He took her hand and kissed it before cranking his truck and following what soon became a caravan of cars leaving the loop and heading for Blackberry Springs Baptist Church.

The parking lot was covered with cars when they arrived, and a swarm of women was buzzing around a long concrete table underneath an open-air shed next to the church. It was fast getting filled with platters, bowls, and casserole dishes, while a smaller table beside it held gallon jugs of sweet tea, ice water, and lemonade. Some of the men had come early to set up folding chairs and spread cotton quilts under all the shade trees around the church.

After Anna and Jesse helped unload Dolly's food and get it on the table, they drifted back together. Standing a little distance from the fellowship table, they tried to take it all in.

"Never saw an outdoor table at a church," Jesse said.

"I never saw anything like *any* of this," Anna said. She looked up at him and smiled. "But I don't mind seeing something new now and again."

Just then the preacher rang a big bell in the churchyard, calling all the worshipers to the service. Jesse took Anna's hand as they went inside together.

After the singing, the congregation formed a long line that snaked around the fellowship table, and then they took their overladen plates and scattered all over the churchyard in search of shade. Anna and Jesse were looking for an empty spot when they heard Joe Dolphus calling to them. "Over here!" He was waving to them from a big oak at the far edge of the lawn.

As Anna and Jesse approached the tree, Si pointed them to a couple of empty folding chairs. All of Dolly and Si's boarders had gathered together, along with two of the "loop girls"— Daisy's shorthand for Alyce, Jo-Jo, and Dolly's other young cousins.

"Hey, y'all!" Alyce waved to them from a quilt where she was sitting with her cousin.

"It's good to see you again," Anna said as she and Jesse settled in.

"Say, Jesse, how long have y'all been married?" Jo-Jo asked out of the blue.

Dolly looked mortified. "Jo-Jo! Where on earth did that come from? Quit your pryin' in the churchyard, honey."

"I'm not pryin'—I just want to know."

Jesse grinned. "Well, that's different, I guess. We've been married . . . four years?" He looked at Anna for confirmation. She nodded.

"How'd you meet?" Jo-Jo asked. "Was it romantic like in the movies?"

"Would you let them alone so they can eat their chicken in peace?" Alyce said.

Jo-Jo rolled her eyes. "Oh, come on. All the other married people around here are so *old*!"

"Dolly, I believe we should take offense," Evelyn said.

"Absolutely," Dolly agreed. "Si, go to Childersburg first thing tomorrow and rent us a room at the nursin' home."

"Oh, y'all know what I mean!" Jo-Jo said as they all laughed at her.

"If y'all are ready for the old folks' home, Dolly, I reckon that puts me in the graveyard," Joe said.

"We can drop you off at the cemetery on our way home," Si answered.

"C'mon and tell me," Jo-Jo pleaded. "How'd you meet Anna?"

Anna felt that old familiar knot in her stomach. She wondered what Jesse was about to say.

"We grew up in the same church and went to the same school." He looked at Anna, whose heart was suddenly pounding. "When we were teenagers, I started finding ways to talk to her without anybody around. Then there was this spring dance, and I just remember looking up as she walked in, and, well . . . that was that."

"I had been waiting for him to notice me since I was about twelve," Anna added, which made everybody laugh.

"That is *so* romantic!" Jo-Jo exclaimed. "Tell us some more."

"No—eat your chicken," Jesse said sternly, but then he smiled.

"You'll have to excuse Jo-Jo," Alyce said. "She has marriage fever."

"Well, can you blame me? I'm already seventeen! All the good ones are gettin' gone! They'll prob'ly all come home from the war married to girls from Italy and France."

"As a veteran myself, I can assure you that there's little time for courtin' when you spend your days in a foxhole," Joe said.

"Well, that's somethin' to hang on to, I guess."

"You would prefer to have a potential beau dodging bullets in a foxhole than pitching woo with a French girl?" Evelyn asked.

"You better believe it!" Jo-Jo said, which brought more laughter from the group.

"Heart o' gold," Alyce said, shaking her head.

Dolly uncovered a plate of sliced cake. "Who wants dessert?"

"Me!" her cousins shouted.

"Dolly, m'dear, you've outdone yourself today," Si said as he passed the cake around.

"Well, I hope it's fit to eat. I was in such a hurry that I'm worried I left out something critical."

"It's wonderful," Anna said as she tasted the cake. "Do you think I could learn how to make it?"

"Why, of course! It's just an old-fashioned yellow cake with Little Mama's chocolate icin'."

"Don't let her fool you, Anna," Evelyn cautioned. "I've watched her make it, and that recipe is *not*, well, a piece of cake. Aren't I clever?"

"You've never cared for baking, though, Evelyn." Harry winked at the group.

Evelyn raised her hand in protest. "Do not bring up the incident of 1937. How was I to know that baking soda and baking powder are not interchangeable?"

"Oh no!" Dolly exclaimed.

"Those biscuits were no thicker than a nickel," Evelyn said, "and about as dense."

"Dolly, whatever you do, keep that woman outta your kitchen," Si said, which brought more laughter from the group as they finished their dessert and enjoyed Sunday dinner on a spring afternoon.

nine

Anna and Daisy stood in the middle of Dolly's attic, amazed by what they saw. It was a real treasure trove, with everything neatly stacked and arranged: old trunks that must have been a hundred years old, headboards and footboards and rocking chairs, a cradle and crib, wooden toys and dolls with china faces, grand old ball gowns that looked like something out of a movie, even a Confederate uniform and rifle.

"Dang!" Daisy exclaimed.

Their morning work done, Anna and Daisy had asked Dolly if they could explore her attic and look for clues about the pirate Chauvin and his bride. Now Daisy was sitting on the floor, looking through a small trunk filled with letters and pictures. Anna was wandering around the attic, trying to decide where to start, when the door to a large cedar wardrobe screeched open.

"Did you see that?" Anna pointed to the open door.

"Maybe it's Catherine's ghost," Daisy said with a grin.

Anna reached into the wardrobe, took out an emerald ball gown, and held it in front of her. "How do I look?"

"Like Scarlett O'Hara. If we dig around up here long enough, we might find Rhett." She walked over to the cradle and rocked it. Lowering her voice, she asked Anna, "Why you reckon Si and Dolly never had kids? They'd be such great parents."

Anna put the dress back and glanced at the attic steps to make sure no one was coming. Then she went to Daisy and whispered, "Jesse and I went walking on Saturday and followed a trail way back in the woods. It led to Dolly's family cemetery. Right next to Si and Dolly's headstone, there was a grave with a little marble lamb at the head and fresh flowers on it."

Daisy stared down at the cradle and ran her hand over the empty blanket inside it. "So sad. Such a sweet lady." Then she looked at Anna. "You and Jesse slippin' off to the woods now?"

Anna shook her head. "I wish. We just went for a walk—but he held my hand the whole way. And we actually *talked*, hallelujah."

"You do realize you're datin' your husband, right? I thought we were gonna take that bull by the horns."

"I know! It's ridiculous! But Jesse's trying so hard. I'm just doing my best to let him find his way back."

Daisy giggled. "Maybe you need to leave him a trail o' satin and lace."

"Stop!"

They laughed together as they renewed their search in the attic.

"Hey, look at this." Daisy held up a yellowed photograph. "Si and Dolly's wedding picture."

"Wasn't she pretty?" Anna said.

"They're strange, ain't they—old pictures? When this one was taken, Si and Dolly were younger than we are now. They didn't have no idea they were gonna suffer heartbreak together, or live through a Great Depression and two wars, or open up their home to people like us. They were just happy and excited to be together—same as Charlie and me, same as you and Jesse."

Anna nodded but couldn't find her voice.

Daisy laid her hand over Anna's. "Be about it, Anna. Be about it."

"Dolly's gonna strangle us!"

"No, she won't—she'll think it's fun!"

Anna still wasn't sure she wanted to go along with Daisy's latest adventure. She'd said the attic was making them sad, and they needed something fun to bring them out of the "mully-grubs," as she called it. She had talked Anna into putting on the green ball gown and coming downstairs to sit for a portrait.

"Hey, Dolly!" Daisy called toward the kitchen. "Come in here and see Scarlett O'Hara!"

"What?" Dolly called back, just before she hurried into the front parlor and saw Anna standing there in the ball gown. "Oh, honey, you look beautiful!"

"Are you sure you don't mind?" Anna was still afraid she had overstepped her bounds.

"I pushed her into it, Dolly," Daisy said. "I thought it would be fun to draw Anna's portrait in the ball gown—you know, as a little present for Jesse."

Anna was so busy fussing with a brooch on the gown that she paid no attention to the look that passed between her friends.

"Why, I can't think of a better activity for us on a rainy afternoon," Dolly said. "But if we're gonna do it, let's do it up right. Y'all pick a spot for the portrait and I'll be right back."

"What about the music room?" Anna suggested. Daisy followed her there and was directing Anna through different poses by the piano when Dolly returned with an armload of supplies—combs, brushes, jewelry, and long black lace gloves.

"Man, Dolly, those are beautiful!" Daisy said as she gently picked up the gloves.

"Wanna try 'em on?" Dolly asked.

"I doubt they'd look right with my overalls."

"Well, we'll be gettin' rid of them overalls one o' these days, I imagine, so go ahead."

Daisy carefully slipped the gloves onto her hands and pulled them up her arms. "Do I look like Princess Elizabeth? Because I feel like Princess Elizabeth."

"Absolutely," Anna said, attempting a curtsy in the ball gown.

"Daisy, honey, you are hidin' your light under a bushel," Dolly said. "Any girl who can pull off lace gloves with overalls is a force to be reckoned with, but we'll deal with that later. Let's us get this portrait a-goin'. Come sit right here, Anna."

Anna sat down on a velvet pouf in the music room, and Dolly began brushing her long auburn hair and pinning it up, then added a delicate pearl tiara. The necklace she had chosen for Anna was a short strand of tiny pearls with a small emerald pendant. Once Anna had on the lace gloves, Daisy and Dolly stepped back to admire her.

"You look *better* than Princess Elizabeth," Daisy said.

Anna laughed. "I feel like I'm playing dress up."

"Why should kids have all the fun?" Daisy said. "Hey, stand there by the piano and kinda rest your right hand on it. Yeah, just like that." She took out her sketchpad and went to work. "You have to promise to let me give this to Jesse. I cannot *wait* to see the look on his face."

"What on earth are you talking about?" Anna shook her head.

"You'll see. Now be still."

⁓◌⁓

"Here he comes!" Daisy had kept watch as the rain finally let up, and Anna helped Dolly cook supper for her boarders.

"Dolly, should I be worried about another woman who's this

85

excited to see my husband?" Anna asked as she checked on a pot roast in the oven.

"I'd keep an eye on her," Dolly said. "I've always thought she was a floozy."

"Y'all just wait—you'll see," Daisy said. "I gotta go."

Dolly winked at Anna. "Come on—let's go get us a good view." They hurried upstairs and slipped out onto the upper porch just in time to see Daisy strolling nonchalantly across the yard.

"Hey, Jesse." She threw up her hand as he got out of his truck, but kept walking down the driveway.

"Hey," he said as he headed for the porch.

"What's she up to?" Anna whispered to Dolly on their perch high above.

Just then they heard Daisy call out. "Say, Jesse, wait up. I got somethin' here you might like to have, now that I think about it."

He turned back and met Daisy by his truck.

"Me and Anna were rummagin' around Dolly's attic durin' the rain today, and I talked her into lettin' me draw her in one o' the fancy dresses up there. Turned out pretty nice. Why don't you take it?"

"Thanks," he said, taking the portrait from Daisy. He didn't take his eyes off of it.

"If you don't like it, you don't have to keep it—you won't hurt my feelin's," Daisy said.

"N-no—she's—beautiful. Your picture's beautiful."

"You mean it?" Daisy asked, as if she were concerned about the quality of her work. "Because I just got these colored pencils, and I wasn't sure I got the right shade o' green for her eyes. You really think I came close?"

"Remind me never to play poker with her," Dolly whispered to Anna.

"They're . . . they're perfect," Jesse said.

"Well, I gotta go," Daisy said. "Y'all have a good night."

She was near the end of the driveway before Jesse seemed to remember himself and called out, "Bye, Daisy! And thank you!"

"C'mon!" Dolly said to Anna. "Let's not get caught. I'll go to the kitchen and you go meet that husband."

Anna paused at the screen door and watched Jesse. He had taken a seat on the front steps and was staring at her portrait, running a finger lightly over the image of her cheek and then her throat. How strange it was to feel like an intruder, watching her own husband absorbed in her image, showing her likeness the affection he could not bring himself to offer in the flesh. She would spare him—not his pride but his wounded spirit, bruised from the sense of utter failure and helplessness that had engulfed him when their farm and all the dreams it held fell apart.

She walked back to the dining room and called his name as she moved toward the front door, giving him ample warning. "Jesse? Is that you?"

He stood up and quickly turned around as she stepped onto the porch. She had taken off her finery but left her hair up, as Dolly had styled it.

"Hey," he said, still holding the drawing.

"Hey." She smiled back. "I see Daisy showed you what she got me into this afternoon."

"What?" He was looking at her just as he had looked at the drawing.

"The drawing," she said, pointing to it.

"Oh! Yeah. She gave it to me. It's beautiful."

"Daisy's really talented."

"That's not what I meant. I meant *you're* beautiful." He came to her, cupped her face in his hand, and kissed her. And then he whispered, "You always have been."

ten

Daisy and Anna hiked down a furrow of the cotton field in front of Lillian's house, where the porch was empty. The cotton was getting tall, but it was still green, its leaves slapping at their legs as they walked to the edge of the field, where red dirt gave way to patches of Johnsongrass, dandelions, and occasional briars. Just a few yards away sat the housekeeper's shack—an unpainted shotgun with a tin roof and rough-hewn logs used as pillars to hold up the roof of the front porch. It was shaded by oaks that no doubt kept anything from growing below, because the yard, if you could call it that, looked bare.

"Dang, this place is creepy—and snaky," Daisy said. "Here, grab you one of these and poke around in the grass before you take a step." She handed Anna a piece of cane from a pile at the edge of the field. "Looks like somebody was plannin' to fish and thought better of it."

They slowly trekked through the weeds, poking about with their canes and watching where they stepped, until they reached the tiny shaded yard, where there was nothing but dirt beneath their feet.

"I can't believe we're actually doing this," Anna said as they stepped onto the front porch. "And I'm mighty glad you thought to bring a flashlight."

Daisy gingerly bounced on the boards of the porch floor, testing to make sure she and Anna wouldn't fall through. "Feels sturdy enough." She pulled open the remains of a screen door—only the frame was left—and then turned the knob on the front door and pushed it open.

Anna followed her into the one-room house, which was lit with morning sunlight. Its sparse furnishings—a rocker by the fireplace, a small table and two chairs in the kitchen—were covered with dust.

"I've seen some small houses in my time," Daisy said, "but this place is a postage stamp."

"Lillian said the woman who lived here cooked and kept house for Andre before he married Catherine, so she probably spent most of her time at his house. I'll bet this was just a place for her to sleep."

"But there's no bed."

"Maybe somebody took it? Hey, I wonder what's in here." Anna pointed to a narrow door next to the stove. She pulled it open, only to find canning jars, mixing bowls, and some kitchen tools. "Just cooking stuff."

Daisy was coming over to have a look when she caught the toe of her sneaker on something and tripped, stumbling a few steps to right herself.

"You okay?" Anna asked.

"Yeah. Looks like an old board curled up a little. Hey, look—there's a whole row o' short ones like it."

Studying the spot where Daisy tripped, they could see the outline of what looked like a small door in the kitchen floor. There was a round hole in the middle of one end, just big enough to fit a thumb.

"What do you make of that?" Anna asked.

Daisy shrugged. "Prob'ly a root cellar. Only one way to find out." She stuck her thumb in the hole and pulled the door up, revealing what was indeed a root cellar down below. "I'll bet you there's spiders as big as a heifer down there."

"What about snakes?"

"Too cold underground."

Daisy aimed her flashlight at the foot of the cellar steps, where she and Anna immediately spotted it—an old-fashioned steamer trunk. They both gasped as they looked at each other, then back at the trunk.

"Oh my gosh, Daisy! What if it's Catherine's?"

"What if it's just the housekeeper's?"

"Well, even that would be something, wouldn't it?"

"How brave do you feel?"

"Not very, but I'm plenty curious."

Daisy started down the steps first, shining her light all around the trunk and on the ceiling overhead to see what might be crawling up there. Spiderwebs were everywhere. "I feel like they're crawlin' all over me!" she said. "Quick, you grab one handle and I'll grab the other—let's get outta here."

The two of them took hold of the trunk and hurried up the steps as fast as they could. Back in the light of the kitchen, they stepped back to have a look. It was very plain. Daisy found an old rag in the kitchen sink and wiped away the cobwebs. Then she went over the trunk with her flashlight.

"Hey, look," she said when the light struck what looked like initials on the latch of the trunk. "E. E. O. Who the heck is that?"

"The 'O' could be for 'O'Dwyer,' but I've got no idea who 'E. E.' might be. Why don't we take it to Dolly's to open it? Don't you feel like she should be with us, just in case there's something special inside?"

"Yeah, you're prob'ly right. It's not that heavy—we should be able to carry it if we stop and rest a few times. Ready?"

The women of Dolly's house gathered in her front parlor, sitting on the floor around the steamer trunk.

"I just can't believe it," Dolly said. "All the times me and Vi searched this house, it never occurred to us to search that ol' shotgun."

"What do you make of the initials, Dolly?" Anna asked.

"Oh, that has to be Esther O'Dwyer. She was Catherine's older sister—much older—and she's kinda famous around here, or maybe it would be 'infamous,' Evelyn? Anyway, when she was in her forties, she left her husband and run off up north with one o' them abolitionists. Fell head over heels with him at a camp meetin' and never looked back. Lucky she didn't have any kids. They said her stern ol' miserly husband was still tryin' to figure out why she left till the day he died."

"Yes, I do believe that would make her infamous," Evelyn said.

"They say she's buried somewhere up in Maryland," Dolly added.

Evelyn looked puzzled. "Why would Esther's trunk be in the Creole woman's house?"

"Well, seein' as how she was a lot older'n Catherine, maybe the trunk's a hand-me-down," Dolly said.

"Ladies, could I make a suggestion?" Daisy flipped the latch up. "Let's open the dang thing."

The smell of cedar chips, tucked into some of the side pockets, wafted out as Daisy lifted the top of the trunk. "Man!" she said as they began examining the contents. "These have gotta be the ugliest dresses I ever saw."

One by one, they pulled out the few dresses in the trunk—all of them severe frocks in gray or dark blue wool or cotton.

"Bless her heart, this underwear's just as sad," Dolly said, shaking her head over a pair of plain cotton pantaloons.

With the trunk emptied of clothing, the women could see what was stored in its interior pockets.

"Even her books were dull," Anna said, handing a few volumes on philosophy and theology to Evelyn, who began thumbing through them.

"Ha!" Evelyn exclaimed. "Don't count Miss Catherine out just yet. Look." The center pages of each book had been ripped out, replaced with poetry by Tennyson, Byron, and Poe. "Our girl was smuggling the Romantics and that madman Poe in her philosophy books," she said. "Well done, Catherine. Well done indeed."

"Hey, y'all, look at this." Daisy presented a plain brown leather journal that had been pushed deep down into a side pocket of the trunk. Opening the book, she looked up at the others, her eyes wide, then began to read.

February 10, 1844

I've never done this before. And I'm not quite sure who I'm talking to. Myself, I suppose? Shall I introduce myself to myself, do you think? How do you do, self. My name is Catherine Elizabeth O'Dwyer, and I am nineteen years old.

All the women squealed and clapped their hands with delight. "Oh my gosh, oh my gosh!" Anna exclaimed. "It's her! It's really her! Keep reading, Daisy!"

Daisy shook her head. "No, it oughta be you, Anna. You oughta speak for Catherine. Here, read it to us."

Anna took the leather journal and began reading.

Sister gave me a set of three journals and said I might find it a comfort to record my thoughts as she has done for many years. She hides her journals from her husband. When I marry, as it appears I am about to do, I hope my husband will not be the sort of man from whom I must hide my thoughts.

My troubles began with a tea party, if you can believe that. It was hosted by a new member of Father's church, Mrs. Bertram Claypool, wife of the recently elected—and very first—mayor of Blackberry Springs. The Claypools are quite wealthy. They have always lived on a plantation by the river, but now that they are the royalty of our little village, they decided to build what they call a townhome in Blackberry Springs.

As they have now joined Father's church, Mrs. Claypool invited all the ladies to tea. Mother has not been the same since. I regret she is often guilty of the sin of covetousness. She cannot rejoice in the good fortune of others for the weight of her own envy. Father is not so much envious as ambitious, and he has a way of bending us all to his will. Sometimes I wonder if he has even read the Bible he preaches from—read all of it as I have, from cover to cover, seeking understanding—or does he merely search the Scriptures for whatever passage he can shape to his purpose? The latter, I think.

What does this have to do with me? Marriage. Father has rarely allowed me so much as a conversation with a boy, and then only under the probing eyes of the church ladies. But ever since the tea party, he has begun speaking of marriage—my marriage—incessantly, just as Mother talks of the Claypool townhome incessantly. It is past time I married, Father said. I owe it to my family to make a good match, he said. And then the suitors started calling on us—most of them old or otherwise uninteresting, but all with land and money. I would rather die than let any of them lay a hand on me, and I pray fervently every night for God's protection.

"Dang, how awful would that be?" Daisy said. "Havin' your daddy try to marry you off to some ol' coot just to get his money."

"I would imagine arranged marriages were common in the South back then," Evelyn said.

"Prob'ly," Daisy agreed. "Still, you'd hope your daddy would think more o' you than to ship you off with somebody you couldn't stand the sight of."

"Girls, be glad you're livin' in the modern age," Dolly said. "But we're holdin' Anna up. Go on, dear. What does Catherine say next?"

February 12, 1844

Dear Self,

Yesterday I was in the dining room, polishing Mother's silver—it actually belongs to the church, but she convinced the ladies it would be better cared for here—when I heard Father welcome someone into the parlor. Next, I heard a man's voice, which I can only describe as the sound of velvet. There was something luxurious about the way he spoke, the way his words glided almost musically from one to the other, and there was a hint of something—I don't know how to describe it . . . foreign?—in his accent. I searched about for a way to get a look at him without getting caught, but there was none.

February 13, 1844

Dear Self,

No sooner had Father said his goodbyes to the man with the velvet voice than Mother was in my room, riffling through my wardrobe in search of a suitable frock for supper tomorrow night. The man's name, it turns out, is Andrew Sinclair. He is the son of a wealthy rice planter from South Carolina and moved here to "establish a base" (Mother's words) for extending the family's holdings into Alabama cotton. He has bought 100 acres, mostly pasture and woodlands, Mother said, and built a home, which no one has been invited to see, on Tanyard Creek. Mother was all but salivating. There had been rumors that someone "substantial" (again, Mother's words) had moved to Blackberry Springs, based on the enormous order for lumber placed at the sawmill months ago and the shipments of furniture from New Orleans that had recently been delivered by train. They had been picked up at the depot by a dark-skinned woman no one knew, driving four fine horses and a large wagon. Someone was building something grand, and that someone was Andrew Sinclair. Now that he had come calling to inquire about church membership, Father "wisely" invited him to supper. It seems I am finally to meet Mr. Sinclair.

"So that's where all o' Little Mama's furniture came from!" Dolly exclaimed. "She always said most of it was here when Granddaddy Talmadge bought the house, and now we come to find out it was shipped from New Orleans! That makes me feel downright uppity. Y'all call me Mrs. Chandler from now on."

"I just can't believe this," Anna said. "It's like Catherine's right here with us."

"Yeah, yeah, keep goin'," Daisy urged her.

February 15, 1844

Dear Self,

   It happened. I met him—the man with the velvet voice. He is quite handsome, I'll admit that—tall with strong

shoulders, and hair and eyes the color of rich, dark chocolate. His hair has a slight wave to it that would make him
look roguish if he weren't dressed in such fine clothes.
And his skin is very tan—bronze really—as if he came
from some exotic place far from our little Alabama town.
I suppose that's what men look like in South Carolina.
Every girl in church will soon be throwing herself at such
a wealthy, handsome bachelor. Why Father thinks he can
marry mousy little me off to him is beyond me.

I was instructed to speak only when spoken to during
supper—nothing unusual there—and Mother seated Mr.
Sinclair directly across from me at the table. Small wonder
she didn't stand me ON the table, walking me back and
forth so that Mr. Sinclair could study my gait and judge
the quality of my bloodline. The only saving grace was
that I sensed Father was not in control of this man, or my
situation. Mr. Sinclair did not blabber on and on, flatter-
ing my parents and making a gaudy show of his wealth.
He was quiet—not in a shy way but in a calculating one,
as if he were taking the measure of us all.

After coffee and cake, Father told me I was excused
from the table, and when I stood to go, Mr. Sinclair also
stood and bowed to me. "Good evening, Miss O'Dwyer,"
he said.

"Good evening, sir," I said. And then I walked in a daze
to my room. I fell asleep hearing it over and over in my
head: his velvet-voiced "Good evening, Miss O'Dwyer."

February 20, 1844

Dear Self,

I realize that all men, especially ministers, are not like
Father. Nor are all women like Mother. I see married cou-

*ples at church who seem to enjoy one other's company—
and to enjoy the free spirits of their children instead of
stifling them. Might I ever be so fortunate as to have that?
I don't know.*

*Andrew Sinclair is politely ignoring the advances of all
the girls at church, including Lavinia Mason, who attracts
boys like horses to corn with her flirtatious eye batting
and flattery. I find that silly. A girl might as well shout,
"Choose me! Choose me!" What of her choice?*

"What indeed!" Evelyn said. "I tell you, the more I learn of
this young woman, the more I like her. My apologies, Anna.
Do go on."

March 1, 1844

Dear Self,

*After three more suppers with Andrew Sinclair—and
you'll find this very stupid of me—I have come to anticipate, with some excitement, his "Good evening, Miss
O'Dwyer." How ridiculous. Perhaps it wouldn't be entirely terrible to marry him—which I am about to do.
Did I mention that? Yes, he has asked Father for my hand,
and Father accepted—accepted but will not allow us one
second alone together. And so I will be walking down
the aisle to a man of whom I know nothing, save "Good
evening, Miss O'Dwyer" and a velvet voice.*

March 15, 1844

Dear Self,

*I have a confession to make. And you must take it to
your grave. I have, for some time, been reading stories and*

poetry that Father absolutely forbids. They are smuggled to me by my cousin Vivian, who, I'm afraid, encourages my rebellious streak. I keep them hidden in plain view. Vivian tears the pages out of her own books when she finishes them and slips them inside something dreadfully boring that Father would approve of. If you should look at my bookshelf, you would think me quite absorbed in philosophy and theology, when in fact I am reading Mr. Edgar Allan Poe with a mix of horror and delight. Also Byron and Tennyson, whom I love. They transport me from this dreary place. Absent those fleeting journeys, I fear I would surely die. "She hath no loyal knight and true, The Lady of Shalott."

"That's the saddest thing I've ever read," Anna said. "She must've been so lonely and unhappy."

"Got a feelin' the man with the tan's about to change that," Daisy said. "Keep goin'."

March 20, 1844

Dear Self,

Sister came to tea today, and afterward she asked Mother if the two of us might enjoy a stroll together, during which she managed to turn my apprehension as a bride-to-be into outright terror. She is much older than I, and we've never been very close. I've always felt like the black sheep compared to Esther, perhaps because I know deep down that all of my good behavior is compelled and not of my own choosing. Now that I consider it, the same might be true of Sister. Sometimes it seems she has escaped the constraints of her marriage by constraining herself even more than anyone else would dare to.

She told me not to fear my wedding night, for it would be over and done with soon enough. I should think of my marriage bed, she said, like any other unpleasant but necessary task, such as hoeing weeds out of the garden. When I begged her for the particulars, she said, "Ladies do not speak of such things—just close your eyes and think of England."

The women of Dolly's house all burst out laughing.

"Close your eyes and think of England?" Daisy howled, lying back on the floor and holding her stomach because she was laughing so hard. "That makes me feel bad for poor ol' Esther," she said. "But I guess she finally found her a decent garden with that abolitionist."

"My land, that reminds me of things my grandmother used to say to me and Violet," Dolly said when she finally stopped laughing. "You know what her courtin' advice was for us girls? 'Always keep both feet on the floor.'"

"You gotta be kiddin' me!" Daisy said. "What does that even mean, Dolly?"

"Well, think about it, honey. Definitely limits the mischief you can get into."

"Anna, you better keep readin'," Daisy said. "I don't think I can take any more advice from Dolly's grandma."

As the women quieted down, Anna resumed her reading.

March 31, 1844

Dear Self,
    The good ladies of the church no doubt think me very fortunate to marry a handsome man with a fine house and deep pockets. But a grand house can hold as much sorrow as joy, and I have no idea which of the two awaits me.

I know only that my own father sold me to the highest bidder like a horse or a cow. He has conveniently planned the wedding for Easter Sunday—one week from today—when, he says, my Easter frock should suffice for a wedding gown and the Easter fellowship will make a suitable reception.

And what of Andrew Sinclair? What is he thinking right now? The ladies at church go on and on about how romantic it is for us to marry after such a brief courtship, but we've had no courtship at all. I've never had so much as a private conversation with the man I'm expected to spend the rest of my life with. He's older than I am—I would guess in his late twenties or early thirties—and quite fine to look at. But I once read that some of the most beautiful snakes in the world are also the deadliest.

There is something secretive about my intended. For all I know, he could be the cruelest man in the county. What happens to a bride on her wedding night if her husband is a cruel man? For that matter, what happens to any bride on her wedding night? I'm too embarrassed to ask anyone but Sister, and she was hardly a comfort.

Anna turned the page but stopped reading.

"Don't hold us in suspense, dear," Evelyn said.

Anna flipped through the remaining pages of the journal. "They're all blank. That can't be where the story ends. It just can't be."

Dolly put her arm around Anna's shoulders and gave them a little squeeze.

"But why would she just stop?" Anna was clearly distraught at leaving young Catherine hanging in her predicament, forced into a marriage against her will.

"Honey," Dolly began gently, "remember what I told you

about the fishermen and what they found in the river? The part you just read was written the week before her wedding—the week before she disappeared. Maybe Catherine and Andre were headed downriver for their honeymoon and had an accident. Maybe she just never got to write any more. There's no way for us to know, really."

Anna's eyes welled with tears as Dolly held her tight. "I know I'm being silly," she said. "But I so wanted a happy ending."

"There ain't nothin' silly about that." Daisy reached over and gave Anna's hand a gentle squeeze. "Your story just got tangled up with hers, is all. And you want 'em both to turn out right. You got nothin' to be embarrassed about."

"Indeed not," Evelyn chimed in. "And I do not believe in abandoning the chain of one's research. The two of you found something that was lost for decades. There is no reason to believe you won't find more. Do not give up on Catherine. There is something special about her. She might surprise us all yet."

"You really think so?" Anna asked, dabbing at her eyes with a handkerchief Dolly handed her.

"I do. Catherine has left us a trail and we must follow it. The next crumb will present itself in time."

"I hope you're right," Anna said.

Evelyn smiled. "I'm always right. Just ask Harry."

❧

"What do you think?"

A couple of days after the women of Dolly's house read Catherine's unfinished journal together, Anna took it to Lillian's house and read it to her. The two of them were sitting together on the front porch as Anna closed the small leather volume and waited to hear what her friend had to say. She was surprised to see Lillian reach into the pocket of her dress, take out a handkerchief, and blot her cloudy eyes.

"You think they drowned, don't you?" Anna felt her own eyes begin to sting.

Lillian shook her head. "No, sweet Anna, that's not why I'm crying. It's just that I find their first real encounter so moving. Think of it! Two complete strangers about to marry one another. Andre so handsome and Catherine so beautiful. And the way Catherine is drawn to him, even though part of her fears him. It's almost too much to take in."

"But she didn't write any more. The journal ends before their wedding day."

"That doesn't mean their story did."

"I don't understand how you can be so sure. I wish you'd tell me so I could be sure too."

Lillian smiled. "Do you really think a pirate, an adventurer, one who had taken all manner of risks in his life and made his living on the mightiest river in this entire country, who could read the currents and sound the depths—you think such a man who had survived every challenge in his path would, in the end, simply drown?"

Anna frowned. "Well, since you put it that way . . ."

"And having saved the entire Presbyterian congregation, including Catherine's father, whom he loathed, do you think Andre would then allow his beautiful young wife to drown?"

Anna reached over and took Lillian's hand. "No. I don't believe that for a minute."

"Then they didn't drown," Lillian said.

"They didn't drown." Anna didn't just say it, she believed it. And there was something about knowing Catherine survived that made her feel like a survivor too.

CHAPTER

eleven

"Joe, I'm ready on this end!" Si called toward the woods. He and Harry had just turned a big wheel that opened a valve on a metal pipe about two feet in diameter. The pipe ran underground from the creek to the back wall of the lake.

"Jesse, you ready on the creek bank?" Anna heard Joe call from behind the trees.

Dolly, Anna, Daisy, and Evelyn were standing together on the porch of the skating rink, waiting for whatever might happen next. Everybody else on the loop who didn't have something better to do had gathered on the boardwalk, no doubt to see if the lake would hold or if they needed to run home and move their valuables up to the attic.

"Jesse's ready!" Joe called.

"Tell him to start the pump!" Si shouted.

"Start 'er up, Jesse!" Joe relayed.

"Lord Jesus, protect us all," Dolly said, and Anna put an arm around her to offer support.

"We didn't miss it, did we?" Jo-Jo shouted as she and her cousins came running onto the porch.

"Haven't missed a thing," Dolly said with a little quiver in her voice. She couldn't seem to stop wringing her hands as they waited for the inevitable blast of water.

Just then everybody heard an engine crank somewhere in the woods. The women gasped at what sounded like gunfire.

"No cause for alarm, ladies!" Si shouted across the lake. "That ol' engine on my pump is just talkin' back a little!"

Within seconds, water from the creek came shooting out of the pipe like a fire hose—more like ten fire hoses tied together.

Si and Harry threw their hats up in the air, and a shout went up from the crowd as if they had all just struck oil. Creek water was gushing into the lake with such force that the stream almost reached the boardwalk on the other side.

"Dang," Daisy said. "That's a real gully washer he's got there."

"Might need to adjust the throttle!" Si shouted, slapping his knee and laughing as he watched the spectacle with Harry and Joe.

"See, Dolly, it's gonna be fine," Anna said. But she kept glancing toward the woods, hoping Jesse would come out soon.

"Well, at least we know the lake won't be dry," Dolly said. "Sure hope we don't flood anybody out. And I sure hope this helps us pay that awful tax bill a little earlier."

Just then Jesse came running out of the woods to join the men.

"Jesse!" Anna cried. "Are you alright?"

He was laughing with the men—all of them slapping each other on the back—but even from the porch, Anna could see that her husband's face, his clothes, and even his blond hair were black with soot. She went running off the porch and along the far bank of the lake.

When she reached Jesse, he opened his arms, gave her a big smile, and said, "Kiss me?"

Anna giggled. "Who *are* you? All I can see are teeth and eyes!"

"That engine of Si's—she smokes a little."

"Apparently," Anna said, looking him over.

"Just how big is that engine on your pump, Si?" Daisy asked as the women joined the others at the pipe.

"Took 'er off a Ford tractor—just temporarily, o' course. Soon as we start makin' money on the lake, I'll get me an engine for the creek and put my tractor back together again."

"Think ya mighta overshot the horsepower," Daisy said as they watched the column of water spray the lake and begin puddling in the center.

"We won't worry too much unless the water goes to white-cappin'," Joe said.

"There isn't any way your engine could start a fire in the woods, is there?" Anna asked Si.

Si opened his mouth to answer, but then he frowned, scratched his head, and said, "You know, you make a good point, Anna. In all the excitement, I didn't even think about fire. Seein' as how Jesse's gonna need to jump in the slough and clean up anyhow, reckon you could fetch him some clean clothes and a little picnic lunch? If y'all could watch the engine for a coupla hours while I make sure everything's runnin' fine here and get me a bite to eat, I'll relieve you this afternoon, and then I can hire a coupla the older boys on the loop to sit up with her tonight. Would that be alright?"

"Sure."

"Just come get me up at the house when you're ready to change shifts."

Anna looked at Jesse's soot-covered face. "I think I'll see if Dolly can spare some soap—and maybe a scrub brush."

"Well, I can't hear myself draw with that ol' Ford runnin' full throttle," Daisy said. "I'm goin' home."

Slowly the crowd dispersed, with Si and Dolly's crew heading to the house for lunch and Jesse starting for the creek.

"I'll be back!" Anna called to him.

"Hey, bring one of your mother's quilts with you so we'll have something to sit on for our picnic, okay?"

"Okay!" Anna waved to him and smiled as he disappeared into the woods. She actually felt butterflies in her stomach— just like the first night he'd picked her up for a date. How silly was that?

"That oughta do it," Si said as Dolly joined him on their front porch.

"Do what?" She could see that he was watching Anna make her way to the woods, carrying a quilt over one arm and a basket that held lunch and Jesse's clean clothes in the other.

Si winked at her. "That engine's on a platform in the middle o' the creek. It don't need watchin'."

twelve

Anna followed the trail to the creek, past the smoky engine still chugging away, and deep into the woods. She was nearing the slough, where noise from Si's engine was distant and blessedly muffled, when she heard the sound of splashing water. Jesse's smoky clothes lay in a heap beneath a sprawling oak, which cast its shade onto the beautiful natural pool that Si and Dolly had shown them. Anna set down her basket and spread the quilt.

At first Jesse didn't see her beside the tree. He was a few yards from the bank, standing in a sunny spot with his back to her. The water hit him just below his shoulders. After tipping his head back into the water, he reached up to run his hands through his hair. Anna had always thought his arms and shoulders were beautiful. Hard work had chiseled them with strength, and she loved the feel of them.

He turned around and caught her staring at him. For a moment, he stared back. But then he smiled and said, "Sure looks hot up there on that bank."

Anna smiled back at him.

"Want to come in?"

She looked around. "What if somebody catches us?"

Jesse scanned the woods around the slough. "All clear."

"Turn around."

"I'm your husband!"

"I know, but it's broad daylight!" Anna argued back.

"Okay, okay, I'll turn around."

Anna hid as best she could between the oak tree and a cane-brake encircling part of the slough and laid her clothes in a neat stack. Then she scanned the woods one last time, got a running start, and jumped into the slough before anybody could see her.

Jesse was laughing when she wiped the water from her eyes and opened them. She had to stand on tiptoe when she reached him.

"Did you peek?" she asked.

"Absolutely," he said. "Are you touching bottom?"

"Barely—another step and I'll be swimming."

"Remember how to swirl?" He held his arms out with his palms up.

Anna smiled and laid her arms over his. They held on to each other, both of them laughing as he pulled her through the water in a circle around him.

"Think your pirate and his lady ever did this?"

"I hope so," Anna said. "I'd hate to think Catherine missed out on it."

Jesse stopped, but they kept holding on to each other, still at arm's length. "Anna," he finally said, "I've been such a—I mean, I've thrown away so much of our time together—I'm so sorry for the way . . ."

"I don't want you to be sorry," she said. "I just want you to let me back in. It's so lonely out here without you, Jesse."

He pulled her to him and held her close as she buried her face in the curve of his neck and released a year's worth of sadness. He stroked her back and her long, wet hair, letting her cry all of their hard times into a sunlit pool deep in the Alabama woods.

As Anna's tears subsided, Jesse's hands were no longer comforting but reclaiming. The waters of the slough reflected a kiss, long and deep, before Jesse carried Anna to her mother's quilt and the two of them let the tall pines drink in their kisses and sighs and whispers.

PART 2

The Return

May 1, 1944

Dear Violet,

It sure was good to get your letter yesterday. I was so happy to hear from you that I made up my mind to get up extra early this morning while the house is quiet and write you back.

Vi, you just don't know what your encouraging words meant to me. You always know exactly what to say to make me think I might not be losing my marbles after all.

You won't believe who stopped by yesterday—Vern Ingram. Him and Si's always been like brothers. I know they miss one another now that they live so far apart. Remember Vern and Ouida's boy, Reed? He had those beautiful eyes? Well, Vi, he's all grown up and been through a terrible ordeal in the war. Near about lost his leg and can't hardly walk. Has awful nightmares and keeps to himself all the time. Can't get his mind settled after all he's been through. Vern said Reed wants to come back to the loop. Says he's just not adjusting with his family all around him, and he never did take to north Alabama—remember they moved up there when Ouida inherited that farm? So he's coming to stay with us. He was such a sweet little thing when he was a child. And such a comfort to me after we lost our precious Samuel. Pray for me, Vi—pray that I'll know how to help this lost boy.

On to happier news. I'm tickled to death that y'all have found you a church and made some nice friends. And Vi, friends are everything when you're away from family. I'm more convinced of that every day. You know that young couple from Illinois I wrote you about? Well, they turned out to be good people. She's just a dear little thing named Anna. Her husband, Jesse, came here with a chip the size of all creation on his shoulder. But Si's working on him, and Jesse's coming around. He's a good boy. Just had his pride shot to pieces by the same hard times that forced us to turn Little Mama's house into a hotel.

Anna has got to be friends with Daisy Dupree. I told you about Daisy—the one that's done lost her husband to the war, bless her heart. I see a real special friendship between those girls. They remind me of us way back when. They've both got all excited about that ol' pirate tale you and me used to love so much—Anna especially. I can't figure out why it's so important to her to find out about our Catherine and Andre, but it passes the time and gives us something to talk about. You know me, I'm always happy for something to talk about.

We've all gone to really liking that college professor from Chicago—Evelyn. Now, Vi, would you ever in a million years have thought your sister would be friends with a college professor? I sure appreciate the way she reins in her education so the rest of us don't feel so stupid. That must take a lot out of her.

Oh! Si got rid of that awful couple from Reno. I can't begin to tell you that story on paper, so you'll just have to come home on the Fourth and hear all about it.

One last thing. I know I cried like a teething toddler when you left for Georgia. And no matter how many friends I make, there's nobody can ever fill your shoes. But you've got to live your own life, honey. I see that now, watching Daisy and Anna try to find their way without *their families. And I just want you to know that as long as you're happy, I'm happy. Be happy over there in Georgia, precious Violet.*

Kiss the young'uns for me and give Wiley a hug.

Your loving sister,
Dolly

thirteen

"Guess we better get one of these beds moved down," Anna said. "Which one, do you think?"

Daisy surveyed their options. "Those old iron beds always squeak. And they weigh a ton. What about that kinda plain cherry one over there? That looks like somethin' a man would like—and somethin' we could carry without killin' ourselves."

The two of them carried first the headboard, then the footboard, and finally all the pieces of the frame down the attic steps. Si had already moved the mattress and had it airing in the sun, as Dolly requested.

"Oh, this is really pretty," Anna said when they finally had the bed down and could see it better in the light. She got some polish and dust rags from beneath Dolly's sink, and she and Daisy cleaned the bed from top to bottom. Then they went to find Dolly and report their progress.

They abruptly stopped in the doorway of an empty bedroom in the back corner of the house, right behind Si and Dolly's room. The only furniture it held was a rocking chair by a tall window. Dolly was sitting in the rocker, blotting her eyes with an embroidered handkerchief. Anna and Daisy looked at each other before Daisy went straight to Dolly and knelt down by the rocker.

"You okay, Dolly?" Daisy asked.

Looking down at her, Dolly forced a smile and nodded.

"You ain't gotta pretend with us," Daisy said as Anna came over and knelt down on the opposite side of Dolly's chair.

"I thought I was past it after all these years," Dolly said as she began to cry.

Daisy took her hand. "Anna and Jesse stumbled onto the little headstone with the lamb. This used to be a nursery, didn't it?"

Dolly sniffed and nodded.

"Dolly, I'm so sorry," Anna said.

"Look, I don't know if I'll ever have babies," Daisy said, "but if I do, I'll be a better mother because o' you. You mother all of us, Dolly. It's just that, well, your babies all drive, and some of 'em have steady jobs."

Now Dolly was laughing and crying at the same time. She reached down and hugged both Anna and Daisy. "Y'all are just so precious to me," she said as she tried to regain her composure.

"Dolly, are you sure you want to put Reed in this room?" Anna asked. "If you're worried about the rest of us upstairs, we can handle it fine. We could help you fix up the Clanahans' old room so it's not so drafty, and he could stay up there with the rest of us."

Dolly dried her face with the handkerchief and shook her head. "Thank you, honey, but no. I can't explain it, but sometimes this ol' house speaks to me. I know that sounds crazy. But it's tellin' me that Reed needs this room—this one in particular—just as surely as it told me that you and Jesse needed mine and Violet's. Reed was always such a sweet and lovin' boy. If it wasn't for him runnin' in and outta my kitchen back then . . . The thought of a child like that bein' thrown into somethin' so horrifyin' that it disturbed his young mind—well, it just breaks my heart. He might think he wants to be all alone, but I don't believe that. I mean to keep him close—close as I would my own—well, you know."

"Then me and Anna will get to it," Daisy said.

"Thank you, girls. I don't know what I'd do without you."

"Good luck gettin' rid of us," Daisy said, which made everybody laugh.

"Dolly, that door on the back wall—it looks new," Anna said.

"It is. I had Si put it in. And I've asked him to build a little screened-in porch off the back—nothin' fancy, just big enough to hold a rocker and a twin bed. I thought it might help Reed to have a little outside space of his own and a private way in and outta the house."

"You always think of everything and everybody." Anna patted Dolly's hand.

"You're mighty thoughtful yourself, honey—both o' you girls."

"What you need us to do next?" Daisy asked. "If you don't mind my sayin', this room might need a little paint touch-up."

"Sweetheart, that's like sayin' Si's ol' tractor needs a little engine tune-up."

Daisy looked around the room. "Why don't you just let me and Anna make this our project?"

"That's a great idea!" Anna agreed. "You won't even have to come in here till it's ready."

Dolly smoothed the handkerchief across her lap. "You girls are mighty kind. Do you think you could make it look . . . completely different? I think that might help."

"Done," Daisy said as Dolly slowly folded the handkerchief into a neat square.

"You girls fix Reed a nice room, and I'll cook him some good food, and we'll just hope Little Mama's house can put him right."

fourteen

Si and Dolly were sitting in their porch swing, enjoying a Sunday afternoon breeze, when a black Ford pickup came slowly around the loop and pulled into their driveway. As the truck door opened and a tall young man with a walking cane stepped out, they went to greet him.

"Last time I saw you, son, you were a couple o' feet shorter," Si said as he shook Reed's free hand. "And you didn't have all them muscles. It's mighty good to see you."

"Thank you, Mr. Chandler."

"None o' that. You're all grown up. We're just plain ol' Si and Dolly."

Dolly took Reed's hand and held it between hers. "You prob'ly don't remember me, but I remember you," she said. "I always thought you had the prettiest eyes I'd 'bout ever seen on a child—and you still do."

"They've seen a lot." Reed looked down, as if he needed to protect Dolly from his wartime visions.

"We know, honey. And if you decide you want to talk about any of it, we're right here. But if you don't, ain't nobody in this house gonna push you."

"I 'preciate that."

"You go on in with Dolly, and I'll grab your suitcase," Si said.

"I can carry it," Reed said.

"I know you can, but I'm hopin' you'll let an ol' fella show off for his best girl."

Reed smiled. "Okay. Go on and show off for Miss Dolly."

He took a duffle bag from the truck seat and let Si carry his larger suitcase. Dolly led him to his room, with Si following close behind.

"I'll let Dolly get you settled," Si said as he set the suitcase at the foot of Reed's bed. "Whenever you like, you and me can dip a line or light a pipe and have us a good visit."

"I'd enjoy that. And thank you."

Si patted the young vet on the back. "We're the ones oughta be thankin' you. Get yourself comfortable and we'll talk later on."

Dolly sat down on the edge of the bed next to Reed, who was surveying his room. "I figured I'd be upstairs with your other boarders," he said.

"You're not just another boarder. You're like family to us. I thought you might be more comfortable here, where you've got your own door in and outta the house right there." She pointed to the new door. "There's a little porch if you want some fresh air and outside space to yourself. But I think once you get to know ever'body here, you'll feel right at home with 'em. And if you decide you'd be happier upstairs, there's still an empty room up there."

Reed took another look around and gestured to the new door. "Y'all put that in just for me?"

Dolly nodded. "We figured there'd be times when you wanted comp'ny and times when you didn't."

He gazed at her for a moment and then squinted slightly. "You used to cut me two or three pieces o' your chocolate cake even though I only ate the icin'. You let me scrape off all the chocolate I wanted, without eatin' a bite o' the cake."

Dolly clapped her hands together and laughed. "I can't believe you remember my chocolate cake!"

"Why'd you do that—let me scrape off the icin', I mean?"

"Because you dearly loved it, and I didn't see any reason to make a sweet child like you eat somethin' you *didn't* want just to get somethin' you *did* want."

"What'd you do with the cake—once I had scraped it clean, I mean?"

Dolly leaned toward Reed like a conspirator passing state secrets. "Fed it to Si's huntin' dog. Ol' Blue gained a few pounds every time you came over."

Reed smiled and reached into his shirt pocket. "I need to pay you my rent."

"You don't owe us a thing. We're tickled to have you."

"I 'preciate that, but I can't stay if you won't let me pay my way."

"Well, alright then." She took his rent money and stood up to go. "I reckon I need to get out o' your way and let you unpack."

"Don't go—I mean, don't feel like you have to go."

Dolly sat back down with him. "If you remember my chocolate cake, what else do you remember about this ol' place?"

The room was quiet while he thought about it. "I remember a creek and a pretty pond—way back in the woods?"

Dolly smiled. "That's right. The Tanyard Creek is right behind the lake—that's how we filled it up, by pumpin' creek water into a big hole Si dug. And the pond you're thinkin' about is the slough offa the Tanyard. Si and your daddy used to carry you fishin' there all summer long."

Reed thought again for a minute. "Still got my sword?"

Dolly reached under the bed and pulled out a small toy sword made from a piece of broom handle painted silver, with a homemade hilt. "Aye, Cap'n Chauvin," she said.

"I can't believe this." Reed shook his head as he took the

sword and held it like a precious artifact that might disintegrate before his eyes. "Hard to believe my hands were ever small enough to do battle with a sword this size."

"I never saw a young'un take to that ol' pirate story the way you did," Dolly said. "You spent many a rainy day up in my attic, capturin' enemy ships and pilin' up loot."

"Didn't you rig me up a treasure chest?"

"Oh, I'd forgot about that! We took the little trunk I had when I was a child and stuffed most of it with a blanket. Then we piled some ol' costume jewelry and silver-plate dishes on top of it. You'd always bring me a present from your treasure chest when your ship docked in the attic."

Reed smiled. "Sorry you had to act excited when I gave you back your own stuff—and I'm sorry I never found the real treasure."

"That's okay, honey. You just keep lookin'. No better way to pass a rainy day than lookin' for lost treasure."

Reed studied Dolly's face like a road map back to his childhood. "You doctored my knee when I fell offa my bike in front o' your house."

"Oh, that was a bad, bad tumble you took." Dolly shook her head at the memory of all that blood on a child's leg. "I was worried your mama might have to carry you on to the doctor, but you healed up."

"That was a long time ago."

"Yes, son, it was. But you can still mend. You've just got some deeper cuts this time, and they're gonna take a while."

"What if they never get better?"

"I won't believe that. I've got faith in the Lord, and I've got faith in you."

"I'm doin' my best. But I don't seem to be gettin' anywhere. You promise you'll let me know if I get to be a burden so I won't ruin everything here?"

"You're not gonna ruin a thing. Just give 'em a chance, Reed. They're all real good people. And I know you've been keepin' to yourself quite a bit since you got back, but that's not good for you, honey—not all the time anyhow. I think I maybe under-stand why you couldn't go home. If I was your mama, I might want so badly to get back the boy they took from me that I'd put all kinda pressure on you to get well—without even meanin' to. I know you can't be that boy I used to know, but you can be a good man—and a happy one."

Reed stared at the floor. "Hope so."

"Would you like to have supper with the rest of us tonight? Most nights I cook and we eat at the table, and then whoever's here for lunch gets a sandwich. But on Sundays I flip that around because I think ever'body ought to have a nice family dinner after church, so we break out the sandwich bread on Sunday nights."

"I think I might need to just get my bearin's tonight, if that's okay?"

"'Course it is. I'll bring you somethin' at six unless you're hungry now?"

"No, ma'am—six'll be just fine. And thank you. I'll get my-self to the table in the mornin'."

"We eat breakfast at six too, but now, if you change your mind and don't show up, I'll fix you a plate. Nobody's gonna hurry you, honey."

"Thank you—for everything. And if you'd do me one more favor—could you ask Si to keep his gun cabinet locked? Some-times those flashbacks . . . well, they're awful real, and I just don't wanna take a chance . . ."

Dolly nodded as she reached over and wrapped her hands around his. "Are you too grown to hug?"

"No, ma'am."

They put their arms around each other and held on, just as

they had so many times when he was a child, shyly peeking into her kitchen in search of chocolate cake.

Reed stepped off the porch Si had built for him and looked around. It was all coming back—the way his footsteps echoed on the wood floors of the old house with its towering ceilings, the sound of a breeze stirring the pecan trees, the sense of security he had always felt on this old loop. He was twelve when they moved away, and he had never felt at home anywhere but here. Even when he was overseas, he longed for his family and an escape from the horrors engulfing him, but not for the farm his mother had inherited, a place where he had always felt like an alien.

Slowly making his way out of the yard and around the loop, he spotted a small, neatly kept cottage. The old woman sitting on the front porch beckoned to him. His bad leg was especially bothersome today, stiff and sore from the long ride.

"Hello!" the woman called.

"Hello," Reed answered, trying to remember her. He could tell from the clouds covering her eyes that she couldn't see him. "I know you." He said it out loud, though he didn't mean to.

"Yes, I expect you do. Join me while you consider it."

Steps were especially hard for him when his leg locked up, but he managed to climb them and sit down next to her. Gradually the fog shrouding his happiest memories began to clear, and he could see his childhood self standing on this very porch.

"You're Miss Lillian!"

"Yes!" She laughed, still staring straight ahead.

"You used to make me tea cakes."

"Then you must be young Reed."

"How did you know?"

"Of all the children on this loop, you loved my tea cakes best of all. I made a big batch every week just for you."

"But why? Why'd you do that for me?"

"Can you not remember yourself?"

"Ma'am?"

"Have all your memories of that long-ago boy faded away?"

Reed felt like he had just taken shrapnel to the gut, and he was silent for a moment before he finally answered. "Yes, ma'am. I have a hard time rememberin' him at all."

"Well, we must help you get him back."

"You really think you can do that?"

"I know it to be so. You are wounded. I can hear it in your gait and in your voice. You need not explain the how or the why unless you wish. But you must not give up on healing. There is healing to be had here, young Reed."

"I wanna believe that."

"Then do! And here is where to begin. Nothing soothes like flowing water. Go into the woods and follow the Tanyard to its shallows. Sit down on the cool earth and listen to the creek splash against the rocks. Go now. Then come back someday soon and tell me what became of it."

"You want me to go to the creek right now?"

"Yes! No time like the present. Be on your way, and fare thee well."

Reed was befuddled but, for reasons he couldn't explain, felt compelled to do as she said.

"I'll be back," he said as he left the porch. "Is there anything you need?"

"No, young Reed. Just the pleasure of your company now and again."

"Bye for now."

Lillian waved. "Goodbye."

Reed stood on the porch of the skating rink and looked out over the water. It was so clean and clear. He thought about the great lake he had crossed in Tunisia, a place that would've been beautiful if war hadn't sullied it. Si's lake and roller rink were closed on Sunday, but Reed could imagine what this place must have looked like just yesterday, with all the swimmers and skaters swarming it. He walked to the far end of the porch, stepped onto the trail, and followed it to a creek he had loved as a child but barely remembered now.

This place was paradise. Deep woods and clear, flowing water, a mossy carpet along the water's edge, and birdsong—constant birdsong. That was something he hadn't heard in the desert. But he refused to let his mind go to those dark places right now.

Limping alongside the creek, he made his way to the shallows and spotted a girl leaning against a tree and holding a book in her lap. In the Army he had learned to move silently, but his limp had robbed him of stealth, and the girl looked up when his bad leg snapped a few twigs underfoot. He could see he had startled her. He seemed to startle a lot of people since he'd gotten back.

"Hey," she said.

"Hey," he said, giving her a smile and a wave so she wouldn't be scared.

"You must be Reed."

"How'd you know?"

"Not many guys your age left around here, so I figure you must be Dolly's vet."

"How'd you know I was comin'?"

"Me and Anna—she lives with Dolly and Si—we got your room ready. You like it?"

"I do."

"You wanna sit?"

"I'll try—pretty stiff today." Reed limped over to a tree next to the girl and began a familiar process—figuring out how to manage simple movements that he once did effortlessly, automatically even.

She seemed to guess his dilemma. "Hey, you know what you could do? Hook your cane over that real low limb right there and hold on to it. That way you won't have to try and bend your bad leg while you lower yourself down. And then you can use it to pull up. I'll help if you need me to."

Reed followed her advice and managed to get comfortable against the tree, facing the girl and stretching out his long legs.

"You handled that real good," she said.

Reed looked at her. She was beautiful. Creamy skin, smoky green eyes, a dimpled smile, and not a drop of makeup—she didn't need any. Her caramel hair was cut short, which suited her. And on a Sunday, when most girls would have on a dress, she was wearing overalls.

"You know who I am, but I don't know you," he said.

"I'm Daisy. I board on around the loop with Ella Brown, but me and Anna are friends, so I spend a lotta time at the Chandlers'."

"Nice to meet you, Daisy."

"Same here."

"What you got there?" He pointed to the book, which she turned around so he could see—a drawing of a young woman with flowing blonde hair, wearing a long dress and sitting on a mossy rock in the middle of the creek.

Reed was impressed. "That's really good. Who is it?"

Daisy shrugged. "Just guessin' at what a girl who lived here a long time ago mighta looked like."

"Can I see it up close?" he asked. Daisy handed him her sketchbook. He studied the portrait and then said, "Catherine?"

"*You* know about Catherine and Andre?"

"Even got my own pirate sword," he said as he handed back

the sketchbook. "Dolly made it for me out of a broom handle when I was little. And it was under my bed when I got here."

"That is just like her to keep a broom-handle pirate sword all these years."

"You draw for a livin'?"

"No, I just enjoy it. And it kinda settles my mind. You got anything to settle your mind?"

"I've been considerin' hard liquor."

Daisy grinned. "That won't get you nothin' but a headache." She was looking at him, not the eye-batting way girls did when they used to flirt with him, but like an object—like that mossy rock in the creek. "Don't take this the wrong way," she said, "but you've got the strangest eyes I've ever seen."

Daisy was throwing him completely off balance. "I'm not sure what to say to that."

She actually laughed out loud. Reed couldn't remember the last time he had made a girl laugh.

"Maybe that didn't come out right," she said. "I mean they're strange in a good way. They're kinda blue and kinda silver all at the same time. I'm not sure I can match that color, but I'd like to try. You mind if I draw 'em while we talk?"

Reed frowned and blinked at her. "You wanna draw my eyes?"

"Yeah. If it makes you feel weird, just tell me and I'll stop." Daisy settled back against the tree and stared at his eyes. She appeared to be taking dimensions.

"What should I do while you . . . do that?" he asked, trying to keep his eyes open.

Daisy was laughing again. "You can blink, silly! You don't have to be super still or anything. I'm just tryin' to figure out that color."

Reed relaxed against the tree and looked at Daisy. "So what brought you here?"

She kept looking back and forth from his eyes to her sketchbook. "The war. My husband, Charlie, enlisted, so I moved here from Mississippi and got a job at the plant." Just as he felt a dip in his spirits to learn that she was married, Daisy paused for a moment and then asked, "You know any tail gunners over there?"

Now it was Reed who was searching her eyes. They didn't have that hopeful look women always gave him when they asked if he had seen their husbands overseas. "Why? You lose one?"

Daisy nodded. "What you reckon that was like—for Charlie, I mean?"

Reed picked up a smooth twig from the ground and studied it as he absently twirled it through his fingers, carefully considering what he should tell her. He had seen the shattered remains of fallen tail gunners. The ones who didn't go down with their planes were usually unrecognizable when they were pulled out of there. Finally, he looked up and gave Daisy his answer. "Quick. It woulda been real quick."

Daisy seemed relieved and returned to her drawing. "Sometimes I see Charlie. It's like he just appears in the strangest places, lookin' as real as you do, but only for a few seconds."

"What's he doin' when he appears to you?"

Daisy studied Reed's eyes again and made a few strokes with her pencil before looking up at him. "Nothin' much. Last time, he was at the curb market, just walkin' through the tomato bins with his hands in his pockets. But then he disappeared into the squash."

"Does he ever say anything?"

"No. And he never looks at me either. You think I'm crazy?"

"Oh yeah." Again he made her laugh. Oddly, Daisy's laugh brought him more satisfaction than anything since he'd gotten home. "You're not crazy. You just miss him."

Daisy shook her head as if she were trying to shake off the ghostly appearances of her dead husband. "Why don't you tell me your story? It'll take your mind offa bein' stared at."

"You want me to tell you about the war?"

"Is that your whole story?" Now she wasn't looking at him like an artist scrutinizing an object, but like someone who would see straight through any smoke screen he threw out.

"Feels like it sometimes. Everybody here—they remember me as this little kid. If they knew what I had to do over there, I doubt they'd want me under the same roof with 'em."

"Dolly said you were a medic."

"That's right."

"Medics save soldiers' lives—what's wrong with that?"

"When you're a medic, well . . . sometimes I had to kill theirs to keep 'em offa me long enough to save ours, and that kinda killin' don't usually happen at a distance."

Daisy leaned forward to get a closer look at his eyes. She made a few strokes with three different pencils and then looked up. "There's a real important word in what you just said. And it's *had*. Sometimes you *had* to. And if you hadn'a done what you had to do, you'd be layin' in the ground like Charlie. So would a lotta other soldiers."

"You believe in bein' direct, don't you?"

"I'm sorry. Was that rude?" Daisy seemed worried.

"No, it's great. Everybody around me's been walkin' on egg-shells since I got back. I don't know how to put 'em at ease because I'm not at ease myself."

"I follow that," Daisy said, picking up a piece of charcoal and returning to her drawing. "Women usually end up talkin' about their husbands and kids when they get together, and I ain't got either one. They get all jittery when they're complainin' about their men and remember mine's gone."

"You plannin' to stick around here?"

Daisy sighed and looked up. "I don't know. I think I'm waitin' on somethin' to happen, but I got no idea what it is."

"I follow that." Reed grinned as he mimicked her response.

Daisy rolled her eyes. "Now you're makin' fun o' me."

"No, I'm not—I promise I'm not. I just know exactly what you're talkin' about."

"How 'bout you? Think you'll stay a while?"

"Long as I don't make any trouble for Si and Dolly. Truth is, I haven't been where I wanted to be since I was a kid. Kinda nice to take a minute to breathe and maybe figure out what to do next."

Daisy made a few final strokes with a piece of charcoal and studied her sketchpad. "Just so you know, I went over to the lib'ry in Childersburg and read up on battle fatigue. Some o' those soldiers end up killin' themselves. Or killin' their own family members 'cause they think their brothers and sisters are Germans or Japanese." She looked up at Reed. "But you're not gonna do that."

"How do you know?"

"Because I can see it." She turned the portrait around and held it up.

Daisy had drawn his face and dark hair in charcoal but his eyes in vivid color. It was like looking into a mirror and staring at a stranger all at the same time. The man in the drawing looked so . . . kind. Reed didn't feel kind after everything he had been forced to see and do. It was like the war had dislocated him from himself. The Alabama boy who'd left and the combat medic who'd returned couldn't seem to figure out how to live peaceably in the same body—or the same mind. He was a real Humpty Dumpty: all the king's horses and all the king's men couldn't put him back together again.

Daisy closed the sketchpad and relaxed against her tree. "Can you tell me about your leg? Not how you got hurt—I reckon you don't wanna think about that—but what the doctors say?"

Reed rubbed his knee and tried to bend it. "This is pretty much it. They don't think I'll ever walk any better than I do now."

"You gonna go with that?"

"They're the doctors, so I reckon they know. They gave me these exercises that might loosen it up, but I can't do 'em without help, and I can't afford to pay a nurse, so I guess that's that."

"I'll do it."

"What?"

"I'll help you."

"I can't ask you to do that."

"You didn't ask me. I just told you I would."

"That's mighty kind o' you, but I can't let you—"

"Oh, for heaven's sake," Daisy interrupted him. "Men are the most aggravatin' creatures on earth. I used to keep a house and help run a farm, but now all I do is draw. And help Dolly whenever she needs me. I got a lotta time on my hands, which I don't much care for. There's such a thing as too much time to think."

Reed considered her offer. Why would a pretty girl like Daisy want to spend her time with a worn-out soldier who walked like a grandpa? But she seemed completely sincere. "You promise you'll tell me if you get tired of it?"

"Sure."

"Will you let me pay you?"

"Of course not. We'll start tomorrow mornin' after breakfast. And we'll have to do your exercises on your porch. Dolly doesn't allow what she calls 'single unmarrieds' in any of her bedrooms."

Reed smiled. "That doesn't surprise me."

"Hey, you better get goin'. It's gotta be close to six, and you know what that means over at Dolly's."

Reed reached up and started to pull himself up by the cane hanging overhead but lost his grip and slipped back down. He leaned back against the tree and closed his eyes in disgust.

"Wait a minute," Daisy said. She came over and got on her knees beside him. "Use my shoulder as a prop on this side and pull up with your cane on the other."

"What if I hurt you?"

"Then I'll holler and you'll stop if you don't want me to smack you."

Reed had to smile, as foolish as he felt for being unable to do something as simple as stand up. Holding on to Daisy's shoulder gave him just enough leverage to grip the cane and hoist himself off the ground.

"See?" Daisy said, standing up and dusting off her knees. "Problem solved."

"Thanks. You headin' home too?"

"Guess so. Lemme grab my sketchbook and I'll walk with you."

As the two of them slowly made their way out of the woods, Daisy offered Reed some advice. "By the way, you might wanna steer clear o' the slough on Saturday afternoons."

"How come?"

"Because Saturday's about the only time Anna and her husband, Jesse, have to be alone. The slough's their love nest."

"Roger that."

Daisy grinned up at him. "It's bad enough you got a bum leg. Wouldn't want you to see somethin' that might make you go blind."

fifteen

Reed awoke to the sound of footsteps overhead. He looked at the alarm clock on his nightstand. Five fifteen. Everybody must be getting ready for work. Sitting up, he began the painstaking process of putting on his clothes. His leg was always especially stiff in the morning, which made it difficult to get his pants on, but somehow he managed. By the time he finished shaving in the downstairs bathroom that Dolly had invited him to share, it was almost six.

Cane in hand, he made his way through the old house, stopping now and again to run his hand over a lamp or a painting he remembered. He had no trouble finding his way to the grand dining room in the center of the house, which was alive with conversation as Dolly's boarders gathered for breakfast.

Faced with a roomful of strangers, he had a sudden urge to run for cover. The only thing holding him there was a fascination with the whole scene before him—the idea that, while people like this were gathering around a dining room table and talking about the weather, some soldier was bleeding out on the battlefield, screaming for his mother. Artillery was booming and tanks were rolling and battle-hardened troops were cursing their green lieutenants. Any minute now, some soldier would get blown to bits and leave a shattered young widow to raise his fatherless children.

Just as his heart began its familiar pounding, Dolly called his name. "Reed! Come and join us, honey!"

He could only hope his lips didn't quiver when he tried to smile as the men all greeted him and shook his hand. Harry and Jesse introduced Reed to their wives.

"You're Daisy's friend," he said when he met Anna.

She looked surprised. "How do you know Daisy?"

"I took a walk by the creek yesterday afternoon, and she was sittin' on the bank with her sketchbook. She told me the two o' you got my room ready. Thank you."

"You're welcome. I hope it's comfortable?"

"Perfect."

"Anna, honey, will you help me get everything on the table?" Dolly called from the kitchen door.

"Well, now, I might not be able to boil water, but I can carry food," Evelyn said as she followed Anna into the kitchen. The men took their seats, and the women brought Dolly's breakfast to the table: scrambled eggs, country ham, homemade biscuits and pear preserves, sausage gravy, creamy grits with fresh butter, a pitcher of cold milk, and coffee.

"Did Daisy show you any of her drawings?" Anna asked Reed.

"Yeah, she's really good." He didn't tell them about the portrait she had drawn of him. Somehow that seemed too personal.

"Before I forget, I have news to report," Harry said. "I picked up a *Talladega Daily Home* yesterday, and you'll never guess who was on the front page."

"FDR," Evelyn said.

"Well, of *course* he was there, but who else?" Harry said, looking around the table. "Nobody wants to guess?"

"Out with it," Evelyn said.

"Our very good friends the Clanahans from Reno, Nevada!"

Everybody around the table looked stunned, except for Reed, who had no idea who they were talking about.

"Who are the Clanahans?" he asked Joe. Dolly had seated the two of them next to each other.

"The most detestable twosome you ever did see," Joe explained. "Boarded here for a coupla weeks till they finally pushed Si too far and he run 'em off with his shotgun."

"What on earth were those two doin' on the front page o' the paper?" Dolly wanted to know.

"They had been arrested!" Harry said with relish.

"What!" Dolly exclaimed.

"Can't think of anybody I'd rather see locked up," Si said.

"Well, they're out on bail now," Harry said. "The newspaper said they were caught attempting to vandalize the property of a coworker who accused the not-so-honorable Mr. Clanahan of stealing parts from the Army factory."

"Si, reckon we oughta be worried?" Dolly asked.

"The men o' the house can keep an eye out for anything suspicious, Dolly, but I doubt they'd show up here. They've done seen the business end o' my shotgun once. Doubt they'd wanna eyeball it again."

"Still makes me nervous," she said.

"No need," Si assured her.

"I didn't mean to worry the ladies," Harry said. "Pay me no mind, Dolly. I just wanted us to have an opportunity to rejoice together at the thought of those two behind bars."

"Well, we've rejoiced, so let us move on," Evelyn said.

"Reed, are you a fisherman?" Joe asked.

"Used to be. It's a little tricky now—kinda hard to get in and out of a boat or stand for very long."

"Well, that just gives Si and Harry an excuse to rig somethin' up for you," Joe said.

"Perhaps pulleys could be involved," Harry suggested.

"Si's gonna want something motorized," Jesse said with a grin.

Evelyn shook her head. "Reed, I am afraid Si brings out the mad scientist in my husband, so you will just have to excuse them both. Perhaps you can be a positive influence. Joe and Jesse have proven absolutely useless, as they merely fuel the fire and get right on board with whatever contraption the other two dream up."

Everybody laughed. Reed smiled and looked around the table as the morning chatter went on. There were no anxious stares telegraphing, *Please tell us this is the day you'll forget the war and turn back into the boy you used to be*. Most of these people had no idea who he used to be. He could breathe easy—really easy—for the first time since he'd shipped out.

What if she doesn't show? Reed never considered that possibility until he had changed into a T-shirt and his old high school gym shorts. He was sitting on the edge of the twin bed on the little porch Si had built for him when he heard an engine turning over and over. He could tell by the sound of it that it wasn't going to crank.

Grabbing his keys, he made his way outside and found Anna at the wheel of Jesse's truck, trying the ignition for him while he looked under the hood.

"Can I help?" Reed asked.

"The others already left, and the foreman will fire me if I'm late," Jesse said. "If you've got any ideas, I'd be grateful."

Reed took a look under the hood. "Can you turn it one more time, Anna?" He listened to the engine turn over and over. It wasn't going to fire. "That don't sound like a quick fix, Jesse. Tell you what—take my keys. You can drive my truck to work and I'll see what I can do with yours this afternoon."

"I couldn't do that, man."

"Where am I gonna go? It'll give me somethin' to do. Get outta here so you won't be late. Just set my toolbox outta the back before you leave."

"Thanks—really, thank you," Jesse said. He and Anna started for Reed's truck, but then he stopped, turned, and came back. "I just want you to know—I tried to go. They wouldn't take me."

Reed shrugged. "You're goin' where they sent you. Same as the rest of us."

While Anna said goodbye to Jesse, Reed hobbled back to his porch and found Daisy standing at the screen door.

"What's with that?" She was pointing to the bedsheet Dolly had tacked over the only wall of screen wire that was visible from the loop road.

"Hey," he said. "Come on in."

As Daisy stepped inside, he sat down on the bed and explained the sheet. "When I told Dolly you were gonna help me, she tacked that up there—said the gossips on the loop might talk, so she'd just put a stop to it before it started."

Daisy shook her head. "That's Dolly. She's right, though. When you live someplace where nothin' happens, people talk about anything they can get their hands on. I'm guessin' that's why both doors to your room are wide open?"

"Yep."

Daisy pulled the porch rocker beside the bed and sat down. "So tell me what we're doin'."

He handed her a couple of sheets of paper with exercise diagrams printed on them. "The idea is that if you help me do these for a while, I might get to where I can do 'em myself. And then if I do 'em long enough and often enough, my leg might get closer to normal so I can stop walkin' like I'm one step away from the old folks' home."

"I follow that," she said, which always made him smile. "Looks like you're supposed to be lyin' down for the first one."

As Reed lay down and stretched out on the small bed, Daisy scrutinized his bad leg for the first time. "Dang," she said.

"The answer is no. You cannot draw my leg."

"I didn't say nothin' about drawin' it."

"But you were thinkin' it."

"Okay, yeah, I was thinkin' it. I don't mean to be an oddball. It's just that drawin' things helps me understand 'em, you know?"

"I don't think you're an oddball. But there ain't no way you're drawin' this mangled mess."

He knew how his leg must look to her. It was covered with long, jagged scars where another medic and later surgeons had worked to save it after shrapnel tore it to pieces. His knee was especially bad.

Daisy studied the first exercise on the papers he had given her. "This first one looks simple enough. I'm just supposed to lift your leg a little bit off the bed and help you bend your knee in toward you."

Standing by the bed, Daisy put one hand under Reed's knee and the other under his ankle and lifted his leg a few inches off the bed. But his knee wouldn't bend at all. "You can push a little harder," he said. He could tell she was being as gentle as possible as she tried to push down on his ankle and up on his knee, but he still felt a sharp pain and winced.

"Hold on a second—stay right there." Daisy lowered his leg onto the bed and went into the house.

It was so depressing to think about walking like this for the rest of his life. At twenty-one, he was looking at a lot of years walking like an old man and being of no use to anybody. Just as he felt himself beginning to choke in what he privately called The Dust Storm, Daisy came back onto the porch. She was carrying a wet towel.

"Let's try somethin'," she said, wrapping the towel around his knee. It was warm, bordering on hot, and it felt wonderful. "Just let that sit there for a minute. While we wait, why don't you tell me somethin' you remember about Dolly from when you were a kid."

He stared up at the ceiling as he remembered. "First time I ever took my bike out by myself—hadn't been ridin' for more than a coupla days—I got a little full o' myself and came around that curve out there way too fast. Hit some gravel and went tumblin'. Tore my knee up. Kinda rattled me too, because I wasn't even cryin' when Dolly came runnin' across her yard. Guess she had been in the garden or somethin' when it happened. I remember just lyin' there, lookin' up at the sky—prob'ly in shock now that I think about it—and Dolly scooped me up and ran in the house with me. Laid me down right on her kitchen table, put some dish towels under my head, and went to doctorin' my leg and wipin' my face with a cool towel. I musta passed out because all I remember is that coolness on my face and then wakin' up with my knee all bandaged and Dolly hoverin' over me."

"So this knee thing with you has been goin' on for a while."

Reed looked at her and smiled. "You could say that."

"Tell me another one. How 'bout somethin' that don't involve blood."

"That's easy. Dolly's chocolate cake . . ."

As Reed started talking about Dolly's chocolate icing, Daisy loosened the hot towel around his knee and began to gently move the stiff joint up and down, ever so slightly. He told her how the icing tasted like fudge and Dolly never made him eat the cake.

"Sounds like her," Daisy said. "'Course, she coulda saved a lotta eggs by just makin' you a pan o' fudge."

"Yeah, but that wouldn'a been near as special. There was

somethin' about knowin' I was supposed to eat that cake but didn't have to. I figure Dolly knew that."

"Well, look at you," Daisy said.

While he was focused on Dolly's cake, Daisy had managed a small bend in his knee. He could see it. He could feel it.

"Don't try to do a bigger bend," she said. "Just try to repeat the little one a few times." She helped as he repeated the first bend four or five times and ended with a slightly deeper one before he needed to rest. She sat down in the rocker beside him.

"Daisy, thank you. I really mean it. How'd you know to try the towel?"

"Daddy always kept horses. You'd never try to work a horse with cold legs, so I figured . . ."

"In other words, you just took me to the vet?"

"Next time you get a rabies shot."

The two of them were still laughing when Dolly came through Reed's room and onto the porch.

"What's all this commotion I hear? Y'all are havin' too much fun to be gettin' much done."

"Hey, Dolly," Daisy said. "Reed here just figured out that I'm usin' Daddy's ol' horse-trainin' tricks to make his knee bend again."

"Well, I reckon anything that works on four legs oughta work just as well on two. Anybody want lemonade?"

"Sure," Daisy said.

Dolly went into the kitchen for a minute and then came out with three glasses. Reed sat up on the edge of his bed to make room for her.

"Hey, Dolly, where's Anna?" Daisy asked.

"Over at the lake helpin' out. She's been settin' up the concession stand right after breakfast and watchin' over the shallow end, where the little ones play. Jo-Jo and the other girls were all too happy to volunteer as lifeguards for the deep end, just so all the boys will see 'em in that tall chair with the big umbrella. They always look like they just stepped outta the beauty parlor when they climb into that chair."

"I'm guessin' Jo-Jo's a regular?"

"Oh my land!" Dolly said. "If that young'un don't soon find herself a husband, she's gonna run us all crazy. Reed, you better not poke your head outta this house if you don't wanna get swarmed with husband-huntin' girls."

He glanced down at his leg. "I don't think I'm what they have in mind."

"Well then, they're just plain stupid!"

"You tell 'em, Dolly," Daisy said. "Reed, you musta been one fine kid for Dolly to take up for you like that."

"I don't remember much about him," Reed said, "but if he keeps me on Dolly's good side, he's aces."

"You just wait," Dolly said. "I'm gonna introduce the two o' you to each other."

"We prob'ly oughta put some ice on that knee to keep the swellin' down." Daisy got out of her rocker and headed for the kitchen.

Reed winked at Dolly. "Don't I get a sugar cube?" he called after Daisy.

"No," she shot back. "But you can graze in the backyard if you want to."

sixteen

Joe Dolphus pulled two folding chairs from the bed of his truck and set them up under a patch of shade.

"This place looks familiar," Reed said.

"I 'magine Si and your daddy brung you here one time or another. Si said it was prob'ly a waterin' hole for horses back in the day, but he stocked it with catfish and bass years ago, and they still bite pretty good."

Reed had been at Dolly's for several weeks now, but this was the first time he'd had an opportunity to go fishing. He and Joe unloaded fishing rods, a small cooler, and a tackle box, then cast their lines and settled in.

"I can't think of a thing in the world I'd rather do than drop a hook in the water," Joe said.

"Me neither. I never cared much for huntin', but I always loved to fish. I'll do about anything that gets me on the water."

"You ever think o' buildin' you a cabin or somethin' on the river?"

"Never did before, but now it seems like anything's possible—anything or nothin'. Can't make up my mind which."

"I remember feelin' the same way when I came home from

the first World War. That don't help much, but maybe it's somethin'."

They saw a fish jump a few yards away from the spot where they'd cast.

"Now, I think that's just plain mean-spirited in a fish to do somethin' like that," Joe said, which brought a chuckle from Reed. "You an' me oughta commit ourselves to landin' that rascal in a skillet this very day."

They reeled in their lines and cast again where the fish were jumping and then sat quietly, watching the ripples roll across the water and listening to the cicadas.

"Daddy kept tellin' me I'd be fine." Reed broke the silence but kept watching his line in the water. "And I don't mean him any disrespect, but he spent his war workin' for a general at a command center in London. He was never on the front line. It's different up there."

"Yes, son, it is. It's mighty different up there."

"Si told me you were at the front. Where'd you serve, if you don't mind my askin'?"

"In France. At the Marne."

"Against the Germans."

"That's one word for 'em."

Reed smiled at Joe. "We came up with a few ourselves. Guess they had some choice names for us too."

"I don't know why some men can come home and go back to business like it never happened," Joe said. "Me—I couldn't. It was awful hard for a long time. But I was lucky to have Margaret. She was a lovin' wife and a patient woman. Stood right by me. Took us a few years to leave the worst of it behind—all the nightmares and the flashbacks. You gotta work through 'em on your own time, Reed. Don't let nobody tell you it oughta be this way or that. You helped defend your country, an' you can be proud o' that for the rest o' your life. But them captains ain't around when your ghosts go to walkin'. You gotta face them rascals down the best way you know how. If you'll take an ol' man's advice, find you a helpmate. Find you a good wife who'll see you through—and who'll let you see her through. Ain't nothin' better." Joe pointed to Reed's cork. "Wup! Looka yonder—you 'bout to let one get away."

Reed felt the tug on his line, let the hook set, and reeled in a big catfish. He put it in a basket and cast again. "I just can't help wonderin' . . . if the damage is permanent."

"Son, anybody that goes through combat comes out of it with permanent damage—if he's lucky enough to come out of it at all."

"I'm not talkin' about flashbacks or nightmares or stiff knees. I'm talkin' about . . . I don't know what to call it."

Joe nodded. "You're wonderin' if you're still a decent human bein'."

"I didn't have to kill many, but I had to kill some. And what I felt when they were comin' at me, tryin' to end me so they could get to friends o' mine who were already bleedin' and sufferin'—well, it scares me to think about it."

"I know that feelin'."

"Aren't we s'posed to love our enemies?"

"S'posed to. But that's a mighty hard thing to do when they're runnin' at you with a bayonet."

"Near impossible."

"Lemme ask you somethin', Reed. If you was to look up and see a little German boy—one barely big enough to walk— toddlin' toward the edge o' that pond, what would you do?"

"Get there quick as I could—make sure he didn't fall in."

"But he's a German. Might grow up to fight your children one day."

"Yeah, but right now he's just an innocent kid—same as any kids I might have."

"Maybe you don't hate your enemy as much as you think you do."

Reed felt a tug on his line and reeled in another fish.

"You're doin' all the catchin'," Joe said. "I don't think I'm gonna fish with you no more."

Reed smiled at him. "You keep sharin' your wisdom and I just might share my catfish with you."

"I'm from Mississippi, Reed. You couldn't shut me up if you tried."

seventeen

After weeks of working with Daisy, Reed was now adding exercises on his own. He had asked Dolly if he could install an overhead bar on the porch ceiling so he could do chin-ups. He was determined to get himself fit again—for what, he had no idea.

Holding on to the back of the porch rocker, he raised his bad knee up as much as he could. Not yet hip high but getting closer. He repeated the movement several times, pushing himself as hard as he could.

"You fixin' to fire me?"

He looked up to see Daisy standing at the screen door. "Actually, I was gonna double your salary. What's two times nothin'?"

Daisy laughed and came onto the porch. She had worn her bathing suit under her overalls and was carrying a towel she had brought from Ella's. Reed had on a T-shirt with his swim trunks. He grabbed a towel from Si and Dolly's bathroom and a pocketknife he kept on his nightstand.

"I'm goin' swimmin'—what you got in mind?" Daisy asked, pointing to the knife.

"I know it sounds strange—prob'ly is strange—but I still like to know I could defend myself if I had to. You mind?"

"You can't do much damage with a pocketknife."

148

"You can if you know how."

Daisy looked at the knife and then at Reed. She held out her hand. "I'll put it in my pocket."

He handed her the knife and they headed out, taking a rougher trail that led behind the skating rink. Reed wasn't quite ready for the stares of all the swimmers at the lake.

Once they reached the slough, Daisy said, "We can wade in for a coupla yards, but then it drops off real quick."

Reed pulled his T-shirt over his head just in time to see Daisy step out of her overalls, which he now realized were drastically oversized. She had a figure like a movie star and legs like a dancer. It was all he could do not to stare, and he had to wonder why she was hiding all that under baggy denim.

The two of them stepped into the water and waded toward the center. Daisy was right. The water deepened quickly. At first Reed was relying mostly on his arms, but as he began to relax and move his legs, he could easily tread water.

"Feels a lot better than walkin', I'll bet," Daisy said.

"It does. Feels a lot looser. Lemme guess. You've tried this on horses."

Daisy laughed. "No, I never took the horses swimmin'. C'mon. Let's see if we can make it to that big rock by the bank over there."

The two of them swam across the slough to a low, flat limestone outcropping where the creek emptied into it. They propped on the rock, lying on their stomachs and resting their heads on crossed arms like schoolkids at nap time, and let their legs dangle in the water.

Reed was tired but exhilarated. "Man, I love this place," he said as he looked around.

"Never took to north Alabama?"

"No. It's beautiful up there, but it just never felt like home to me."

"You think you'll stay here?"

"I want to. Gotta find a way to make a livin' first."

"What were you gonna do—to make a livin', I mean—before the war?"

"I didn't really wanna farm like Daddy. But I always liked workin' on the machinery. Guess I thought I might be a mechanic."

"Anna says you've got Jesse's truck runnin' like a top. How come you didn't sign up for somethin' like that in the Army?"

"I tried, but they needed medics. When I was in basic, I met several farm boys that ended up medics once the Army decided they might run outta real doctors—guess they figured if we knew how to tend to livestock, we were halfway to takin' care o' people . . ." Reed's voice trailed off, and he felt The Dust Storm begin its awful swirl in his mind.

"Medic!" The bone-chilling screams and the blood and the smoke and the blasts and the sickening smells . . .

"Reed?"

"Medic!" A green lieutenant cowers behind a boulder. The captain who saved the whole unit yesterday collapses into the smoke from an explosion . . .

"Reed? Reed!" Daisy was shaking his shoulder as if she were trying to wake him from a bad dream.

"I'm sorry," he said.

"No, I am. I took you back there with my stupid questions. I'm the one oughta be sorry."

Reed laid his head back down and tried to relax.

The two of them were quiet for a while before he said, "I don't think I'll ever be normal again, Daisy."

"When you figure out what normal looks like, be sure to let me know."

"I call it The Dust Storm—that thing that takes over my mind when I let myself go back there. It feels like a thick, choking blanket that wants to wrap me so tight I can't breathe. I don't know how to free myself from it."

They were quiet again before she said, "I got my own version o' your Dust Storm, just so you know. Mine's more like a black cloud that comes over me whenever I think about what I did to Charlie. Every time I start to feel a little bit happy, here it comes. But I guess that's fair. I really ain't got no right to be happy."

"You wanna tell me why?"

"I sold it. I sold the farm Charlie died tryin' to save—the farm I let him die tryin' to save. I shoulda talked him outta goin', no matter how bad he wanted to. I shoulda pitched a fit or begged and pleaded or *somethin'*. Instead I gave him my blessin'. And I swear it wasn't for the Army pay. I woulda been perfectly happy to move offa that farm and get a job somewhere. But I still didn't talk him outta goin'. It just seemed like it meant so much to him to go. And then after I got that telegram, I couldn't stand the sight o' those fields, knowin' what they cost. So I sold 'em, and I'm usin' the money to hide out here. You're a war hero, Reed, and you're spendin' your time with a real coward."

"You're not a coward, Daisy. And you didn't let Charlie die. Even if you coulda talked him outta signin' up—which you prob'ly couldn't—he woulda been drafted. It was just his time. I saw it over and over—one guy lives and the one standin' a coupla feet away from him dies. Somewhere there's a reason for that, but I got no idea what it is. And if you'd kept that land, what could you have done with it? Worked it all by yourself?"

"I guess not."

"As for that war hero business—there ain't no such thing. There's just the ones that live and the ones that die. Why I came home and a lotta good men didn't—good men with wives and children dependin' on 'em—that's somethin' I'll still be tryin' to figure out when my time comes."

They stopped talking for a while and let the cool water and the warm breeze chase their demons away. Morning sunlight was filtering through the trees and striking the side of Daisy's face. Reed was wishing he could draw as well as she did because her face in the sunlight would've made a beautiful picture.

She caught him staring at her. "What are you thinkin' about?"

"Why do women always ask that?"

"Because we're hopin' one day we'll get a straight answer."

Reed smiled at her. "I was thinkin' I sure hope you don't make me race you back to the bank."

Daisy laughed. "You're lyin'. But no, I won't make you race. Let's dry off and see if Dolly'll feed us."

eighteen

"Mornin', Miss Lillian." Reed climbed the steps to her porch and sat down in the rocker next to her. "I brought you a little somethin'." He set the Mason jar of flowers on the little table next to her.

Lillian closed her eyes and took a deep breath, then smiled and clapped her hands together. "Honeysuckle!" she said.

"Yes, ma'am."

"How on earth did you remember?"

"To tell the truth, I had forgotten how we used to clip it, but the minute I walked past some honeysuckle bloomin' in the hedgerow at Dolly's, I remembered."

"You were an exceptional child, so patient and kind with an old blind woman like me. And you were a very good guide. We used to roam all over this loop together, clipping honeysuckle and picking blackberries by the road."

"I think maybe you and Dolly were the exceptional ones—puttin' up with a worrisome kid underfoot."

"You were never worrisome, Reed. I regret I cannot say the same for some of the girls in our community."

They laughed together about the rowdy loop girls.

"Tell me what has become of the young woman you met on the Tanyard when you first got back," Lillian said.

"You mean the young woman you sent me to find on the creek?"

"I have no idea what you might be speaking of." She was smiling. "How would I have known she was there?"

"Now, *that's* a very interesting question."

Lillian laughed. "Just an old woman's intuition."

"She's fine. And she's been a big help to me. Mighty good comp'ny too."

"Hmm. Well, how about that?"

"Miss Lillian, I've been tryin' to remember everything you told me about Catherine and Andre when I was little."

"The river pirate and his bride? What on earth for?"

"I'm not really sure. I remember playin' pirate in Dolly's attic. She made me a sword from a broom handle and rigged me up a treasure chest. But there's somethin' I'm forgettin'. Somethin' you told me. I can see us sittin' on your porch together. I had my pirate sword, and I had brought you somethin' from my treasure chest at Dolly's."

Lillian smiled. "Yes, your treasure went back and forth between my house and hers many times. You would bring me a silver candy tray or a rhinestone brooch, and I would send it home by Si the next time he stopped by to look in on me."

"But there was somethin' you told me. Somethin' I think was important."

Lillian nodded. "I told you that once Andre had captured all the gold and silver he could ever need or want, he realized he was lacking the one thing of any lasting value. Do you remember what that was, Reed?"

He looked at her and thought about it. "He didn't have anybody to share it with. He didn't have anybody to love."

Lillian reached over and took him by the hand. "Welcome home, young Reed."

nineteen

"Breathe in . . . and out . . . In . . . and out . . . Good. Whatever you're doing, son, keep it up."

Dolly had suggested that Reed see the town doctor so he'd have somebody close by to check on his progress. He had just finished his first exam with Dr. Sesser.

"I'm quite frankly amazed by what you've accomplished in just a month or so, given the prognosis in your Army records," Dr. Sesser said. "You must be pushing yourself mighty hard."

"I had help," Reed said. "A friend worked with me on the exercises that the Birmingham doctors gave me. Now I can do 'em on my own, so I pretty much work my knee all day long, off and on."

"Well, it shows. Are you familiar with Oleander Springs?"

"No, sir, never heard of it."

"Back in the twenties, a fellow was prospecting for oil way down in the southeast corner of the state, but he hit a hot spring instead. There's a resort down there, so you'd have a place to stay. I'm not saying I believe in any healing magic from those springs, but I do think the heat and minerals in the water would be good for your leg if you were to go down there for a few days now and again."

"Thank you. I'll keep that in mind."

"You ever think of going into medicine, now that you've got all that training from the Army? I'm not getting any younger."

Reed shook his head as he stepped down from the examination table. "No offense to you, sir, but I think that might be the last thing I'd wanna do."

The doctor smiled. "I said the same thing when I came home from the trenches. Give yourself time. You'll find it's hard to put down that red cross once you take it up."

Another Sunday morning rolled around. Reed found that he was marking time by Sundays—those especially difficult days he had to make it through before he could begin another week of working toward normal, whatever that was. After the others left for church, he decided to walk across the road to the lake—no cane required, thanks to Daisy, though he still had a slight limp. He took a seat in one of the Adirondacks on the porch of the skating rink.

The whole place was deserted now—Dolly's rule on Sunday—so he could enjoy the quiet. It was still fairly cool in the morning sun, and a breeze was blowing ripples across the lake. Dolly and her boarders were likely settling into their Sunday school lessons right about now—offering envelopes collected, prayer requests shared, "now turn in your Bibles to the fifteenth chapter of John . . ."

What was so threatening about that? Why could he not bring himself to set foot in church when he had gone every Sunday of his life before the war? Deep down, he knew the answer.

It was the soul-bearing enthusiasm of the Baptist church that Reed couldn't handle right now—the conviction that all wounds can be healed once they're laid bare. His wounds wanted salving, not exposure. The well-meaning faithful who would urge his confession would run screaming in horror if they actually heard it. And so he told only God—the same God whose church he couldn't bring himself to approach.

When Reed was home, his mother had pressured him into going to Sunday services with the family as soon as he got back. She thought it would do him good. Instead, it had sent him into a tailspin. Hearing all those hymns he had grown up with—songs of love and grace and forgiveness—set against his visions of dead soldiers piled on top of each other like old toys nobody wanted to play with anymore . . . it was just too much. He had not lost his faith, but he had lost the ability to cope with the powerful emotions it stirred. Church seemed to demand that he contain but not extinguish the fires it stoked. Reed just wasn't up to it.

Dolly understood, and she never said a word to him about church attendance. She just made sure he had a Bible with a bookmarker on his nightstand. Every time she cleaned his room, she would move the marker to a new passage she thought might be of help. There was something comforting about watching that bookmarker move around without any pressure to do anything about it. He did, though. He read every one of Dolly's chosen Scriptures, placing his dog tags on top of the bookmarker each time to let her know he appreciated her efforts. It was a silent and private devotional they shared.

"You sinnin' today too?"

He was surprised to see Daisy coming out of the woods and onto the porch. "'Fraid so. Why'd you skip?"

She took a seat in the chair next to Reed and laid her sketchpad on the porch. "Haven't been since Charlie's funeral. I tried, but I'd always end up cryin' and slippin' out the back. Somethin' about those hymns—they make too much stuff bubble up. What's your excuse?"

"Same as yours."

They sat in silence for a little while, looking out at the water and listening to two doves calling from somewhere in the woods.

"Sundays are strange," Daisy finally said. "They're like a test I know I can't pass. Soon as Friday rolls around, I start to wonder if this'll be the week I go back to church. And the more I think about it, the more knots I get in my stomach. I start seein' myself sittin' in that pew and singin' those songs like we used to. And then I see myself goin' all to pieces right there in front o' everybody, and I know I can't do it. Once I give up on goin', I feel a lot better. Part o' me dreads Sunday, and part o' me looks forward to lettin' go o' those knots."

"Sure you didn't serve with the 34th?"

Daisy smiled. "Pretty sure I'd remember that. You keep in touch with anybody over there?"

Reed shook his head. "You keep in touch with anybody in Mississippi?"

"My brother Mack's in the Navy. I write to him every week. And then once a month, I force myself to write Mama a letter."

"What's Mama like?"

Daisy shuddered. "A bulldozer in high heels."

"I think I know her."

"Would you believe she had all the church ladies bringin' their bachelor sons to my house less than a month after Charlie's funeral? Like I wanted to date. And even if I had, all the boys my age are overseas. Some o' these fellas looked like they had one foot in the grave and the other on a banana peel."

Both of them laughed at the image of Daisy's geriatric suitors.

"Is that why you came back to Alabama instead of stayin' in Mississippi?"

"That and a lotta other things. Charlie and me grew up together. Everywhere I've been, he's been—except here. Had to get away from my ghosts."

"Mine seem to have followed me."

"Is it bad?"

"Sometimes."

"You wanna talk about it?"

Reed looked at Daisy. "People are always tellin' me they know how hard it musta been, seein' all that death over there. But it's not *all* the death—it's the one. That one guy whose expression is etched on your brain, lookin' at you the way somebody looks at you when they know you're the last thing they're ever gonna see."

Again they were quiet, letting themselves be part of the stillness of a Sunday morning when the whole town was someplace else. Stillness was one of the many qualities Reed had come to appreciate in Daisy. She didn't feel the need to do or say something just to fill the empty spaces.

"What's the hardest part o' comin' back?" she asked, something no one else had ever thought to consider. They always wanted to know what it was like over there.

He thought it over. "Tryin' to hide it," he said. "I think I could live with the nightmares if I knew I wouldn't wake up screamin' and scare Si and Dolly to death. And I could handle the flashbacks if they didn't shut my brain down and make everybody around me feel so uncomfortable. It's not just dealin' with the war. It's knowin' that everybody around me has to deal with me dealin' with the war. I feel like I'm under a microscope even when nobody's payin' me any mind."

"I follow that," Daisy said. "For what it's worth, the creek's a good place to hide from the microscope."

"Good to know."

"You can't control what you remember, Reed—or when you're gonna remember it. Other people oughta be able to understand that. I know everybody at Dolly's house does. Anybody that treats you like you're crazy just because you're havin' a hard time makin' the switch from combat to Sunday school—they ain't worth spit, so don't worry about 'em."

"Does Mama know you say things like 'ain't worth spit'?"

Daisy laughed. "No, she don't, and if you tell her, I'll swear you're lyin'."

They were quiet again before he said, "You wanna go somewhere?"

⁂

Reed pulled into a high mountain overlook and came around to open Daisy's door.

"Dang," she said. "Never saw anything like this before."

"Never had Sunday dinner on a mountain?"

"Never even seen a mountain till I moved here."

He grabbed the picnic basket they had packed and one of Dolly's "everyday quilts"—that's what she called the ones that were old enough and worn enough to be used outside.

"Where are we?" Daisy asked as they spread the quilt on a gently sloping, shady spot.

"Hick'ry Mountain. Daddy used to bring me campin' up here when I was little. That's the Cahaba River down there. If it was nighttime, you could see a glow from the lights o' Birmingham over that ridge."

"You need help?" Daisy asked.

"Nope, thanks to you." Reed could now bend his knee enough to sit down without propping himself on anything. They unwrapped leftover fried chicken and white bread that they had found in Dolly's kitchen. Reed opened the Cokes they had bought at the only filling station that was open along the way.

He watched as Daisy took in the view—Appalachian foothills against a blue summer sky, the river way down below, and sweeps of green in between. Yellow wildflowers painted the rolling landscape.

"It's so beautiful," she said.

"At night, it's just as pretty. You can see a million stars, and it's real quiet. You said you'd never seen a mountain in Mississippi, so what's it like where you're from?"

"The Delta—that's farmland around the river—is flat as a pancake. And we don't have red dirt like here. The fields are the color o' coal, and they smell like the river. There's a bunch o' little towns—no big cities—and the food's different on accounta all the people that've come up the Mississippi to work the cotton. You can see little tamale stands next to chicken joints and Italian restaurants across the road from barbecue pits. The music's great 'cause there's so many blues players around."

"I never even heard the blues till I went in the Army. Served with a guy from Indianola."

"I've still got a few o' my records if you want me to bring 'em to Dolly's sometime."

"That'd be great. You sure sound like you love that place to be workin' so hard to avoid it."

"I did love it."

"But not anymore?"

Daisy shook her head. "I don't fit anymore. And I lived there my whole life."

"You fit in Alabama?"

Daisy thought about it. "Yeah. I think I do."

They watched an occasional breeze send a yellow wave across the mountainside as first one patch of flowers and then the next bowed to it. Daisy reached out and picked two dandelions from the grass, then handed one to Reed. "My granddaddy used to say that if you can blow all the feathers off a dandelion in one breath, you can blow all your troubles away. Ready?"

They each took a deep breath and blew, both of them leaving just a few feathery remains.

"We got most of 'em," she said with a shrug. "That's at least a start."

"Progress," Reed agreed. "Hey, next time we come up here, you oughta bring your sketchbook with you."

"That wouldn't be much fun for you. What would you do while I drew?"

Reed smiled. "Admire your fine qualities."

Daisy rolled her eyes. "That ain't gonna take long."

"I don't know about that, now. I think it might keep me occupied for a pretty good while."

Reed could see that she was blushing, but as usual, she joked her way out of any attention she wasn't ready for. "Well, if I'm such a beauty queen, Reed, what am I doin' here on toppa this dang mountain with you when I could be signin' up for Miss America?"

They laughed together on Dolly's quilt, relishing the sunny sky and their patch of shade on a flower-covered mountainside high above their troubles.

twenty

Dolly was nearly frantic. Along with the usual work to be done, she was checking her pantry to see how much cornmeal, flour, sugar, and lard she needed and calculating whether she could keep her boarders fed and still put back some money for the property taxes that would be due before she could turn around.

"Hey, Dolly, you in here?" Daisy called.

Dolly stepped out of the pantry to find Daisy and Reed in her kitchen. "Oh! Bless your hearts! Would y'all mind runnin' to the mercantile for me?"

"No problem," Reed said.

"Got a list for us?" Daisy asked.

Dolly pulled a grocery list, money, and ration coupons out of her apron pocket and handed them to Daisy.

"Ella needs my coupons, or I'd give 'em to you," Daisy said.

"You can have mine," Reed said. "We should be able to get whatever you need."

"Thank you, thank you!" Dolly said.

"Hey, where's Anna?" Daisy asked. "I ain't seen her all day."

"She found an old poetry anthology that belonged to my mother and decided that if she couldn't read any more about Catherine, she'd at least read what Catherine was readin' the last time she wrote in her journal. She's upstairs with 'The Lady of Shalott.' Want me to call her?"

"That's okay. Let her have a little Catherine time. See you later."

Inside the mercantile, Daisy introduced Wally Trimble to Reed. "I don't remember seein' you around here before," Wally said, "but somethin' about you sure looks familiar."

Daisy handed Dolly's list to Wally, who sent his stock boy to bring their groceries to the counter.

"My family lived here when I was a boy, but we moved away a long time ago," Reed explained. "My daddy's Vern Ingram."

"Sure 'nough! Why, I went to school with Vern 'n' Si. Even now I still say their names together the way we all did back then—Vern 'n' Si—'cause they was best buddies all through school. Even left for the Army on the very same day, but they shipped out in different directions. Where'd you all move to?"

"My mother inherited a farm in north Alabama, up around Florence. We moved there when I was twelve."

"Is that right? Well, you be sure and tell your daddy Wally Trimble said hello, okay?"

Reed smiled. "I will." He reached for his wallet as the stock boy delivered their dry goods and lard to the counter.

"Lemme see now, we got sugar an' flour an' cornmeal an' lard . . . that'll be 6-0-9."

Reed stared at Wally and didn't speak.

"Six dollars and nine cents," Wally repeated.

Still Reed didn't move.

"Grab your gear and spread out! We're goin' up!"

"Son?" Wally said.

Reed felt his hands begin to tremble and sweat as he stood frozen, holding the wallet.

"Captain's hit! Medic!"

"Oh, I know what the trouble is," Daisy said, taking the wallet from his hands. "I forgot to tell him I've got Dolly's grocery money and ration coupons, so we just need to get his coupons outta here. There you go, Wally—bet you gave Reed a fright when you quoted him that price. Prob'ly thought we'd have to sweep the store to work off our groceries."

"Ha! Sorry about that, son!"

"I . . . I thank you for the groceries and . . . and next time I'll count my money before I get here."

"There you go!" Wally said. "But now you can always count on me to spot a veteran a few dollars. Don't forget to tell your daddy I said hey."

"I won't."

The stock boy loaded their groceries into the back of Reed's pickup and disappeared into the store. Reed opened Daisy's door for her and closed it but couldn't take his hands off of it. He feared that if he turned loose, he might go sailing off into oblivion.

"How 'bout I drive?" Daisy said.

He nodded, handed her the keys, and climbed into the passenger seat as she slid beneath the wheel. She drove in silence as Reed stared out his window, letting the hot summer wind blow in his face.

When Daisy stopped the truck, he came out of his haze and looked around. "Where are we?"

"Saxon's."

"We're in Childersburg?"

"Yeah."

"Why?"

"Because now that I know how much money you've got squirreled away in that wallet, you're gonna buy me a chili dog and a milkshake."

Reed tried to smile. "Always knew you were a gold digger."

"Fork it over. What you want?"

"Whatever you get'll be fine."

Daisy took his money and walked to the front window to order. She had situated the truck away from the parking lot, under the shade of tall pine trees facing the river. How had he crossed over without even noticing?

When Daisy came back, she spread napkins on the truck seat between them, laid out their chili dogs and French fries, and set their milkshakes on the floorboard next to the gearshift.

Reed took a bite of his chili dog. "Oh man," he said. "I forgot how good these are."

Daisy nodded. "I know. They get all over you, but it's worth it."

They were quiet for a while, enjoying their food and watching the river glide by. Finally, Daisy spoke. "I read about 'em, you know—the places they sent you. Kasserine Pass and that awful hill—the one they call 609."

Reed felt an adrenaline rush just hearing the name. "I don't think . . . I can talk about it."

"No need to. I just wanted you to know that I understand what happened back there at the store. I won't ever know what you went through on that hill or at that pass, but I get what happened at the store. And I don't want you to feel weird about it."

"Hard not to feel weird when you act crazy."

"Hard not to feel crazy when you act weird—like wearin' overalls every day o' your life."

Reed had to smile. "About those overalls o' yours . . ."

"Don't *you* start on me too. I catch enough flak from Anna and Dolly. Let's just say these are my version of a black dress."

"I'm not complainin'."

They sat together in silence, watching the noontime sunlight on the river, before she said, "You look real tired, Reed."

"I feel tired. Every time I go back there in my mind, I just feel so . . . defeated. Like I'll never get offa that bloody hill as long as I live. I just wanna forget it. I want that so bad."

"How long were you over there?"

"Two years."

"And how long have you been back?"

"Since January."

"But you're already walkin' without a cane."

"Because you worked with me so much."

"And I almost never see you go back there in your head."

"Usually happens at night."

"But still—don't you think that's at least somethin'?"

Reed reached down and took a sip of his milkshake but didn't say anything.

"Maybe forgettin's too big a mountain to climb just yet," Daisy went on. "Maybe you could just learn how to handle rememberin'—a little bit at a time. That ain't gonna be an easy climb either, so you gotta give yourself time."

"Daisy, what on earth are you doin' here with me? You've had enough troubles of your own, and now you're takin' on mine."

She sighed and looked out at the river. "I used to spend a whole lotta time doin' what other people expected me to. But now, I don't do anything I don't wanna do. And I don't go anywhere I don't wanna go. Life's too short." She turned to face Reed. "I'm where I wanna be or I wouldn't be here. How 'bout you?"

She was giving him that look again—like the first time he'd met her on the creek and she had stared at him as if she could read his mind.

He nodded. "Me too."

"Guess we better get Dolly her delivery?"

"Guess so."

"You wanna trade places and drive?" she asked as the two of them stuffed chili dog wrappers and napkins into a paper bag.

More than anything right now, he wanted to make her laugh. "You're doin' okay, I guess—for a girl."

It worked, thank heaven. Daisy laughed. "Watch it or you'll be ridin' back there with the lard."

They drove back over the bridge they had crossed together, retreating to the safety of Dolly's house.

twenty-one

Dolly found Anna pacing in the hallway, stopping now and again to peek inside the parlor doorway, where she could see Reed, sitting on the front porch, through the front window.

"Honey, what on earth are you doin'?"

Anna motioned for Dolly to follow her into the kitchen. Once they were out of earshot, she told Dolly what she was up to. "I'm trying to work up my nerve."

"To talk to Reed?"

"Not just talk to him—ask him a favor."

"Sit down, honey, and tell me what's goin' on."

"You saw Daisy's truck when we pulled up the other day."

Dolly shook her head. "That ol' clunker's gonna strand her in the boondocks one o' these days."

"I know! But she'd rather die than ask for help. So I figured I might ask. Reed has Jesse's truck running like a top. And since Daisy's been helping him with his exercises so much, I really don't think he would mind taking a look at her truck, do you?"

"Why, heavens no. It would give him somethin' useful to do, which I bet he'd enjoy."

"And then there's the other thing . . ."

"What other thing, honey?"

"Well . . . I might be getting my hopes up too soon, but I think there might be a little spark between them."

"Well, get on out there, honey. Let's help 'em fire it up!"

Anna went onto the porch, where Reed was looking through some old magazines. "Could I talk to you for a minute?" she asked.

"Sure."

She took a seat in the rocker next to him. "I need a favor. Actually, Daisy does, but she's got way too much pride to ask. It's that truck of hers. We went to the store together the other day, and I thought we'd have to push it home. You were such a help to Jesse when he had engine trouble that I was just wondering . . ."

"Want me to take a look?"

"Would you? But now, there's a catch. You'll have to offer because she'll never ask. Just tell her I blabbed. I'll let Jesse know that we might have to move."

Reed had forgotten about hydrangeas. When he pulled into Ella's driveway, Daisy was watering two that flanked the front steps. The backyard of his parents' old house on the loop had a big bank of them. Reed had always loved their mop-head blooms in the summertime. When he was a little boy, Dolly had taught him how to dry them to make a bouquet for his mother so she could still enjoy at least a faded shade of their colors, even after the weather turned cold.

"Hey," Daisy said, shutting off the garden hose.

"Hey."

She looked wary of him, walking slowly to his truck and watching as he lifted a toolbox out of the back.

"This is not a social call," he said. "I'm here on business."

"Anna sent you down here to look at my truck, didn't she? I tried to tell her it's just a little moody, is all."

"How 'bout I give it a listen? I won't do anything else if you don't want me to."

Still Daisy hesitated.

"C'mon," he coaxed her. "I'm bored. This'll give me somethin' to do."

He followed Daisy into Ella's backyard, where she had parked her '29 Ford under a shade tree. Nobody could afford new vehicles during the Depression, and now that the war was on, nobody was making them, not for civilians anyway. Only veterans could buy anything new. Everybody else just had to keep patching up whatever they were driving when the whole world went crazy.

Reed lifted the hood and tried his best not to react to what he saw—hoses and belts that needed replacing, a leaky battery, oil everywhere . . .

"What you think?" Daisy peered under the hood next to him.

"Why don't you crank it for me?" he said.

She climbed into the truck and managed to get the engine going after several false starts. Right away, Reed could hear that the truck had a serious case of piston slap. The exhaust was shot. The radiator was about ready for the junk heap. Parts were mighty hard to come by these days, but he figured he had earned the right to take any veteran's privileges offered him and put them to work for Daisy.

"Okay, you can shut it off."

The engine kept running.

"Go ahead and shut it off."

Still the engine ran.

"Daisy?" Reed stepped around to the driver's door and saw her sitting there, staring at the steering wheel with tears rolling down her cheeks. Through the open truck window, he reached across her and shut off the ignition.

Daisy didn't move.

"Let's go sit for a minute." He opened the truck door, took her by the hand, and gave her a gentle tug. She climbed out of the truck and let him lead her to a porch swing hanging by long ropes from the sprawling oak she had parked beneath.

"You prob'ly think I'm a blubberin' idiot," she said, swiping at her face with her hand.

"No, I don't. But I think there's somethin' about this truck I don't know."

Daisy sighed. "It's just one more thing, you know? Just one more reminder."

"Of Charlie?"

"Of everything. Of every dang thing."

"I follow that," he said, which made her smile.

"It was so hard there at the end. Charlie was killin' hisself tryin' to keep worn-out tractors runnin'. I kept tellin' him I was scared this ol' truck was gonna strand me on some lonesome road, and he kept promisin' to get to it. Seems so silly now, the stuff we worried about—tractors and pickups and a piece o' land. Dirt. We spent all our time strugglin' to save dirt. Why couldn't we see how silly that was?"

"Got no answer for that one. I'm as sure as I've ever been about what matters and what don't, but I wish like the daylights there'd been another way for me to figure that out."

"Me too."

"We sound pretty depressin'. Wanna come help me shop for parts and drown our sorrows in motor oil?"

Daisy smiled up at him. "Sure. I'm a cheap date."

❧

"Is this the right one?"

"That's it." Reed took the wrench from Daisy and finished tightening the last bolt on a radiator they had scavenged from a local junkyard. Apparently, some poor fella had just put a new one on his pickup when he got creamed from behind. Luckily for Daisy, the radiator and most of the engine parts Reed needed were spared.

"Never thought I'd say this about a radiator, but I think it's beautiful," Daisy said.

"Compared to the one I took out, she's a stunner."

"And that thing right there—that's the carburetor?"

"Mm-hmm. Why all the curiosity about engine parts?"

Daisy shrugged. "Just figure I prob'ly need to learn about 'em so I can take care o' things myself."

Reed wiped his hands on a shop towel and watched her studying the engine. "As much as you help me, is it really so hard to let me help you?"

"Oh, I didn't mean it like that. I 'preciate everything you're doin'. I really do. It's just—well, it's sinkin' in that I'm by myself now. Took me a year and a half, but I finally got the message. I can't bawl like a baby every time I get piston snap."

"Uh, ma'am, that's piston *slap*."

Daisy had to laugh at herself. "You oughta be over there with all those beauty queens at the lake instead o' stuck here with an ol' widow woman."

"Well, A, I'm not stuck; B, Jo-Jo gets on my nerves; and C, what are you, ol' widow woman—all o' twenty?"

"Twenty-one."

"Same as me. We can go to the ol' folks' home together. Wanna get a hamburger on the way?"

They climbed into Reed's truck and headed for Saxon's across the river.

"Hey, what time is it?" Daisy asked.

Reed checked his watch. "A little after one."

"You mind if I turn on the radio?" She turned the knob and carefully adjusted the dial till Reed could hear the unmistakable sound of Delta blues. "This is about the only reminder o' home I still like," she said.

"Well, if that song ain't appropriate, I don't know what is," Reed said as a tune called "Feisty Little Mama" came over the airwaves.

Now Daisy was laughing. "Yep, that's me alright. 'Course, you'd prob'ly change the title to 'Annoyin' Little Mama.'"

Reed couldn't resist taking his eyes off the road for just a second to see her dimpled smile and the summer wind blowing her short hair. One of these days, he would need to do something about that. But for now, they could just enjoy an easy drive to a burger joint in a sunny Alabama town, far from the war that brought them together.

twenty-two

"Dang, it's fixin' to come a toad strangler!" On a Sunday afternoon, Daisy came running into Dolly's house just seconds before a light summer drizzle escalated into a downpour.

"Here, honey, come in the bathroom and dry off." Dolly handed her a towel, which Daisy used to dry her sketchbook and blot the mist from her face, arms, and hair—anything her overalls didn't cover.

"Come on in here with us," Dolly said. "Harry's about to play us some of his music."

Daisy followed her into the music room, where Jesse, Anna, and Reed had gathered around Harry, sitting at the old Victrola with a stack of records.

"Welcome, Daisy!" Harry said. He set a disc onto the turntable, gave the crank a few turns, and set the needle down. "You are just in time to hear Robert Johnson."

Daisy sat next to Reed on a loveseat by the front window. Through the crackle of the old disc came the signature guitar riffs of the Mississippi Delta.

Harry closed his eyes and absorbed himself completely in the music until the last lick. Then he shook his head and said, "I find it incredible that one who grew up in utter destitution and isolation could create such music—and spin such an inventive yarn about the universal crossroads of good and evil."

"Actually, Harry, it was a real crossroads," Daisy explained. "It's in Clarksdale."

"Do you mean people believe it to be literal—that he truly stood at a *physical* crossroads and sold his soul to Satan himself?"

"Right there where Highway 61 crosses 49. But now, just 'cause it's a real place, that don't take nothin' away from your universal good and evil idea. I like that a lot."

"I should've come here years ago." Harry played them several more of his records—Son House, Muddy Waters, and Bessie Smith. Then he said, "I have a fine idea! Here's one by Memphis Minnie—I hear it's a dance favorite in Mississippi, should any of you young people feel inclined to cut a rug."

Dolly, who was standing in the doorway, clapped her hands together. "Oh yes! You all have a dance, why don't you."

Harry put another disc on the Victrola, and a bluesy number called "Kissing in the Dark" began to play. "How about it, Jesse and Anna?"

"No way." Jesse laughed. "I'd fall all over myself."

Reed looked at Daisy, who was tapping her feet to the rhythm. "Wanna show 'em how it's done?" He stood up and held his hand out to her. Daisy looked too surprised to do anything but follow his lead as they danced a kind of slow jitterbug to Memphis Minnie's blues.

Dolly saw Little Mama's curtains begin to stir, and their subtle dance—just a slight flutter around the windows—made her smile.

When the record ended, Daisy was laughing. "Where'd you learn to do that?"

"That guy from Indianola I told you about. Guess I picked up a few things. Sorry about the clunky leg."

"Hey, teach us!" Anna said.

Jesse shook his head. "Anna, no! I'm a klutz on the dance floor."

"Oh, come on!" She stood up, took Jesse by the hand, and pulled him out of his chair.

"Come on and what?" Evelyn came into the music room.

"Evelyn, you're just in time!" Harry shouted. "We are about to get a lesson in Delta dancing. Come here and let's have a go!"

"Harry, you have lost your mind," she said. "I feel you have a right to know."

"Ha! You cannot dissuade me, Evelyn. We are about to dance!"

Reed and Daisy taught them all a few steps before Harry started the record again.

Dolly looked on with a smile as the three couples danced together in Little Mama's music room: Harry and Evelyn approaching each move with academic determination, counting the beat out loud and correcting each other along the way; Jesse and Anna, laughing and stealing a kiss every time they missed a step; and Reed and Daisy, who seemed unaware of everybody else as he pulled her much closer than before, letting his arms linger around her and his cheek lightly brush against hers, before spinning her away from him now and again.

There hadn't been so much life in the old music room for a long time. Suddenly, the sheer curtains blissfully billowed away from the tall windows as if they too wanted to dance. Si would blame it on a breeze, but Dolly knew better. Little Mama's house was happy this summer afternoon.

twenty-three

"We gotta talk."

Anna had just handed a lake customer his Coke and potato chips when Daisy appeared out of the blue. She seemed agitated, pacing in front of the concession stand.

"What's the matter?" Anna asked.

"I can't talk about it."

"But you just said we have to talk."

"We do. I just don't know if I can. Any chance you can get away for a minute?"

"Hey, Evelyn," Anna called. "Could you relieve me for just a few minutes?"

"Absolutely!" Evelyn answered from one of the Adirondack chairs on the porch, where she was reading in the shade. "Perhaps I'll find that trading in Coca-Cola is my true calling in life."

"Thanks, Evelyn." Anna turned over the cash box. "We won't be long."

"Take your time."

Daisy led Anna off the porch and down the path to the creek. They stopped beside its shallows, where Anna sat down on a boulder near the bank. "Tell me what's going on," she said.

"I don't know." Daisy kept pacing back and forth, now and then shaking her hands out as if she were trying to loosen a cramp.

"Well, you're making me dizzy. If you can't quit that pacing, take off your shoes and let's at least have a cool wade in the creek."

They left their shoes on the bank and stepped into the soothing waters of the Tanyard. Its currents seemed to calm Daisy as she and Anna slowly walked along together.

"It can't be all that bad, can it?" Anna finally ventured. "Won't you give me just a little hint?"

"You swear, and I mean *swear*, not to tell a livin' soul—not even Jesse?"

Anna frowned. "I tell Jesse everything."

"Well, you can't tell him this."

Anna crossed her heart. "Okay. I promise."

"It's Reed."

Anna jumped up and down and squealed. "I knew it! I just knew it!"

"Knew what? There's no 'it.'"

Anna sighed. "Daisy, just tell me."

"Well . . . we've been spendin' a lotta time together. But I'm not an idiot. I know we're just friends and we're helpin' each other along. There's absolutely nothin' more to it."

"If you say so."

"I ain't thought in that direction since Charlie died."

"I know."

"And pretty boys like Reed don't go for girls like me. They go for beauties like Alyce."

"Now stop right there. Have you *ever* looked in a mirror? You're every bit as pretty as Alyce without even trying—*and* hiding in those overalls."

"I'm not hidin'!"

179

"Are too. Keep talking."

Daisy stopped walking and watched the water swirl around her legs. Then she looked up at Anna and said, "Do you remember the very first time Jesse kissed you?"

Anna smiled at the memory of it. "Of course I do."

"You remember that split second right before—when somethin' changed between you and you could feel it? You knew it was about to happen, but before you had time to think about it, it happened?"

Anna nodded and smiled.

"Well, that's how it was with Reed when we were dancin'— that split second before somethin' happens, only nothin' happened."

"What if it had? How would you feel about that?"

"I got no idea."

"Don't you imagine he's spent enough time with you to know that?"

"You really think men get that kinda stuff?"

"Reed would. He's special, Daisy. As sappy as I am about Jesse, even I can see that."

"What am I gonna do?"

Anna put her arm around her friend's shoulders. "Just let it happen, Daisy. And stop telling yourself you don't deserve it."

twenty-four

Reed was glad to have a project to occupy his mind. He had promised Dolly that he would give Si's old Ford a tune-up, and he was looking forward to staying busy with it all day. As he reached into his toolbox and grabbed a couple of wrenches, he could hear but couldn't see Anna and Daisy laughing and talking somewhere in the tall rows of pole beans out in the garden. It was nice, the connection between the two of them. Friends like that didn't come along every day. He of all people knew that.

He had just popped the hood on the Ford when he got that feeling he used to get right before an ambush. It was like walking into a familiar room where a lamp or a picture had been moved. You could sense that something was off before you figured out what it was. That's how Reed felt now, standing in Dolly's yard, which had always seemed so safe. Something was coming. Something was about to happen and it wasn't good, but he couldn't gauge what or when.

Just then he heard a scream from the garden.

"Daisy!"

Reed ran toward the scream and got there just in time to see Daisy hit the ground, clutching her bleeding foot as a copperhead slithered away. Reed grabbed a hoe propped at the end of the row and killed the snake. Then he took his knife from his pocket and knelt down by Daisy, who was crying and breathing hard.

"Daisy, listen to me. You're gonna be fine, okay?" He turned to Anna. "Quick, go call Dr. Sesser."

Anna didn't move. She was staring at the knife in his hand.

"Anna! I'm not gonna hurt her. Please get the doctor!"

She backed away from them and ran to the house as fast as she could.

Reed took off his T-shirt and used the knife to cut a wide strip off of it. He tied a tourniquet a few inches above the bite on Daisy's ankle, which was already turning red and swelling.

"Daisy, I need you to slow down. Breathe with me." Reed locked eyes with her, guiding her to slow her breathing down. "In . . . then out . . . In . . . then out. That's it. Good, Daisy."

"It—it feels like—like fire," she said, struggling to control her breath.

"I know. I need to get the venom out. I'm gonna make a little cut. It'll only hurt for a second. You ready?"

Daisy nodded. She cried out as he cut a slit between the fang marks on her skin, put his mouth over the wound, and sucked the venom out of her ankle, spitting it onto the ground over and over. When he thought he had gotten as much as he could, he wiped his mouth with the T-shirt, then cut off more strips of cloth and bandaged the cut. Daisy tried to sit up but fainted from pain and fright.

He picked her up and started for the house. Anna met him on his porch and held the door open as he carried Daisy into his room and laid her on the bed, propping her up on pillows.

"Doctor's on his way," she said, staring at the seeping bandage on Daisy's foot.

Dolly came running into Reed's room. She began to cry at the sight of Daisy lying there, snow-white and still, with red smears on the white makeshift dressing Reed had made.

"What should we do? How can we help her?" Dolly was clearly distraught.

"Keep her still and quiet so her heart doesn't race and speed up her blood flow," Reed said. "We need to prop her up with pillows to keep her heart above the bite. She'll prob'ly start to have chills before the doctor gets here, so go ahead and get her into some dry clothes—those are sweaty from bein' in the garden. I'll step out and let you and Anna take care of her."

"I'll get her some of my things," Anna said. Reed quickly grabbed a shirt for himself and followed Anna out of his room. Before he disappeared into Dolly's bathroom, Anna took him by the hand and said, "I'm sorry." Then she ran upstairs.

Reed shut the door, sat down on the edge of the tub, and put his head in his hands. The sight and smell of blood had brought it all back—wounded buddies he couldn't reach, still more he could barely keep alive. Fire and smoke and death all around. He wanted to scream. Or curl up on the floor and sob like a baby. But now Daisy was the one with a fight on her hands, and she needed his help. So he did what he had done during battle after battle—prayed a silent prayer for strength, took some deep breaths, and soldiered on.

Reed's bedroom door was closed by the time he collected himself, so he walked through the house to the kitchen but found no one there. He went into the backyard and circled around to the small porch off his room, where he saw Dolly, Si, Anna, and Evelyn standing together, waiting to hear from the doctor.

"Reed, honey, come here and sit down," Dolly said.

"I'm okay," he said.

"C'mon, we'll all sit with you." Dolly motioned for him to sit next to her on the bed, along with Evelyn and Si, while Anna took the rocker.

"Any word?" Reed asked.

"No, honey," Dolly said.

All three women looked like they had been crying—Anna most of all. They all sat in silence, anxiously waiting for news.

At last Reed said, "Here he comes."

"How do you know, honey?" But before he could explain to Dolly how acute his hearing had become in combat, the doctor opened the door and stepped onto the porch.

"What you think, Doc?" Si asked.

"I think she's mighty lucky she was with an Army medic, or she wouldn't be with us for long," the doctor answered. "From the look of the bite, that was a full-grown snake with a lot of venom. But I think Reed stopped it before it went to her heart or her brain. The next two hours will tell. If she looks like she's going into shock or starts having hallucinations, we'll need to get her to a hospital. If not, then she's in for some pain and swelling and maybe some tissue damage around the bite. She'll probably be nauseated when she wakes up."

"Can't you give her anything for the pain?" Dolly asked.

"Not for two hours. I gave her a mild sedative, but the medicine I'd need to give her for that kind of pain can cause hallucinations itself, so before we do that, we need to make sure she's not having any from the bite. Reed, I'm assuming you know how to administer morphine?"

"Yes, sir."

"Then I'll leave her medication and some syringes on the nightstand. If she hasn't had any hallucinations by exactly two o'clock—and not a minute before—give her a dose, then continue that every four hours for the next two days, or as long as she thinks she needs it. That's a good field dressing you did. I put a fresh one on, and I'll leave what you need to change it till I can get back over here."

"Thank you," Reed said.

184

"I'll come by to check on her at the end of the week unless you need me before then."

"God bless you, Dr. Sesser," Dolly said. She and the others stood to thank him, then she went with Si and Evelyn to see him to his car.

Anna followed Reed to Daisy's room. The fever and chills had begun. Daisy's face was flushed and beaded with sweat, while her body was shaking.

"She's cold," Anna said. She ran upstairs and came back down carrying her mother's quilts that she had brought from Illinois.

As Reed helped her spread the quilts, he considered explaining that Daisy's chill was coming from the inside, a place quilts couldn't warm, but thought better of it. He could see that Anna needed to feel like she was helping. And he tried to push from his mind all the times he had seen soldiers die from the trauma of being shot or burned before their actual wounds had time to kill them.

Sitting down at Daisy's bedside, he blotted her forehead with a cool cloth. Anna climbed onto the bed, lying down on top of her mother's quilts and putting an arm around Daisy to keep her warm. The two of them there, huddled together against the world, brought back painful memories of another friend, one Reed had clung to and lost on a battlefield far from home. He felt his eyes begin to sting and the familiar racing of his heart as a wave of sorrow threatened to take him under.

❧

"Hey, Jesse," Reed said softly as his upstairs neighbor came into the room, setting a supper tray from Dolly on top of Reed's chest of drawers.

"How's she doing?" Jesse asked.

"Pretty quiet now. She gets restless about a half hour before every dose o' morphine, but she's easy now. Pull up a chair."

Jesse carried a small chair closer to Daisy's bedside, where Reed was still sitting.

"What about that one?" Jesse smiled and pointed to Anna, fast asleep. Reed had covered her with a light throw when it started raining and cooling off early in the evening.

"Hasn't budged."

"They're joined at the hip, those two. I don't think I've ever had a friend as close as they are. You?"

"Just once."

Daisy stirred and mumbled, "Catherine . . ."

"Guess she's dreamin' about Catherine and her pirate," Reed said.

"Lucky for both of us ol' Andre's dead—that guy woulda been some serious competition." Jesse nodded toward Daisy.

"Ain't nowhere near that," Reed muttered.

Jesse smiled and said, "For now." He gave Reed a pat on the back as he stood up to go. "If I can help you, just come and get me."

"Reed!"

He had nodded off in the rocking chair Dolly brought him and now awoke with a start to see Daisy sitting straight up in bed.

"Reed!" she called again, which woke Anna.

"I'm right here," he said, sitting next to her on the bed.

"Reed!"

"What's the matter with her?" Anna sat up next to Daisy. "She's not having those awful hallucinations, is she?"

"Not from snake venom." Reed took Daisy's face in his hands and looked into her eyes. "I think she's still asleep—just with her eyes open."

"Can people do that?"

"Seen it a few times."

"Reed!" Daisy called one more time.

"Daisy!" He gave her shoulders a gentle shake. "I'm right here."

For just a second he saw her eyes focus as if she were fully conscious. Then she frowned, shook her head, and said, "You wanna go somewhere?" With that, she fell straight back in the bed and was asleep again.

Anna and Reed looked at each other, then back at Daisy. And then they both started laughing—that giddy, uncontrollable laughter that comes with mind-numbing exhaustion.

"You mind if I go upstairs?" Anna asked when they finally settled down.

"You can't do anything for her till she wakes up. Go get some rest."

"Can I bring you something from the kitchen?" Anna asked at the bedroom door.

"Thank you, but I had plenty from Dolly's tray."

Anna picked up the tray on her way out and closed the door quietly behind her. Reed checked his watch. One o'clock in the morning. He carefully filled another syringe, blotted Daisy's arm with alcohol, and gave her the shot that would see her through till daylight. She was sweating off her fever. They would have to change the bed in the morning, but for now he let her rest.

His leg was throbbing. Sitting up all day without stretching it had made it so stiff that he could hardly stand, let alone walk. As exhausted as he was, the spot Anna had vacated became irresistible. Taking off his shoes, he limped to the other side of the bed, stretched out on top of the mountain of quilts covering Daisy, and fell asleep.

twenty-five

Reed sat bolt upright in bed. The window shade had somehow loosened itself and rolled up with a loud *whap* in the wee hours of the morning. Daisy was still sound asleep. Something was off. Something was out of place. He checked his watch—3:00 a.m. Earlier in the evening, he had opened the back door to let in a breeze from the screened porch. That's where the trouble was. Out there.

He quietly stepped onto the porch and listened. Movement— in the woods maybe? When he turned on the outside light, it stopped. Silence. He stood there and listened, but it was gone. Just to be on the safe side, he closed the door and locked it before lying back down and falling asleep.

Dolly looked out the window and peered into the early morning darkness. She and Si were getting dressed for their morning chores.

"Somethin' wrong, Dolly?"

She clasped her hands together beneath her chin and gave a little shiver. "I can't shake the feeling that somethin's . . . I don't know . . . goin' on out there."

"Like what?"

"That's the trouble—I got no idea. You know what worries me the most, Si? Little Mama always said bad things come in clusters. That means more's comin'. Why'd somebody as special as Daisy have to be number one?"

"Why anything, Dolly? We don't get to see the whole map. We just have to cover our stretch o' the road best we can." Si kissed her on the cheek and offered her his arm. "Shall we make our way to your skillets and my milk cow, madam?"

Reed woke up and looked at his watch—5:30 a.m. He turned over to find Daisy awake and staring at him, groggy but wide-eyed.

"What in the . . . Sam Hill . . . happened?" she asked, her words slurring from the drugs.

"Nothin' happened—I mean, well, a lot happened—I just got really tired and had to sleep for a while." He got up as quickly as he could, limped around the bed to Daisy's side, and sat down next to her.

"You're walkin' . . . terrible."

"I know." Reed laid his hand on her forehead to see if she was still hot.

She was looking around, trying to get her bearings. He could tell she was still in a morphine fog. Suddenly, her mouth flew open. "What am I . . . doin' . . . in your broom—I mean, your *room*?"

He blotted her face with a cool cloth. "You've been fightin' a fever since yesterday afternoon, but it looks like it finally broke. Do you remember a snakebite?"

"A *shnake* bite? When did . . . what?"

"Yesterday. When you and Anna were in the garden."

Daisy rubbed her eyes as if that might help her focus. She

looked at Reed and thought for a minute. "It bit me . . . on my foot?"

"That's right."

"Hurts."

"I know. I did what I could for you and then Anna called a doctor. He told me to give you morphine every four hours to keep the pain under control. You're due for another shot right now."

"Wait . . . I'm so blurry."

"Okay. But you need to let me know before it gets really bad."

Daisy nodded. She was frowning at him as if she were trying hard to figure out something on his face. "Can we back up?"

"Sure."

"Me and Anna were pickin' beans . . ."

"That's right."

"Snake bit me."

"A copperhead."

"It hurt . . . real bad . . . burned."

"Are you hurtin' bad now?"

Daisy shook her head. "I was . . . scared . . . You said . . . breathe slow."

Reed nodded.

"And you cut me."

"To get the poison out."

"How'd . . . how'd I get here?"

"I carried you."

"Musta . . . hurt . . . your leg."

"I really didn't have time to think about that. Here, while you're awake try to drink some water." Reed raised her up in the bed and let her lean against his shoulder while she drank as much as she could, then got her settled back down on the pillows.

"Why . . . am I . . . in here?"

"This was just the quickest place I could find to lay you down. After the doctor saw you, Dolly and Evelyn and Anna stayed in here with us till suppertime. Then Dolly and Evelyn left, but Anna slept next to you till about one o'clock this mornin'. I sent her off to bed to get some rest till you woke up. Those are her quilts you're buried under."

Daisy gave a weak smile. "She always . . . wants to make it butter . . . I mean batter . . . Dang . . . my foot hurts, Reed."

He was giving her another shot when Anna came into the room. "I'm your relief," she said. "And I'm kicking you out. Go get some breakfast."

"Yes, ma'am." Reed left Daisy in her friend's care. He could hear the morning chatter as he approached the dining room. Once again he struggled with the strangeness of it—pain and morphine in one room, coffee and conversation in the next—and wondered if he would ever be able to reconcile the two.

<hr />

"Anna?" Dolly softly called as she opened the door to Reed's bedroom, where Daisy was sound asleep and Anna was blotting her forehead with a damp cloth. "Honey, I've got somethin' for you."

"What is it, Dolly?"

Anna could see that Dolly was holding a small package about the size of a shoebox, wrapped in plain brown paper.

"Looka here," Dolly said. The package had "To Anna" written across the top.

"For me? Where did it come from?"

"I don't know. It was on the front porch when I went out to water my ferns." Dolly handed the box to Anna.

"Let's see what's inside." As Dolly sat down in a rocker by the bed, Anna tore the paper off the package. She opened the box, and her hand flew to her mouth. "Oh my gosh, Dolly, could this possibly be what I think it is?" She reached into the box and pulled out a leather journal. "I don't think I've got the nerve to open it."

"Sure you do, honey."

Anna opened the book and read, "'April 20, 1844. Dear Self . . .'"

For a split second, she and Dolly stared at each other, but then they were both hugging, trying to contain their excitement so they wouldn't make too much noise and wake Daisy.

"Oh, honey, I'm so happy for you!" Dolly loudly whispered.

"But Dolly, who gave this to me? There are no markings on it anywhere."

"I don't know, but that don't make it any less real. You gonna read it?"

Anna thought it over. "No. Not until we can all read it together. Not until Daisy's up to it."

Dolly smiled. "You're a mighty good friend to have, Anna. Your mama raised you right."

twenty-six

"Well, good morning—actually, good afternoon," Evelyn said from her chair by the bed as Daisy rubbed her eyes.

"Hey, Evelyn." Daisy looked around. "What time is it?"

"A quarter after twelve. How do you feel?"

"Like a train hit me. I think . . . I think I'm done . . . with that morphine."

"Well, I imagine we should consult Reed about that."

"Is he . . . is he here?"

"Yes. He's in the kitchen. The others are at church."

"Is it Sunday?"

"That's right. May I do anything for you—some water perhaps?"

Daisy nodded and let Evelyn help her sit up and take a drink. "I think I want to . . . stay up for a while," she said when Evelyn tried to help her back down.

Evelyn fluffed Daisy's pillows and put an extra one behind her back for support.

"Thanks," Daisy said.

"Do you feel as if you might become nauseated again?"

"Again?"

"Oh, yes, dear. You've had quite a time with nausea."

"I think I'm okay right now."

They heard a car in the driveway, and soon the church group was surrounding Daisy.

"How do you feel?" Anna asked, sitting down on the bed.

"Wonderful," Daisy said. "How do I look?"

"Gorgeous."

"Liar."

"Miss Daisy, it's mighty good to see you awake and full o' mischief again," Si said.

"Oh, honey, we've been so worried!" Dolly shook her head.

"I'm sorry."

"You don't have nothin' to be sorry for," Si said. "Where's Reed?"

"Cooking lunch for everyone," Evelyn reported.

Dolly and Anna said it at the same time: "Reed can cook?"

"Yes, he can," Reed said as he stepped into the bedroom. "But nothin' like Miss Dolly, so don't expect too much."

"Hey, I've got an idea," Dolly said. "Let's all go fix us a plate and bring it in here with Daisy. Reed and Daisy, I'll fix both o' yours. It'll be just like a picnic, only without the bugs."

"Why, that's a fine idea!" Evelyn agreed.

"If y'all will excuse me from the festivities, I promised Dolly I'd carry a Sunday plate up to Lillian," Si told them. "Think I'll take one for myself and keep her comp'ny for a little while."

"Joe and I can deliver Ella's lunch and look in on her," Harry said.

Everybody else headed for the kitchen as Reed sat down by Daisy. "How we doin'?"

"My whole foot . . . kinda feels . . . like it's on fire."

"You're about due for a shot."

"That morphine just makes me so . . . so crazy-headed. Are you gettin' any sleep at all . . . havin' to doctor me every four hours?"

"Sure."

Daisy stared at him for the longest time. "I might be dead if it wasn't for you."

Just as he was about to answer, they heard the others coming.

"Here you go," Dolly said. "Anna, honey, how 'bout pullin' that little table there by Daisy's bed." She set two plates down on the table as Reed brought in some chairs.

Anna brought tea for everybody and climbed into the bed next to Daisy, propping against some pillows and holding her plate in her lap.

"I prob'ly don't smell so good," Daisy said.

"That's okay—I'll stay upwind."

Daisy looked around the room and pointed to something on Reed's chest of drawers. "Hey, what's that doin' in here? Y'all been rereadin' Catherine's journal to pass the time?"

"I've been dying for you to wake up so I could tell you," Anna said. "That's not the same journal we all read together. It's the next part of Catherine's story—her second journal."

"Where'd you get it?"

"Well, that's the really strange part. It just appeared on Dolly's front porch, wrapped in brown paper with my name on it."

"But . . . where'd it come from?"

"We don't know, honey," Dolly said.

"Did y'all read it?"

"We did not," Evelyn said. "We all agreed that we would not read one word until you could enjoy it with us. We entrusted the journal to Reed to keep us honest."

"Did you read the rest of it?" Daisy asked him.

"Just a little bit." Reed handed the journal to her. "I think it'd make me blush, though, to read it with you ladies."

"What are we waitin' for?" Daisy said. "Here, Anna—let's make Reed blush." She passed the journal to Anna, who began to read.

April 20, 1844

Dear Self,

My wedding was everything I knew it would be—wholly orchestrated by Father for Father. Andrew and I said our vows immediately following the Easter Sunday sermon—

"Anna, read that date again," Daisy said.

"April 20, 1844."

"You know what that means?"

"No, what?"

"The last time she wrote was at the end o' March, and she said she was gettin' married in a week. She's writin' this on April 20."

"Then they didn't drown on their wedding day!"

"Bingo."

"Oh, I just knew it!"

"We're real happy for you, honey," Dolly said. "Now keep a-readin'."

Andrew and I said our vows immediately following the Sunday sermon—which Father mercifully cut shorter than usual. I wore a frock I didn't like, to marry a man I didn't know, so we could both pretend to be happy as all the church ladies fluttered around us and insisted we have some of this cobbler or that pie. I could barely swallow.

There was one moment, though, that Father couldn't control. Nor could I. After he pronounced us man and wife, he nodded to Sister Phipps, the organist, to begin the recessional, but she wouldn't do it. Instead she began gesturing to Father—no doubt trying to get him to say, "You may kiss your bride"—when Andrew, in one smooth motion, took my face in his hands, bent down, and softly kissed my mouth. The congregation applauded, and Sister Phipps began her recessional. I was so stunned that my new husband had to offer his arm and lead me out of the church just to get me moving again. I had never been kissed before—except on the cheek by cousins and aunts and uncles. Never by a man outside the family. And never on the mouth. It was so warm. And fleeting. Did I like it? I don't know. I think so. It happened so quickly. This much I'm sure of: it did not feel like hoeing the garden.

The women laughed with delight.

"Now I did read that part," Reed said. "What's hoein' the garden got to do with anything?"

The women all looked at each other and burst out laughing again.

"That's it," he said. "I'm not man enough to stay in here with y'all."

They all laughed once more as he fled to his porch.

"We were mean to scare him off like that," Daisy said.

"Isn't it just so romantic?" Anna said.

A collective sigh went around the room.

"We're gettin' distracted, y'all," Dolly protested. "Keep a-readin', honey."

Anna turned the page and continued.

When the fellowship finally ended and we prepared to leave, Andrew escorted me to his carriage, took my hand, and helped me in. It was so confusing. All this time, I had been half drawn to and half terrified by the man being forced upon me, yet whenever he touched me, whenever I felt the warmth of his skin against mine, I wasn't afraid at all. It made no sense.

The congregation threw their rice when we left the church, and then . . . silence. Not two hours ago, the man sitting next to me on that carriage seat had kissed me—his mouth and mine touching, sharing breath—and now we were strangers again. How can that be? How is it possible for the space between a man and a woman to expand and contract so?

Andrew looked down at me as if he had heard what I was thinking. "If I ask you a question, Catherine, will you tell me the truth?" he said.

I couldn't find my voice just then, so like an idiot, I only nodded.

And then he asked me, "Is it anger or fear that you're trembling to contain right now?"

Never in my life had a man asked me what I was feeling or thinking. I looked down at my hands, which were indeed trembling in my lap, and considered my answer. For whatever reason, it was important to me, in that moment, to tell my husband the truth.

Finally, I looked into his chocolate eyes and said, "I thought I might die of both at the church. But my anger is all for Father, not for you. I am afraid, though, of what I don't know. That's it, truly—I'm afraid of what I don't know."

Andrew stopped the carriage and looked at me, searching my face as if he needed more information and would eventually find it there. In that moment, I had to ask him why, with every pretty girl in the church flirting with him, he had chosen me.

"Men are forever trying to kill or cage the most beautiful things they find," Andrew said. "I'd rather set them free."

"But you bought me," I said.

"No," he said, "I paid your ransom."

Once we reached the edge of his property, he drove the carriage off the main road and stopped before a tall iron gate. He jumped down from the carriage, opened the gate, and gave the horses a command I couldn't understand. They dutifully walked through and stopped on the other side of a fence that began a few yards north of us and stretched as far as I could see to the south. Andrew climbed back in, and we followed what looked like a new road through the woods.

In a clearing on the banks of Tanyard Creek, he stopped the carriage again, turned to me, and said, "You have nothing to fear, Catherine—least of all me."

And then he told me the most incredible story. A year ago, there was a great convention of Presbyterian ministers held in Montgomery. Our family traveled there with Father. As he and the other ministers held camp meetings on the Alabama River, Andrew had passed through on a paddle wheeler bound for Mobile. It dropped anchor just a stone's throw from Father's camp.

I remember walking along the riverbank, enjoying a rare moment of freedom and wishing with all my might that I could board that beautiful boat. All the while, Andrew was watching me from the upper deck. Something about me caught his attention, he said, and he had called to a porter to fetch him a telescope. He was looking at me through that lens as I sat on the bank, tossing rocks into the water and watching the ripples roll out to nothingness, before Mother interrupted my reverie. She was carrying a small bowl of turnip greens, which I loathe. She had noticed, she said, that I hadn't taken any during the afternoon meal. Did I want to appear ungrateful to the hands that prepared them? Did I think myself above *eating them? She handed me the bowl and said she intended to stand there and watch me swallow every bite.*

Mercifully, one of the ladies called to her about then, and she had to leave me to my own devices. I waited till she was out of sight and then threw the horrible greens into the river.

Andrew watched the whole silly scene from the upper deck of that fine boat. He said he made up his mind, watching my face as I threw those greens into the water, to learn my identity—which wasn't difficult, given Father's position in the church. Andrew had already decided to leave the "vagabond life," as he calls it. And so he thought he might as well settle in Blackberry Springs—and find me.

Can you imagine? The whole time Father was trotting me out to the supper table, trying to convince Andrew of my worth, my suitor already knew what he meant to do. He had known all along.

Now here we were, a year later, two strangers on our wedding day, making our way home.

"You know everything about me, but I don't know anything about you," I said.

That's when he said the strangest thing. He said he didn't think anyone knew me because Father hadn't allowed me to show myself. He told me bluntly that he despised Father for that.

I admitted that I despised Father too, and that I was praying about it. He said I should devote my prayers to a worthier subject. I told him I believed he had secrets—a specific one, actually—something I could feel but could not name.

For a moment, he looked not so much at me as inside me—as if he were probing my heart and soul to determine whether he could trust his own wife. Abruptly, he stood up and climbed down from the carriage, then held his arms up to me and asked me to walk with him.

He lifted me down and took my hand. We began following the creek deeper into the woods. Never in my life had my heart raced so. Was he about to tell me everything or nothing? Had he truly ransomed me, as he said, or was he about to murder me in the woods? I had just married this man without knowing enough about him to gauge whether he might actually do away with me. But he was holding my hand, and I loved the strength of his long fingers around mine. I loved the height of him and the way he looked down at me. I only wished that I knew what was about to happen.

"Daisy?" Anna stopped reading. Daisy had become restless, moving around in the bed as if she couldn't get comfortable, and pulling the covers up tighter around her.

"We've tired her out," Dolly said. "Ever'body, come on and let her rest. Daisy, honey, don't you worry. We'll send Reed right in." She ushered Evelyn and a reluctant Anna out of the bedroom.

"Don't you think I should go in there and see if I can help?" Anna asked Dolly in the kitchen.

Dolly shook her head and smiled. "Let's see what comes o' lettin' the two of them get through this together."

twenty-seven

Sitting down at Daisy's bedside, Reed laid his hand on her forehead and felt the heat. Then he held her wrist and found her pulse, timing it with his watch. "Pain's pretty bad?" he asked.

Daisy nodded.

"It's my fault. I shoulda made you take somethin' earlier."

Daisy gave him a weak smile. "Good luck tryin' to push me around."

He smiled back at her and prepped a syringe.

"Will you stay with me till I go to sleep?" she asked.

"I'll stay with you after." He swabbed Daisy's arm with alcohol and gave her the shot that would stop the throbbing in her foot and let her rest.

Reed waited until she was sound asleep and then started organizing a tray of bandages and supplies so he could dress her wound while she couldn't feel anything—and also to keep her from seeing it. Snakebites always looked horrendous.

Folding back the covers at the foot of the bed, he was startled by what he saw—blood and infection seeping through Daisy's bandage. The wound had likely abscessed and would need to be excised. He hurried into the kitchen and found Dr. Sesser's number by the telephone, only to learn from the nurse that the doctor had just left to deliver twins.

After returning to Daisy's room, he opened the bottom drawer of his chest of drawers and pulled out the backpack he had carried across battlefield after battlefield. He'd thrown his medals aside but held on to the lifesaving tools that had allowed him to earn them. He didn't know why exactly, but he couldn't let that canvas bag go. The smell of it instantly stirred up The Dust Storm, constricting him so tightly he couldn't—

"No!" he said out loud. He could stew in the war later, but right now Daisy needed all his skills, and he prayed they would be enough.

He removed the instruments he would need, carried them into the kitchen, and sterilized them. He paused to listen for the women, who were all in the front parlor. That was good.

Reed locked both doors to the bedroom to keep Anna or Dolly from walking in on what he was about to do. He took out one of the last three IV bags in his kit, "overlooked" by the buddies who had packed up his gear when they shipped him home, and started a morphine drip. It would keep Daisy completely unconscious while he worked. He put a stack of clean towels under her infected foot and began.

twenty-eight

Anna was sitting on the bed next to Daisy, holding her friend's hand. For two days now, Daisy had barely stirred. The feverish red of her cheeks would fade to white as her temperature climbed and dropped over and over again. That, at least, had stopped. Daisy was now breathing easy, and her long sleep appeared more restful than before.

"There's something wrong, isn't there, Reed? Why did she start running a fever again and sleeping all the time? And why are you checking her pulse so often? Please tell me."

"I didn't wanna scare you, but her wound abscessed."

"What? When?"

"Two days ago. It was full of infection that had to be, well, removed. And the doctor was deliverin' two babies when it happened. So I didn't have any choice but to do it myself, or she could've—it just had to be done."

"Why didn't you call us?"

"You didn't need to see that, Anna. Dr. Sesser brought over some antiseptic and antibiotics, and I've been changin' her bandage and treatin' her wound several times a day like he showed me. He wanted me to keep her on a higher dose o' morphine till the pain settles down. That's why I'm watchin' her so close—to make sure I don't give her too much."

"You ought to be a doctor, do you know that?"

"Not me."

"Yes, you. If Daisy gets through this, it'll be because of you. You want to go get some breakfast while I sit with her?"

"I really don't wanna leave her till the doctor gets here."

"Then I'm bringing you a breakfast tray."

As Anna left for the kitchen, Reed checked Daisy's pulse one more time, just to be on the safe side.

⁓⊷⊶⊷⁓

"Are y'all plannin' my funeral?"

"Daisy! You're awake! Oh, thank goodness!" Anna was sitting at Daisy's bedside, clutching her hand. All the women of Dolly's house were circled around the bed.

"How . . . how long have I . . . been asleep?"

"Two days," Dolly said.

"We were beginning to think a bucket of water might be required to awaken you," Evelyn said. "Fortunately, it never came to that."

"I'm . . . so crazy-headed," Daisy said, blinking several times as if to clear the fog. "Am I still . . . at your house, Dolly?"

"Yes, honey, you're still at my house, sleepin' in Reed's room."

"Well . . . what about Ella?"

"Joe and Harry have taken good care of her," Evelyn reported. "They check on her every morning and evening—and of course, Dolly has been sending her food."

"Why have I been . . . sleepin' so much?"

"Daisy, it was amazing," Anna said. "We all can't believe it. The wound on your ankle abscessed and had all kind of infection in it that needed to come out, but Dr. Sesser was delivering babies when it happened. So Reed did it. He did surgery on your foot to keep you—to get you well."

"*Surgery?*"

"It's true, honey," Dolly said. "Without tellin' a one of us, that brave boy *operated* on you. And the doctor said it looked like a trained surgeon at the hospital had done it. Said he couldn'a done no better hisself. And he said you're gonna heal up just fine now. That's the only way we were able to pry Reed away from you and make him go upstairs to sleep."

Daisy slowly took in everything the women were saying, and then she began to cry.

"Oh, honey, don't cry!" Dolly hurried to her side. "You're gonna be fine now."

"She's right, Daisy," Anna assured her. "Everything's going to be alright. You'll start getting better now."

"It's not—it's not that," Daisy said as Dolly handed her a handkerchief. "Don't you see? I made him—go back there. Back to all those bleedin' soldiers—an' all his awful nightmares."

"Maybe so, but you did something else," Anna said. "You showed him that he can beat those nightmares. If he had let them take over, that infection could've taken you away from us, and he knew that. You gave him his fight back, Daisy." She took the handkerchief and wiped Daisy's tears away. "You're the bravest person I know."

"I don't feel very brave."

"Well, you are. You want some water?" Anna helped her sit up in bed and drink. "Are you in pain?"

"Not too bad."

"The doctor gave Reed something to deaden your foot so you can start coming off the morphine," Anna explained. "You think you could eat something?"

Daisy shook her head. She looked around the room as the fog in her brain began to clear and spotted Catherine's journal on top of Reed's chest of drawers. "Guess I missed the rest of the story."

"You did not," Evelyn said. "We all refused to read one word without you."

"Really?" Daisy smiled.

"Really," Anna said. "You just rest, and when you're up to it, we'll all read Catherine's story together."

It was pouring outside. Anna had just finished helping Daisy eat a bowl of chicken and dumplings when Evelyn and Dolly came in.

"Honey, does that feel like it's gonna stay down?" Dolly asked.

"I think so," Daisy answered. "Sure tastes good, Dolly."

"Well, you haven't eaten much o' nothin' since you got bit, honey. I 'magine anything would taste pretty good right about now."

"Do you feel as if you might enjoy a story?" Evelyn asked Daisy.

"I think I'm ready for Catherine and Andre," Daisy said.

"Okay, ladies, pull up your chairs." Anna took Daisy's empty bowl away and fetched the journal. She climbed onto the bed and fluffed the pillows behind Daisy's back as Evelyn and Dolly pulled up two chairs. When everyone was situated, Anna began to read.

April 25, 1844

I must apologize, dear self, for all the interruptions. I have had little time to write. Obviously, my husband did not murder me in the woods, or I would not be writing to you now. What he did there was change me.

We walked silently along the Tanyard until it opened into the most beautiful little slough I've ever seen—a sunlit, glassy pool with grand oaks shading the banks.

Andrew took both my hands, turned me to face him, and told me that he did indeed have secrets. A man where he came from was trying to do him in. But Andrew said he regretted nothing in his past, and he promised that no dark shadows of his would ever fall on me. Then he asked me whether I trusted him. I said yes—and I meant it.

Even so, there was something I had to know—was his name really Andrew Sinclair? It wasn't, he said, but for both our sakes I should call him that. And then I asked the hardest question of all—was our marriage even legal if he had used a false name on the license he wrote for Father to sign? His answer astonished me. He had written his real name on the license but had made it so illegible that Father couldn't tell what it said. My father held my husband's unreadable identity in the great wooden cabinet where he kept all the church records in his office. Meanwhile I—Andrew's wife—had no idea who he actually was.

He took a few steps away from me and said, "As long as we're in the confessional, I should admit that I only dressed this way to impress your father, which I don't see the need to do ever again."

He took off his hat and sent it sailing into the slough. We watched it drift toward the creek as he removed his jacket, vest, and ascot, then tossed them into the water as well. He unbuttoned the collar of his white dress shirt, removed his cuff links and pitched them in the water, then rolled up his sleeves.

"Catherine, meet your husband," he said.

"So that's how his cuff link ended up in the belly of a catfish!" Dolly exclaimed. "Y'all, I just can't believe this. Do you have any idea how many years this whole community has wondered what happened to this couple? Go back to that 'meet your husband' part, Anna."

"*Catherine, meet your husband*," *he said.*

"*Hello, husband,*" *I said, which made him smile. I had to smile myself. I told him I'd introduce him to his wife if only I knew who she was.*

"*Would you like to find out?*" *he asked.*

"*Yes,*" *I said.* "*I want to be a good wife.*"

I'll never forget what he said next: "*I'd rather have a happy woman than a good wife.*"

He asked me, to my surprise, if I liked my wedding frock—a high-collared, stiff gray linen dress with a frumpy topcoat. I told him it was a hand-me-down from Sister and that I suspected it would look like a potato sack were it not for the very tight lace collar. He moved very close to me. First he untied my bonnet and sent it sailing into the slough. Next he unbuttoned my topcoat, slipped it off my shoulders, and tossed it in as well. Then he unbuttoned the choking collar of my dress. After pausing to consider the result, he opened another button below it, and another. For a moment, I thought he might keep going all the way down my dress, but then he stopped and studied me—like a painter reviewing his work—and said, "*You can breathe now, Catherine.*" *No, I couldn't. I had stopped breathing the moment I felt his fingers brush against my throat.*

He asked whether I was happy with my hair, which Father insisted that I wear pulled back into a fat braid wound tightly and pinned against the nape of my neck, with a heavy black crocheted net to cover it. Father found blonde hair offensive. I shook my head in response. Andrew asked if he might take it down. I turned my back to him and felt him begin removing pins from my hair, taking care not to hurt me as he freed me of my confines. He threw the net into the slough and continued sliding pin after pin away until I felt the heavy, loosed braid fall down my back. And then his hands were in my hair, unwinding it from every constricting hold till it was completely unbound.

Slowly I turned around to face him. He twirled a strand through his fingers. Then he laid his free hand against the opening he had made in my dress, against my bare throat.

I thought he was about to kiss me again as he had in the church—in fact, I hoped he would—but instead, he sighed, shook his head, and let his hands fall to his sides. "I'm sorry," he said. "I'm getting ahead of myself."

"Holy mackerel!" Daisy said.

"I might need me a Liberty National fan if we keep readin' this," Dolly said.

"Ladies," Evelyn said, "we must not interrupt the narrative flow. Do continue, Anna. We will try to keep quiet till you finish."

Andrew asked if he might show me his favorite spot on the creek and held my hand as he led me there. We leisurely followed the Tanyard farther into the woods, around one bend and then another, until we came to the loveliest little waterfall, where the creek deepened on its way to the river. The pines towered above. All around this length of the creek, the ground was carpeted with emerald moss so thick that it felt like a cushion beneath my feet.

We sat down next to each other on a black wrought-iron bench that looked as if it belonged in drawings I had seen of New Orleans. There beside the falls, we re-

mained quiet together, listening to the water flow over the rocks and rhythmically plunge into the deepening channel below.

Finally, Andrew said, "You think I know everything about you, so why don't you tell me something I don't know?"

"I believe I'm the one most entitled to ask that question," I said, which made him laugh.

And then he offered me a bit of new information: until a year ago, he had made his living on the water.

I was intrigued. How?

But he shook his head and refused to tell me anything else until I reciprocated. He had the most beautiful smile I've ever seen. I couldn't look at it without smiling back.

"Tell me, Catherine," he demanded, "have you robbed the collection plate, daydreamed about stowing away on a riverboat during your Father's sermons—anything scurrilous like that?"

"Much worse," I said. I told him about all the poetry I had read—all secular and some of it romantic in nature.

"Ha!" he said with that gleaming smile. "Good for you! Which devil poets have you dallied with?"

I reported that I had devoted most of my reading to Tennyson, Byron, and Mr. Edgar Allan Poe.

"No Coleridge?" he asked. And then he looked into my eyes and recited in his velvet voice, 'In Xanadu did Kubla Khan a stately pleasure-dome decree: Where Alph, the sacred river, ran through caverns measureless to man down to a sunless sea.'"

I realized, as those exquisite words flowed out of him and into me, that this was as intimate as I had ever been with another human being. But it wasn't close enough. The blackness of my solitary past seemed as if it might devour me, like a great wave swelling ever higher till it rose above my head and crashed over me, pulling me down to the depths and pinning me there.

As he had done before, Andrew seemed to read my thoughts. "Catherine," he said, laying his hand against my face. My own hand was drawn to the open collar of his shirt, and I laid it against his bare skin as he had laid his on mine.

Suddenly, like a crack of lightning, a shot rang out from somewhere across the creek. Andrew, as startled as I was, looked up to see if he could judge where it came from. He told me we must hurry, and he put his arm around me to help me through the woods as we ran back to the carriage.

The horses seemed to sense our urgency and wasted no time making their way along the creek to another new road through the woods, where the way was clear for them to gallop. Andrew kept an arm around me as we sped through the pines. We stopped abruptly when the woods opened onto a lawn and the most beautiful house I had ever seen—graceful and grand, with double porches and lovely scrolled bannisters. It took my breath away.

On the front porch stood a woman. She looked old from where we sat, though I couldn't really tell from the carriage. She was holding something at her side. Andrew stared at her, his lips slightly parted as if he couldn't decide whether to speak. She motioned for him to come. He gave the horses another of his strange commands, and they delivered us to the front steps, where Andrew helped me down.

"What has happened, Appolline?" he asked. The woman standing before us on the porch had skin the color *of cocoa and very pale blue eyes. She looked older than my parents—perhaps in her seventies. At her side, she held a pistol.*

"This the woman?" she asked in an accent similar to Andrew's but much heavier.

Andrew introduced us, and I said, "How do you do," or something equally stupid under the circumstances. The woman said nothing but looked me up and down.

Andrew asked her again—what had happened?

She said something that sounded like "say-fin-ee."

"Alright, I'm breaking my own rule," Evelyn said. "*C'est fini* is French for 'It's finished' or 'It's done.' French would make sense for a man from Louisiana, would it not?"

"You speak French, Evelyn?" Dolly asked. "Why, honey, you're just as smart as a whip, do you know that?"

"Thank you, Dolly. I'll hush now. Go ahead, Anna."

Andrew and Appolline spoke briefly in words I didn't understand. He occasionally glanced at me, and Appolline nodded agreement to whatever he was saying.

Finally, Andrew turned to me and said he needed for me to trust him right now. We had to get Appolline out of Blackberry Springs quickly, but he promised to explain everything as soon as we were safe.

Then he kissed me—quickly but softly—and told me Appolline would help me get ready while he attended to her troubles.

Before I had a chance to say another word, Andrew disappeared behind the house, and Appolline motioned for me to follow her inside. I paused for just a moment before the sweeping staircase. From the entryway with its soaring ceiling, I could see a music room to my right, a

213

parlor to my left, and a grand dining room straight ahead. It was incredible—like something out of a poem.

Appolline motioned for me to follow her into an elegant bedroom with a tester bed. Spread over it were the loveliest dresses and underthings I had ever seen—all of them silk, satin, lace, and fine cotton. There was even a pair of breeches with a white blouse and riding boots. Appolline pointed to them and said what sounded like 'poor voo.'"

Anna paused and all the women looked at Evelyn. "*Pour vous* means 'for you,'" she said. "Go on, Anna."

Women around Blackberry Springs never wore breeches. "Best for now," Appolline said. Then she showed me a skirt that unfastened at the waist and opened up like a cape. "For when people might see," she said. She folded the skirt and put it into a small grip. Then she told me to change while she packed for me.

I stepped behind a silk screen and hurried out of my very Presbyterian clothes. Appolline brought me some of the fine underclothes, along with the breeches, blouse, and riding boots. When I was dressed and stepped from behind the screen, she paused from her work to study me, walking around me in a circle and looking me up and down. She said, "Bébé chose well," and resumed her packing.

None of the fine dresses were going into the grip she was packing. "What about those?" I asked.

She told me I couldn't wear them where we were going and promised that "Bébé" would buy me more. She said we had to think only of life right now.

I followed her back to the carriage and climbed in behind her. Giving the horses the same kind of foreign com-

*mand Andrew had spoken, Appolline sent us on our way
up a dirt road away from the house and across a cotton
field to a small shotgun cottage at the edge of the woods.
She climbed down and began tugging at my trunk, trying
to get it down.*

*She looked surprised when I offered to help. The two
of us carried the trunk onto the front porch and then
slid it inside the house. Appolline opened it and told me
I would never see it again. She asked what I wanted to
take with me.*

*I looked down at the frumpy clothes, all handed down
from my sister and none of them even belonging to me.
I thought of my poetry disguised as philosophy. Surely
there would be no way to carry books with me wherever
we were going. I considered my journal, which would be
impossible to hide with the three of us traveling together.
I would die of embarrassment if Andrew should read any
of it. I removed the two blank journals from the trunk.*

"Nothing else," I said. "I don't want any of it."

*Appolline picked up a rug in the kitchen and opened
a small trapdoor beneath it. "No one will look here,"
she said. I helped her slide everything I owned down the
wooden steps of her root cellar. Covering the trapdoor
with the rug, she said again, "Say-fin-ee."*

"I just can't believe this landed on our doorstep," Anna said,
looking at Daisy. "Hey, what's the matter?"

"I don't feel so good," she said.

twenty-nine

Daisy endured one more bout with nausea before she turned a corner and began improving. She had been walking on crutches, but Dolly insisted she be able to walk without them before going back to Ella's, where she would have to contend with stairs.

"You sure you wanna try to put weight on it?" Reed had one arm around Daisy's waist and was holding his other hand out so she could brace against it. Now that she wasn't in constant pain anymore, and Anna had helped her get a bath, wash her hair, and put on clean clothes, she was getting restless.

"I'm just sick o' this room," she said. "No offense."

"None taken. I'm ready when you are."

Daisy took a tentative step and winced.

"Hurts?" Reed asked her.

"A little. Mostly it's just sore. Let's try to make it to your porch."

He helped her slowly walk into the fresh air of the porch and sit down on the twin bed.

"Prob'ly shouldn't let your foot dangle like that—let's prop you up." He put pillows against the headboard so she could lean against it and prop her feet up on the bed. Then he went

216

into the kitchen and came back with an ice pack, which he laid against the stitches he had sewn in.

"I thought Dr. Sesser told you to come by so he could take your stitches out."

"He did. But I never had stitches before and I'm kinda scared to go."

"I don't think it'll be bad."

"Would you take 'em out?"

"I've had more practice puttin' 'em in, Daisy."

"I just don't think it'll hurt if you do it."

Reed went to the kitchen to wash his hands and sterilize the surgical scissors and tweezers from his medical bag. Then he came out and sat on the edge of the bed, with Daisy's feet in his lap. He blotted the stitches with alcohol and then swabbed a spot just above them, where he gave her a shot of the local anesthetic Dr. Sesser had left to deaden her foot. Just a tiny dose would be all she needed this time.

"Doin' okay?" he asked her.

Daisy nodded, but he knew she was anxious about it. He ran his finger lightly over the stitches. "Feel any pain?"

She shook her head. "Can't feel anything."

Reed began clipping the stitches and gently removing them with the same tweezers he had once used to pull shrapnel out of bleeding soldiers. But this time The Dust Storm didn't kick up. He was too focused on Daisy.

"All done."

Daisy had been looking away while he worked. Now she leaned forward to see for herself. "Painless," she said with a smile.

Reed grinned at her. "My bill's gonna be a doozy." He traced the scar with the tip of his finger, then looked up at her. "I scarred you for life, Daisy."

"You saved my life, Reed." They looked at each other for

a moment before she said, "I need to tell you somethin', and you're gonna think I'm crazy."

He smiled at her and shrugged. "Already leanin' in that direction."

"Pull up a chair. Dolly'll have a conniption if she comes out here and sees two single unmarrieds sittin' on the same bed."

Once Reed sat down in the rocker, Daisy blurted out, "I saw Charlie this mornin'."

"What do you mean, you saw him?"

"I mean I *saw* him, plain as day, standin' right in the back corner o' your room. Has all that morphine made me completely bonkers?"

"You're not takin' morphine anymore. And I don't think you're bonkers. You were seein' him before the snakebite, right? Like that time at the curb market you told me about?"

"Yeah, but this was different. I had to be dreamin', right? Only how could I dream and drink water at the same time?"

"Back up just a little."

"When I woke up this mornin', I was thirsty, so I sat up and took a drink o' water. But then I tried to put the glass back on the nightstand and dropped it—spilled a little puddle on the floor and had to get outta bed to wipe it up. When I got back in bed, Charlie was standin' in the corner o' your room, smilin' at me."

"Was he in uniform?"

"Yeah, his dress uniform. And here's the strange part—well, the even *stranger* part. There was a white dove sittin' on each of his shoulders."

"Did he say anything—Charlie, I mean?"

"Yeah, when he turned the doves loose. He took the first one off his right shoulder, cupped it in his hands, and said, 'I had to go, but you didn't send me.' Then he lifted it up and said, 'Fly now.' It circled above the bed three times, and every time it went around, some of its white feathers turned all these beautiful colors. When all the feathers were rainbow colored, the ceiling opened up and the dove flew out to a bright blue sky. Then Charlie took the second dove off his left shoulder and held it in his hands like before. It was wearin' somethin' around its neck—an eagle on top of a cross hangin' from a red, white, and blue ribbon."

Reed knew exactly what a Distinguished Service Cross looked like. He had discarded two of them in a drawer back home. The mention of them was like a kick in the gut, which Daisy must have sensed, like always.

"You want me to stop?" she asked.

"No, keep goin'."

"Charlie said, 'Heaven is deacon's joy. Let him go.' And then he lifted up the dove, and it flew straight up before glidin' back down and flutterin' past that bottom drawer in your chest of drawers. Then it took off through the hole in the ceilin' and into the sky. When I looked back down, Charlie was gone."

Reed felt his eyes stinging, his heart racing, and his stomach churning. The Dust Storm, he feared, might swallow him for good this time. He was taking deep breaths, trying to keep calm, but they were coming faster and faster as his ears began to roar, and he felt like his head was spinning. He held it in his hands to try to stop the unnerving motion.

"Reed? Reed!"

When he finally got a grip on himself, Daisy was sitting on the edge of the bed with her hands on his shoulders. He was struggling for normal breath, like a runner who had finally finished a race he always knew he couldn't win.

"You need to tell me," Daisy said.

He shook his head, as if the thought of letting her near the images in his mind would surely do them both in.

Daisy laid a pillow in her lap. "Lay your head down here

and stretch your legs out that way." At first he only blinked at her. She calmly repeated her directions, patting the pillow and pointing to the bed so that Reed could understand.

"Your foot," he started to protest.

"Don't worry about that right now."

He lay down on his side with his head in her lap and curled up on the bed. She stroked his hair as he struggled to calm down.

"I think you need to tell me about the deacon in heaven," she said. "You can stop if it gets to be too much. But do the best you can, and we'll see if it shows us a way outta that storm o' yours so you don't have to dread it comin' anymore."

Reed was finally breathing normally again. The porch was silent while he found his voice. "Not *the* deacon . . . just Deacon. My best friend in the Army. A Yankee boy from Long Island."

"Y'all were close like me and Anna?"

Reed nodded. "He knew a lotta things about the world, and I knew stuff about the land. We stuck together, him and me . . . all the way from boot camp to the troop ship . . . all the way onto that bloody hill . . . kept each other alive . . . kept each other from crackin' up."

Reed was quiet for a while before Daisy helped him along. "You lost Deacon on that hill, didn't you?"

"He got hit real bad . . . pinned down out in the open . . . maybe ten yards from me. I crawled out there to him . . . dragged him behind what little cover we had. Did all I knew to do. 'Hold on, buddy,' I said. He looked straight at me . . ."

As Reed's voice trailed off, Daisy coaxed him again. "What did he say when he looked straight at you?"

"He said, 'What for?' And then he was gone. Just gone. That's when I got hit. It felt like my leg was full o' fire, and then I woke up in a field hospital."

"Go back to that 'what for,'" Daisy said.

"It's the part I can't get outta my mind. What did he mean?

That he knew I couldn't save him? That he didn't see any reason to hold on—any reason to live?"

"Remember what you told me about it bein' a soldier's time? Maybe Deacon just knew it was his time."

"What if I'd moved faster—got there quicker? Was I too worried about my own hide? I turn it over and over in my mind till I wanna scream."

"Reed, you wouldn'a been thinkin' o' yourself when your friend needed you. You just ain't wired that way. No matter what you did or didn't do, it was the best you or anybody else coulda done. Whatever you mighta done different wouldn'a changed anything. It's awful and it don't make sense, but it was just Deacon's time."

Reed turned to lie on his back, his head still in Daisy's lap. Looking up at her, he said, "You really think that was Charlie you saw?"

"Who else would know about Deacon? And I'll tell you somethin' about Charlie. He wasn't perfect, but he never lied. If he says Deacon's happy in heaven, I believe him."

Reed laid his hand against her face. "Then I'll try to believe him too."

thirty

Reed wasn't sure why he felt so lonesome. He had arranged for this trip to Oleander Springs weeks ago, on his doctor's recommendation. And now that it was time, he didn't want to go. All he could think about was Daisy and the way she had looked at him when she held his head on her lap and told him about Deacon. The last thing he wanted to do right now was put miles between them, but anything that might help him heal was worth enduring.

Oleander Springs wasn't far from the Florida line. Palm trees aside, something about it reminded Reed of an Army base—or maybe an Army hospital. He had driven through the iron gates of the resort around two o'clock in the afternoon. The sprawling, single-story white motel had green shutters and wrapped around two outdoor pools—one with steam rising above it like a fog, the other a cooling, blissful blue. Guests could relax in one till the heat overcame them and then splash into the bracing waters of the other.

Reed checked in, put on his bathing suit, and made his way to the warm, spring-fed pool. Easing into the soothing water, he took a seat on a ledge about two feet below the surface and relaxed, trying to clear his mind.

Looking around the pool deck, he saw what could've been one picture postcard after another: a young dad standing waist deep in the blue pool and holding his toddler, her back against his chest and her legs dangling over his arm as she kicked her feet in the water; a couple sitting together on a park bench, studying a road map; three elderly ladies wearing cotton dresses, straw hats, and sandals over white-socked feet, sitting side by side in lounge chairs with umbrellas to shade them. None of it seemed real to Reed. It was as if he were in some kind of bubble—or maybe everybody else was. He could see them and hear them. But he couldn't touch them. He wasn't even sure he wanted to.

As he watched the toddler nestled in the safety of her daddy's arms, gleefully kicking her chubby little legs and giggling with every splash, he ran his hand along his own scarred leg hidden beneath the water and thought of another child he'd once held in his arms. He had clutched her against his chest as he sprinted from a bombed-out church, across an open field, to a Red Cross truck, where a nurse took her from him. That little girl, with her curly black hair and dark, sad eyes, couldn't have been more than three years old. Her legs had dangled over his arm just as the little girl's legs dangled over her father's in the swimming pool. Reed had no idea what had become of her. He didn't even know her name. But he could still see her little hand clutching his shirt as he ran through the blasts and the smoke with her. So much trust in a stranger. So much suffering for a child . . .

"I'd bet a shiny nickel you're a war hero."

Reed turned to see what Daisy would call a beauty queen sitting next to him—full makeup and perfectly styled shoulder-length blonde hair. He had been so preoccupied with the poolside tableau that he hadn't heard her glide onto the bench next to him.

223

"Just a vet," he said with a polite smile. With his leg underwater, he looked normal, and he knew what was coming—the flirty tilt of the head, the eye batting and flattery . . .

"I'm Natalie."

"Nice to meet you, Natalie. I'm Reed."

"You must be *so* brave," she said with a pageant-worthy smile and a head tilt.

"Just glad I made it home."

"Well, don't be shy! Tell me all about it. Where were you?"

"North Africa and Italy."

"Did you get to meet General MacArthur?"

For half a second, he considered explaining the geography of the war, but then she probably wasn't listening to anything he said anyway. Girls like Natalie were usually too busy plotting their next move to get bogged down in anything as mundane as conversation. "Sorry to say I didn't," he said.

Here came the eye batting. "Well, now, after all you've been through, I just might have to let you take me to dinner."

There was a time when he would've obliged a girl like Natalie. But now the thought of spending the evening with her made him tired. And for reasons he couldn't explain, it would feel like cheating on Daisy. Telling Natalie he had a girl back home would do no good. The Natalies of the world were usually confident in their ability to take any guy away from any girl. He needed an escape hatch.

"That's mighty kind o' you," Reed said. "I have to stay in the pool a little while longer—Doc's orders. He wants me to keep my left leg strong since they have to take the right one off next week."

"What?"

"Got hit pretty bad over there. Both legs. There's a slim chance they can save the left one, but the right one's a goner."

"Oh."

224

"What time did you wanna have dinner?"

"You know what?" she said, shaking her head. "I am such a goose. I forgot all about a family to-do that Mama roped me into. We'll do it another time, okay?"

"That sounds great," Reed said, knowing he had seen the last of Natalie as she scrambled out of the pool.

"Hey, man, you mind if I pick up where you left off?"

A few minutes after Natalie sprinted away from him, a guy about Reed's age took her place in the pool.

"Be my guest," Reed said.

"Where'd you serve?"

"Thirty-fourth infantry."

"USS *Pillsbury*."

Reed nodded. He didn't want to be rude, but he didn't want to swap war stories either.

"Bobby Stillwell." The sailor offered Reed a handshake.

"Reed Ingram." Reed shook his hand.

"Strange, ain't it?" Bobby said. "Girls like Natalie flirtin' around a swimmin' pool when all hell's breakin' loose over there."

"It's strange alright."

"Well, I ain't over there no more, hallelujah, so I mean to make up for lost time. See you around?"

"Sure." Reed looked on as Bobby strategically bumped into Natalie at the other end of the pool. He saw her head tilt and imagined her eyes batting. Watching the two of them made him feel lonesome and homesick. Right now he would've given anything to talk to Daisy.

As he climbed out of the pool and dried off next to a lounge chair, he could hear a couple of teenage girls loudly whispering to each other about his leg. He knew how it looked, but he was through hiding it. If people back home didn't want to see the war, they could look away.

And another thing—he had absolutely no desire to be here.

⁓◠⁓

Supper was served buffet style in the dining hall, which was a wood-frame structure as big as a barn. Tall windows overlooked a lake rimmed with boat docks and fishing piers. A screened porch held outdoor dining space for those willing to brave the south Alabama heat.

Reed half considered skipping supper altogether so he wouldn't have to deal with a dining hall full of chatter, but it had been a long day and he was hungry. Most of the other guests had already been served by the time he stepped up to the long buffet table. Three colored ladies wearing immaculate, starched white uniforms were dishing out catfish, fried chicken, pot roast, hush puppies and cornbread, green beans, coleslaw, baked potatoes, squash casserole, fried okra, and banana pudding. He thanked them for his heaping plate of catfish and found an empty table for two beside one of the windows overlooking the lake.

The fish was perfectly fried—golden brown with nothing but cornmeal for a crust—and the hush puppies were light and airy. This was the kind of food he had dreamed of on long, hot days at the front, with nothing but K rations and water to sustain him.

Looking around the dining hall, he spotted all the people he had watched at the pool—the dad and his toddler, plus a wife and two older children; the couple; the three ladies. There were others, most of them families with kids, all with mouths moving.

"Daddy, can we go to the amusement park tomorrow?"

"You'd think, at these prices, they could keep it cool in here."

"I just love the food, but why couldn't we get a table with a view?"

"I'm calling the manager about that blown lightbulb in our room. I mean, at these prices . . ."

Reed found himself tuning in to a conversation on the porch, which he could hear through the open window.

"You must be *so* brave!"

"Aw, it was nothin'."

"How about taking a girl for a walk under that full moon out there?"

Natalie and Bobby Stillwell. Reed didn't even have to look out the window to identify the mouths attached to those voices. What would it be like to go through life like Bobby and Natalie—one refusing to work the puzzle, the other completely oblivious to it?

"Something tells me you'd love to serve your country."

Reed looked up to see a wiry man in plaid pants and a red golf shirt standing over his table. "'Scuse me?"

Without invitation, the man took a seat at Reed's table. "You just strike me as the kinda young man who wants to give something back to the US of A."

"Think I already did."

"Oh, I'm not talkin' about military service. I can tell by lookin' at you that you've served. But now it's time to serve again."

"I don't mean to be rude, but I'd just like to have a quiet supper."

"And wouldn't we all? But how can we sit quietly by while our veterans suffer?"

Reed stared at him and debated whether to forsake his food just to get away.

"That sufferin' is needless—*needless*. And *you* have the power to stop it. United America is prepared to sell *all* veterans—we're talkin' every branch o' the service—a top-notch life insurance policy at unbelievable discounts. And we need vets like you to spread the word—wear your uniform, take our beautiful red, white, and blue sales kit to your brothers in arms, and help them get the security they so richly deserve."

"Don't you think we needed that insurance before we left?"

"Wouldn'a been cost effective—too much risk. But now—*now*—why, we can make a real difference in the lives of our servicemen. And we consider it our patriotic duty to get our life insurance into their hands."

"Get away from me."

"Now hold on, son."

Reed spoke very calmly. "I'm not your son. And if you don't get away from me, I'm gonna hit you—right in the face."

The insurance man turned beet red and kept babbling about his patriotic duty as he backed away from the table.

Reed finished his supper as quickly as he could and headed for the walkway around the lake. He was skipping rocks off the water and enjoying the moonlit night when he saw Natalie and Bobby walk down the hill from the dining hall, hand in hand, and climb into a rowboat. He could hear Natalie giggling and flirting—"You better stop that, sailor!"—as Bobby rowed them across the lake.

The best thing Reed could say about Oleander Springs was that he planned to leave it behind early in the morning. He had found no healing here. But now he knew where to look for it.

Reed checked his watch—6:00 a.m. Dressing as quickly as he could, he packed his grip and locked the door behind him before heading to the office to turn in his key. He could see the clerk through the office window, which gave a solitary glow of light this time of morning. No doubt most of the guests were sleeping in.

"Everything okay? Didn't you just get here yesterday?" The clerk looked concerned.

"Yes, ma'am, but somethin' came up back home and I need to get goin'."

"Well, I'm sorry to hear that. Let me just pull up your bill and we'll get you on the road."

As the clerk did her paperwork, Reed looked out the office window at the two swimming pools. The warm one was especially steamy in the dim dawn light, the cool morning air mixing with heat from the mineral spring below. Through the steamy mist, something caught his eye—something off, something not quite right. He opened the office door to get a better view, then suddenly turned to the clerk and yelled, "Call an ambulance!"

"What for?" The clerk hurried around her desk and out the office door just as Reed, fully clothed, jumped into the steaming pool. Seconds later, he climbed back out, dragging a body behind him.

"Oh, dear heaven!" the clerk cried as Reed turned over the body and tried pumping on the man's chest to force the water out of his lungs. "What do I do? Who is that? Oh, this is just awful!"

"Call an ambulance!" Reed shouted again, bringing her to her senses enough to dial the telephone.

Reed kept up his efforts, staring in disbelief at the young man he was trying to revive—the man with the alabaster face and blue lips and set eyes staring into nothingness. Another sailor lost at sea.

⁓◦◦⁓

Loading his grip into his truck, Reed glanced in the direction of the office and counted three town police cars—probably all they had—plus an ambulance and the state patrolman who had taken his statement and the clerk's. A crowd of onlookers had gathered outside the office, their voices pecking at Reed like mean chickens in a barnyard.

"Oh, it's just awful . . . so young . . . The policeman said he did it on purpose . . ."

thirty-one

"Daisy, is something the matter?"

"No, why?" She was propped against a tree at her favorite spot on the creek when Anna found her.

"You just haven't been yourself since Reed left for that resort." Anna sat down next to her and tossed a rock in the creek.

"Got a lot on my mind, I guess."

Anna tossed another rock in the water. "You miss him?"

Daisy put her face in her hands and shook her head. "What am I gonna do, Anna?"

"Well . . . I imagine you'll go on a few dates and then realize what a waste of time that is and get married."

"Stop!"

"You know you've thought about it. You'd be crazy not to."

"I just never thought o' myself as somebody that somebody like him would think about."

"Come again?"

"You know what I mean. Reed's perfect. War hero perfect. And I'm such a mess."

"No, you're not. You've just been pretending to be so men would leave you alone till you didn't want to be alone anymore."

"Anna, I knew Charlie my whole life. I've known Reed—what—a heartbeat?"

"Catherine fell for Andre the minute she heard his voice."

"Yeah, but Reed's not a river pirate, and I'm no moony-eyed preacher's daughter, so it's a little different. Then there's the other thing."

"What other thing?"

"Well . . . Charlie and me . . . we knew each other since we were kids. And we started datin' in junior high. It was just always so . . . comfortable, I guess. I never *fell* in love with Charlie, I just always *loved* Charlie. And now Reed comes along. I mean, Anna, ka-wham! I'm prob'ly just bein' stupid. Bet there's a bunch o' beauty queens at that resort just a-smilin' at him right now."

"The important thing is, do you think he's smiling back? Tell the truth."

Daisy shrugged and didn't answer.

"Honestly, Daisy, the only two people on this loop who aren't already making wedding plans for you and Reed are you and Reed."

Daisy smiled at her. "You can be so dang aggravatin'."

thirty-two

Reed pulled into Ella's driveway and found Daisy watering flowers in the backyard.

"Hey," she said, shutting off the garden hose and dropping it at her feet.

"Hey," he said with a smile as he walked toward her.

Daisy frowned. "I thought you were gonna be gone a lot longer."

"Didn't work out that way."

"You wanna sit for a minute?" She led him to the swing in Ella's backyard. "So did you meet any beauty queens at that resort?"

"I did."

"Figured as much."

"She asked me where I was stationed. When I told her North Africa, she wanted to know if I got to meet General MacArthur."

"But he's in the Pacific."

"Thought about explainin' that, but I don't believe she was listenin'."

"Bet you took her out anyway."

"I was goin' to . . . but she insisted on wearin' her crown to dinner and I didn't wanna get stared at."

"Are you *serious*?"

"No." Reed laughed. "Another vet did the honors."

"You sorry about that?"

"I'm sorry I went down there. I'm real sorry about that."

"How come?"

Reed rocked silently in the swing before he told her. "He killed himself, Daisy."

"Who?"

"The vet who went after the beauty queen at the resort. A sailor. He sat down right next to me in the pool. Said he was puttin' the war behind him and wanted to know if he could try his luck with her since I wasn't goin' to. I saw 'em laughin' and talkin' in the dinin' hall. Saw 'em kissin' in the moonlight. And the next mornin' I had to fish his body out of the pool. That sailor went on a date with a pretty girl at Oleander Springs and then drowned himself in its healin' waters. What you make o' that, Daisy? What are we s'posed to make o' that?"

"Pull back, pull back! Cover the medic!"

"No!" Reed woke himself up screaming it. He was wet with sweat and gasping for breath, his heart racing, his hands trembling. He could've sworn he heard footsteps outside, like someone running on the loop, but it had to be part of the nightmare.

The one saving grace was that the stillness of this summer night had driven him out onto his porch, putting two doors between his torment and the sweet couple who had given him refuge. He was miserably hot and longed to splash cold water on his face, but even that might wake Dolly and Si. He stepped outside, walked across the yard to the lake, and jumped into the shallow water.

The moon was high and full. He threw water onto his face, chest, and back, relishing the blessed coolness as his heart slowed its fitful beating and he could breathe again. He knew what had brought this on. That sailor's suicide, for one thing. He couldn't seem to shake it. And he never should've joined the others around Dolly's radio, listening to reports from the front. It was a miracle any of the guys made it into France, let alone took it from the Germans who had dug in—just like they had dug in on that bloody hill.

Hill or village, victory or defeat, Reed believed the consequences for a soldier were the same: memories. Vicious, horrifying, haunting memories. Even when he wasn't consciously wrestling with them, he always knew they were there, lurking in the shadows of his mind, waiting for the perfect moment to ambush his sanity. All those voices from the war, coming over the airwaves and into Dolly's parlor, had awakened the slumbering specters that never really left him.

After climbing the steps out of the water, he stood on the porch and listened. Something about the skating rink seemed disturbed. That's the only way he could describe it. Reed walked the length of the porch and stepped off the back, following the path toward the creek for a short distance. He stopped and took a deep breath. The smell was faint but unmistakable. Gasoline. And this time he knew he wasn't dreaming. This time he wasn't imagining a battlefield conjured by a radio broadcast.

A few more steps and his foot struck metal. It was a gas can, almost full, no doubt dropped by whoever fled when they heard him coming. He took one more look around the woods, then picked up the can and headed back to Dolly's. Whoever intended mischief here was gone for now. But they'd be back. Trouble like that always came back.

thirty-three

Both banks of the creek were lined with people as everybody on the loop gathered to watch the annual seining of the Tanyard for the Fourth of July fish fry. They stood just beyond the slough, where the creek deepened on its way to the Coosa River, waiting for Slick Harper to begin his journey.

Slick had the best bass boat on the loop. The men had attached a great net to the back, with ropes long enough to keep it a few feet back from the trolling motor that powered the boat. A couple of teenage boys—the strongest swimmers in the community—were in the boat with Slick. Once the net began to fill, they would jump out and swim alongside, holding it up so the weight of the fish couldn't pull it down.

"Ready, boys?" Slick called.

Away they went down the Tanyard as the crowd let out a cheer.

"You ever seen this done before?" Jesse asked Reed and Daisy.

"A few times," Reed said.

"They used to do it every summer back home," Daisy said.

"Is it a certain kind of fish that they'll cook?" Anna asked.

Reed shook his head. "Best I remember, they cook whatever they catch—just throw it all in one big pot and fry it up."

"That's how they do it in the Delta." Daisy winked at Reed

and added, "One time they hauled in a long-winded Baptist preacher."

"What!" Anna exclaimed.

Daisy kept a straight face. "Personally, I didn't think it was Christian to fry him, but we were a little short on fish that year."

"Fry him?" Anna looked horrified. "They fried a *person*? Why, that's just horrible! How on earth—"

Daisy couldn't hold it in any longer. The couples were still laughing together when Slick's boat disappeared from sight.

"Guess we'd better get to the house and help Dolly," Daisy said.

"I ought to shove you into that kettle of oil for making me believe such a crazy story," Anna said.

"I'll bring the tartar sauce," Jesse said.

༺ⱷⱷⱷ༻

Dolly's yard was like a beehive, with men frying huge batches of fish and dumping them onto newspaper spread over make-shift tables made from plywood and two-by-fours. Quartered watermelons were everywhere, and Dolly had filled washtubs with ice to hold big jugs of lemonade and sweet tea. All the women of the loop had brought cakes and pies, potato salad and coleslaw.

"There are people here I've never seen before," Anna said, looking around Dolly's yard at all the families, colored and white, who were sitting on quilts spread over the grass and sharing fried bream, catfish, crappie, and hush puppies. Anna, Jesse, Daisy, and Reed had found spots in the rockers on Dolly's front porch.

Across the road, the lake was overflowing with swimmers, some of whom drifted over in their bathing suits, drawn by the aroma of fried fish. As usual, Dolly fed everybody in sight and had some of the teenagers carry Si a plate.

237

"It really stinks that Dolly's sister couldn't come," Daisy said.

Anna shook her head. "I know. She's been hoping all summer to see Violet today."

Batch after batch of fresh fish went into the kettle in Dolly's yard until finally the protests of "I couldn't eat another bite" and "I'm full as a tick" started drifting through the crowd, which began to disperse.

At sunset, Si closed up the rink but let the swimmers keep enjoying the lake if they wanted to. He invited Jesse and Reed to join the other men of Dolly's house at the well house while the women helped Dolly clean up.

"Hey, Miss Dolly, looka here what Mr. Harper done gimme!" A scruffy boy of about twelve came running to show Dolly his treasure.

"Why, that looks like a piece o' silver, R.W."

"Mr. Johnson says I can sell it. He says it's what they call a cuffed link, and it's real silver."

Dolly turned it over in her hand.

"See?" the boy said. "Got the letter 'S' on it. Ain't that somethin'? Looks real old."

"It sure does, honey. Don't you lose it now. And I wouldn't go flashin' it around too much."

"I won't. Bye, Miss Dolly—and Mama says thank you for all the food you sent home."

"You tell her she's more than welcome. And you remember our little secret?"

R.W. smiled. "Yes'm. If our cupboards get bare, I'll slip and tell you."

"That's my sweet boy!" Dolly hugged R.W. before he ran off with his treasure, and then she turned to Anna, who looked stunned.

"Do you ever feel like Catherine and Andre are going to walk

238

into your parlor and sit down with us for tea?" Anna asked. "They just seem so . . . so *real* to me."

"Honey, they *were* real. And anybody who was, always is to the people that love 'em."

"Hey, where's Reed?" Daisy was standing with Anna and Jesse on the boardwalk at the lake, where everybody on the loop had gathered after dark to watch Si's fireworks display.

"He had to go," Jesse said.

"But why? Jesse—somethin' the matter?"

"It was the fireworks. They were giving him a lot of trouble. He slipped away a couple of minutes ago—didn't want to ruin it for you."

Boom! Another burst of color exploded in the sky, bringing cheers from the crowd.

Daisy froze until Anna squeezed her hand and told her, "Go!"

Daisy ran back to Dolly's house and found Reed on his porch, sitting on the edge of the bed and holding a pillow around his head to try to block out the sound. He jumped when she sat down next to him.

"I don't want you to see this, Daisy," he said. "This one— it's real bad."

"I know."

"You should go."

"I ain't goin' nowhere." Daisy took the pillow away from him and put it in her lap, just as she had when he'd told her about Deacon. "Lay your head down and put your feet up."

Reed squinted at her as if he couldn't quite make her out.

"Lay your head down right here," she repeated, patting the pillow in her lap, "and put your feet up on the bed there." She pointed in the direction she wanted him to go.

Reed obeyed her, appearing too shaken and drained to do

anything but follow a command. Daisy stroked his hair as if he were that little boy with a skinned knee Dolly had tended long ago.

"Just breathe," she said as he flinched with each boom and flash of light. "Nobody's shootin' at you, Reed. And I ain't goin' nowhere."

thirty-four

Jesse all but ran to his truck the minute the whistle blew in the lumberyard. It was quitting time on Thursday, with just one more day till the weekend. As he turned onto the loop and rounded the bend to Dolly's house, he started looking for Anna on the front porch, but she wasn't there.

He parked his truck and walked to the porch, where he was greeted not by Anna but by Dolly. "Jesse, honey, thank goodness you're finally home," she said, leading him to the porch swing.

"Is something wrong? Is something wrong with Anna?"

"Anna's fine—I mean, she's not sick or anything—but honey, she got a big heartbreak today."

"One of her brothers?"

"No. Her friend Lillian. Si found her dead this morning. He got worried when he didn't see her on her porch all day yesterday and went in the house to check on her. He said it was like she knew. She was dressed nice and had her hair pinned back and was layin' in her bed on top o' the covers. She left a package addressed to Anna on her bedside table."

Jesse shook his head. "She'll have a really hard time with this."

Dolly nodded. "Lillian was a great comfort to her when— when y'all first moved here."

"You mean when I was acting like a jerk."

"Oh, honey, I didn't mean it that way."

"It's okay, Dolly. It's the truth. What should I do?"

"Go upstairs and be with Anna. I don't know if she's opened Lillian's package yet, but she hasn't come down since she got the news. Daisy stayed with her for a while, but you're the one she needs right now. I'll bring y'all a tray up tonight so she don't have to come to the supper table."

As the two of them stood up from the swing, Jesse did something he had never done before. He hugged Dolly. "Thank you," he said. "Thank you for taking care of her—and not just today."

Jesse opened the door to the room he shared with his wife and found her curled up on the bed with her back to him. She didn't move. He slipped off his work boots, lay down beside her, and put his arm around her. Anna awoke with a start and turned to see him there beside her. She dissolved into his shoulder as he put his arms around her and held her.

"I just can't believe she's gone," Anna finally said. "I mean, I know she was old, but still . . ."

Jesse kissed her forehead and ran his fingers through her hair. "I'm sorry. I know she was your friend."

"More than that."

"Tell me."

"I felt like—like she had some sort of gift. Like whenever she told me to go somewhere or do something and I did it, something good would happen."

"And you liked her pirate stories."

"They weren't just stories to me."

He rolled her over on the bed so that she was lying on her back, looking up at him. "It's alright, Anna. You can tell me."

"Well . . . I guess I met Lillian . . . at a time when . . . when I really needed her."

"Because you didn't have me."

"I didn't mean—"

"I know what I did. And I know how wrong I was." He bent down and kissed her. "Tell me about Lillian. Tell me why her stories mattered to you."

"I guess . . . I guess I feel like we're connected somehow— Andre and Catherine and you and me, Reed and Daisy. I just really want to believe in happy endings—for all of us."

"I want that too," he said as he kissed her again.

Neither of them heard Dolly leave a tray outside their door and quietly slip away. And they didn't see the heavy old doorstop slip away from its catch and anchor itself to the floor.

⁀◦◦⁀

Morning came, bringing with it the sunny promise that everything would be back to normal. But it wasn't, not for Anna anyway. She asked Jesse if he wanted to open Lillian's package with her. He put his arms around her and said, "I have a feeling that's something you need to do by yourself. But if I'm wrong, just hold on to it till I get home tonight and we'll open it together."

Jesse wasn't wrong. She needed one last visit alone with Lillian. After the breakfast dishes were done, she retreated to the upper porch and sat down with Lillian's package. It was wrapped in brown paper, with an envelope tucked under the string around it. Anna slid the envelope free and opened it, unfolding a letter written on fine ivory note paper.

Sweet Anna,

If you are reading this letter, which R.W. was kind enough to write for me, then I have left this mortal plane. I divine that my crossing will upset you, and I want you to

243

know that you should shed nary a tear for me—save one or two we may cry together for our temporary parting. All of my people are on the other side now, and I want you to know that when my time came, I was ready to go. I was feeling the pull of that heavenly current, and I had no desire to row against it. My days here have passed; my days there are beginning. I must sail on.

I wanted you to have some books that are very precious to me—one I'm leaving you now, the other I had delivered to your doorstep a little while ago. Think of us rocking together on my porch when you read them, and know that I intend to ask the Almighty if I might look in on you from time to time.

Eventually you will learn how I came to possess my little tomes. For now, just enjoy them and believe that I will eternally treasure our time together. You have filled an old woman's last days with comfort and companionship.

Persevere, dear Anna. Persevere. Read every word. All will be well.

Love,
Lillian

Anna folded the letter and put it back in the envelope, then cried once more for her lost friend.

Anna was blotting her face at the washstand when she heard a knock at her door and opened it to find Daisy standing there.

"You okay?" Daisy asked as she came in.

"I'm alright. Just sad. Guess I'll feel that way for a while."

Daisy followed Anna to two rockers on the porch outside her room. "You still haven't opened it?" She pointed to the package.

Anna shook her head. "I read the letter, though." She handed it to Daisy, who read it through.

"She says she's the one who left you Catherine's journal on the doorstep? But where'd she get it? And how'd she get it onto Dolly's porch?"

Anna shrugged. "Don't know, but she says we'll be able to figure it out. She told me one time that her parents were friends with Catherine and Andre, so that's probably how she got the journals."

"You don't wanna talk about it right now, do you?"

"I just feel—I don't know—kind of hollow on the inside. I guess I really should open her package, though. Will you do it for me?"

Daisy picked up the package, untied the string around it, and pulled away the brown paper.

"That's really old," Anna said as Daisy unwrapped a wooden box about the size of a shoebox. Carved into the lid and sides were flowers that looked like daffodils.

Daisy opened the box and pulled out a small, leather-bound book. Turning to the first page, she read, "'April 2, 1847. Dear Self . . .' It's her, Anna. Lillian's left you the rest of Catherine's story. But we don't need to read it now."

The two friends sat quietly and rocked together on Dolly's porch, looking down at all the laughing swimmers splashing in the lake below, oblivious to what was lost.

thirty-five

Reed stood before the mirror hanging above his chest of drawers and straightened his tie. Miss Lillian's funeral was today, and while he had no idea how he would get through a church service, he felt he owed it to her—and to Anna—to go.

He threw his suit coat over his arm and stepped outside into the shade of Dolly's pecan trees. It was overcast and breezy today, which mitigated the heat, but it would be sweltering by the time they left the cemetery. Reaching through his truck window, he laid his coat on the seat.

Something caught his eye—movement on the loop road—and he looked up to see Daisy, wearing a navy dress and heels, walking up the driveway. Reed had never seen her in a Sunday dress. She hadn't noticed him standing among all the parked cars and trucks of Dolly's boarders.

He watched as she stopped about halfway up the driveway and turned around, as if she were considering a retreat, then stopped again. Before she could flee, he went out to meet her.

"Daisy?"

She was struggling for breath and fanning herself with her hand. "I think I'm havin' some kinda spell."

"Can't breathe, hands sweaty, heart beatin' ninety to nothin'?"

"How'd you know?"

"I reckon you can get battle fatigue from fightin' ghosts as well as Germans. You'll be okay. Just try to take some real slow, deep breaths. Come on over here in the shade." He put his hand against her back and escorted her to a glider under the trees. "Sit right there and I'll get you some water."

Reed went into the house and came right back out with water for Daisy. He sat down next to her as she took a few sips. "Better?"

Daisy nodded. "I don't ever remember feelin' that scared. I'd prob'ly be runnin' down that road if you hadn'a showed up when you did."

"Can you run in those shoes?" He tried to lighten the tension.

"If I'm scared enough, I can run in roller skates."

"Try to take your mind off it. I know—you told me y'all have been readin' some more about Catherine and Andre. Tell me what happened next. That oughta distract you."

Daisy kept taking deep breaths. "We got as far as the wedding and some serious ooh-la-la, but then I started feelin' sick again. And with Lillian gone, Anna says it makes her sad to read the journal. Dolly put it in your room for safekeeping until all of us are ready to keep goin'."

Reed grinned at her. "Define 'serious ooh-la-la.'"

⁂

Daisy, Anna, Jesse, and Reed stood together in the church-yard. Reed saw Daisy looking at the front steps as if they were the highest mountain she had ever tried to climb.

"You mind if I sit in the back?" she asked Anna. "I'm just not sure . . ."

Anna gave Daisy a hug. "You sit wherever you're comfort-able. The minister asked me to read Lillian's favorite Scripture, so we have to sit up front. If you need to leave, just go. Reed can stay with you so you won't be by yourself."

247

Anna and Jesse went into the church. Daisy looked up at Reed, who offered her his arm. "We can do this for Anna," he said, escorting her up the church steps and onto a back pew, where they waited for the service to begin.

Reed remembered this little church—the dark wooden pews, the stained-glass windows, the old velvet chairs where the preacher and song director sat behind the pulpit. Even the smell of the wax they used on the hardwood floors was familiar. The crowd was sparse, no doubt because most everybody who knew Miss Lillian was already dead.

Her open casket was at the altar. Even if Daisy hadn't been with him, Reed wouldn't have walked down the aisle to look at her. He wanted to remember her alive, not "looking natural."

As the organist began playing "How Great Thou Art," the choir filed into the loft, and the undertaker closed Lillian's casket.

"O Lord my God, when I in awesome wonder . . ."

The longer the choir sang, the more Daisy fidgeted with her hands, which Reed could see were shaking. He put his arm around her shoulders and laid his free hand over her trembling ones. She looked up at him and tried to smile but couldn't manage it.

Trying to keep Daisy from falling apart was having the odd effect of calming Reed's own anxieties. He leaned over and whispered to her, "Close your eyes and go to the creek."

Daisy closed her eyes. After a few minutes, he felt her hands relax beneath his, and she was breathing easier. That got her through the hymns and prayers. But now Anna was about to read. The sound of her friend's voice seemed to pull Daisy back into the church. "For I am persuaded, that neither death, nor life . . ."

Without realizing it, Daisy had leaned closer and closer into Reed as Anna spoke, until her head was resting on his shoulder. He put both arms around her and held her tight, knowing all too well what she was feeling right now—the kind of unbridled panic that makes you want to dig a hole wherever you are, jump in it, and never come out. Luckily, they were the only ones sitting in the back of the church, or the ladies would've had plenty to gossip about.

As soon as Anna finished and the preacher took the pulpit, Daisy began to come around. She looked up at Reed and whispered, "What happened?"

"Nothin' anybody saw," he said. He expected her to pull away from him out of embarrassment, but she didn't. Daisy was too honest and too drained for that. So he kept his arms around her and repeated something he had said countless times on the battlefield. "You're gonna make it outta here—I promise."

After the graveside service, Reed walked with Daisy from the cemetery, where she had stood stoically beside Anna, somehow keeping her emotions in check. The two friends had hugged each other goodbye before Daisy and Reed made their way back to his truck. He opened her door for her and helped her in, then climbed into the driver's side. They sat there silently for a few seconds before they turned to each other and both said, "You wanna go somewhere?"

thirty-six

"I'll try not to stare like the bumpkin I am," Daisy said to Reed as they stood before a grand department store with a clock on the corner. Both of them needed an escape after Lillian's funeral, and Reed had suggested that since they were all gussied up on a Saturday afternoon, they might as well go out on the town. He had driven to Birmingham and taken Daisy to Joy Young for a white-tablecloth lunch. Now they were strolling downtown and had made their way to Loveman's, where he held the door open for her.

They felt the blissful rush of air-conditioning as they stepped inside. "Dang!" Daisy said as they walked around. Elegantly dressed salesclerks were spritzing perfume and dabbing makeup on eager customers. Mothers were towing impatient kids behind them as starry-eyed young couples asked directions to the wedding rings.

"Those stairs are movin'." Daisy was wide-eyed, watching women in their high heels step onto the stairway that sent them gliding upward, past the mezzanine to the second floor of the store.

"That, ma'am, is the first escalator in the state o' Alabama," Reed said. "Wanna ride?"

"Maybe later. I think I'd rather go up there." Daisy pointed to the mezzanine, where diners were having lunch at the store's own restaurant. She and Reed took the stairs up and stood together at the balcony, watching all the activity below.

"How'd you learn your way around Birmingham?" Daisy asked.

"I used to come here with my buddies in high school. One of 'em had an older brother who'd let us tag along with him and his friends if we didn't get on their nerves. And then when I got outta the hospital, I used to come here a lot. Birmingham's a good place to kinda lose yourself. I think I like extremes. I either wanna be in a big city or on a creek bank. Never been too happy anywhere in the middle. You follow that?"

Daisy laughed. "Yes, I follow that."

"You ever spent much time in a city this size?"

"No. We used to go down to Biloxi and Gulfport now and again, but they're nowhere near as big as Birmingham. Charlie was never interested in much outside the farm and the Delta. But I've always been kinda curious about New Orleans."

"Ever seen pictures?"

"Just in schoolbooks. Kinda doubt they showed us kids the most interestin' parts."

"Prob'ly not," Reed said with a smile. "I served with a guy from the French Quarter, and he used to show me pictures his family sent over. I think you'd wear out your sketchbook there."

"Sure would like to see it one o' these days."

"What else would you like to see?"

Daisy thought it over. "Florida, I guess. Mississippi's got flat water, so I'd kinda like to see ocean waves. How 'bout you? Got anyplace you wanna go?"

"I think I'd like to fish those Louisiana bayous."

"I'd sure like to draw 'em—all that bright green behind those cypress trees."

"You draw and I'll fish. That'll work. Wanna ramble a little?"

They wandered the elegant store with its soaring ceilings, gleaming floors, sweeping stairway, and long glass display cases. The whole place smelled divine, with all the spritzing from the fragrance counter drifting through the store. Eventually they landed in the dress department.

"May I just say there's a dress over here that was *made* for you." A salesclerk had appeared out of nowhere. She was about Dolly's age, smartly dressed, with an authoritative air about her.

"We're not really—" Daisy began.

"Sir, may I ask if you are a veteran?" the clerk interrupted.

"Yes, ma'am," Reed said.

"I thought so. I could tell by your fine posture. Servicemen never slouch. We offer an *instant* discount for our boys returning home. It'll save you a *fortune*. My name is Rhoda. And you are?"

"Reed and Daisy," Reed said.

"Mr. and Mrs. . . . ?" The clerk eyed the wedding band that Daisy still wore.

Before she could protest, Reed answered, "Ingram."

"Come with me."

Daisy was shooting him looks behind Rhoda's back, but he was having too much fun to let her off the hook. The clerk turned her attention back to Daisy. "Floral—that's for you. Many women can't pull it off, but you can—classic bone structure, flawless complexion, hourglass figure. You can handle flowers without looking busy. They'll bring out your lovely green eyes. I've got just the thing right over here."

"But—" Again Daisy tried to protest.

"You heard the lady," Reed said with a grin. "It's right over there."

They followed Rhoda through a sea of racks, straight to a mannequin that held a gorgeous dress—ivory silk overlaid with chiffon in a delicate floral pattern. It was fitted and sleeveless, with a V-neck and a flowing skirt that was slightly shorter in the front. Daisy couldn't take her eyes off of it.

"Rhoda," she finally said, "I can't afford somethin' like this."

"Don't listen to her, Rhoda," Reed countered. "We're loaded. C'mon, honey, just try it on."

Once Rhoda had Daisy situated, she came out to chat with Reed, whom she had seated in a plush wingback chair next to a marble platform in front of a gilded three-way mirror.

"She's a bit reluctant," Rhoda said with her winning smile. "If I may venture a guess, Mrs. Ingram has no idea what she actually looks like?"

"Yes, ma'am, you are dead on the money." He gave her a winning smile of his own, and Rhoda pulled up a velvet stool next to him.

"Might I suggest a few accessories," she said as she sat down, "just little odds and ends to really bring her out? A stylish peep-toe, a hat perhaps, a strand of pearls . . ."

Reed pulled out his wallet. "Load her up, Rhoda."

The salesclerk rushed out to the floor to gather Daisy's accessories while Reed listened to Benny Goodman playing on the store's sound system and waited. In a few minutes, Rhoda hurried back to the dressing room, carrying shoeboxes and hatboxes, with necklaces dangling from her wrist.

Eventually he heard her trying to coax Daisy out of the dressing room. "My dear, you look positively *divine*! Come out here and show Mr. Ingram."

Finally, Daisy stepped through the velvet curtains that led to the dressing room and came out to see Reed. As she often did, she left him speechless. The dress fit her perfectly and did indeed bring out her eyes, as Rhoda had promised. Daisy was wearing the shoes Rhoda had suggested and a simple strand of pearls.

"As much as I love to make a sale, Mrs. Ingram simply does

not need accessories," Rhoda said. "I think simpler is better, don't you agree?"

"I do," Reed said.

Rhoda led Daisy to the platform in front of the three-way mirror. Reed watched her study her reflection as if she didn't recognize herself.

"Shall I . . . ?"

"We'll take it all, Rhoda. Can you wrap up her other things? I don't think she'll want to change back."

Rhoda was beaming. "My pleasure. May I give you my card?"

"Yes, ma'am. And thank you."

As Rhoda left them alone to ring up the sale and package the funeral clothes cast off in the fitting room, Daisy kept looking at her reflection in the mirror. "I don't know her," she finally said.

Reed stepped onto the platform beside her and took her hand. "I do. I met her on a creek bank back in the spring."

Daisy shook her head. "That's not who you met."

"Yes, it is. You just had her all covered up. But I could still see her."

He was gazing at her reflection, and now she was staring at his. "I don't know what happens next, Reed."

"That's up to you. I've known what I wanted from day one."

Daisy kept looking at his image in the mirror. "You've got the strangest eyes I've ever seen," she said very softly.

A reflection of her wasn't nearly enough. Reed turned to face her, slipped one arm around her waist, and held her face with his free hand. He gave no thought to the shoppers passing by or the three mirrors projecting the image of a young vet embracing the love of his life and pouring out, in one lingering kiss, the longing and loneliness that had haunted him since the war.

thirty-seven

The Magic City had put a charm on Reed and Daisy. Outside of Loveman's, he made a half-hearted offer, an escape for her if she needed it: "Just let me know if you want to go home."

Daisy looked up at him and shook her head. Then she took the shopping bag he was carrying for her—the one that held her mourning clothes—and put it in a trash bin on the street corner. He watched as she stared down at the gold band on her left hand before slipping it off her finger.

"What should I do with it?" she asked him.

"Keep it—always. It's part of you."

She gave him a smile he couldn't quite read—maybe grateful, maybe wistful—and put the ring in her purse.

He took her by the hand. "Wanna go for a walk?"

The two of them began a leisurely stroll along 20th Street.

"Can you . . . can you tell me how this works?" she asked him.

As usual, Daisy had thrown him a curveball. "How what works?"

"This." She pointed from Reed to herself and back again.

"Oh. That. Well . . . people been tryin' to figure that one out

since women invented courtin'. Not sure I've got the answer."
They both glanced up as a streetcar whizzed by, ringing its bell.

"Yeah, but I'm *really* in the dark. I never dated anybody but Charlie, and we'd known each other since we were kids. We just kinda . . . grew into each other."

"Can't we do that too?"

"We're all grown up, Reed."

"I follow that." He had broken the tension, and they were finally laughing together. "Look, Daisy, I just wanna be with you—any way that makes you happy. I'm not gonna push you. I'm not gonna hurry you. I just wanna spend as much time with you as you'll let me. How 'bout you?"

She grinned at him and said, "Ditto."

"You have such a way with words."

Reed and Daisy first heard the music as they rounded the corner of 5th Avenue.

"Glory, glory, hallelujah, since I laid my burdens down . . ."

They stopped on the sidewalk and listened as it drifted down the street—music that walked a fine line between churchgoing gospel and juke-jointing blues. The two of them looked at each other and, without saying a word, hurried toward the sound.

The powerful voices, with hands clapping in rhythm, led Reed and Daisy to Kelly Ingram Park downtown, in the shadow of a stately old Baptist church on 16th Street. A tent as big as a barn had been erected in the center of the park, and the folding chairs underneath were quickly filling as worshipers from Birmingham's colored neighborhoods flocked to the park.

"Maybe nobody would mind if we just sat in back for a minute?" Reed suggested.

They found a couple of empty chairs—mercifully stocked with Liberty National fans—on the back row, right beside the aisle.

"Friends don't treat me like they used to, since I laid my burdens down . . ."

"It's weird, ain't it?" Daisy said. "If I was in my own church, listenin' to those old hymns, I'd be havin' a come-apart right about now. But here—I feel safe in this tent."

"Me too. Maybe it's because these folks don't know us from Adam. And that music ain't like nothin' at First Baptist."

Reed and Daisy flapped their fans with everybody else and listened to the singers.

A stage at the far end of the tent held a full choir in bright gold robes, with a soloist standing at a microphone out front. An old upright piano sat on the ground to one side of the stage. The piano player was a tall teenage boy, surrounded by a bass fiddler and two guitar players. A drummer was tucked into a corner behind them. The audience was a sea of flapping Liberty Nationals.

"I feel better, so much better, since I laid my burdens down . . ."

Daisy looked up at Reed. "I think I've been homesick for God."

He smiled at her, lifted her hand, and kissed it. "I follow that."

Daisy became completely mesmerized by the music, but the war had made Reed perpetually vigilant. Part of him was always keeping watch. This time he sensed it before he saw it—a peculiar movement in the aisle.

"Daisy, look." He pointed to an unaccompanied white child, probably nine or ten years old, walking slowly down the aisle toward the stage. She had fair skin and curly blonde hair that flowed all the way down to her waist. Her cotton dress, which reached to her ankles, was plain but brilliant white. No adult came after her.

With every few steps she walked, another row of heads turned on either side of her, but she kept looking straight ahead, like a bride making her way to the altar to meet her intended. The choir kept on singing, the worshipers clapping and shouting, as the child reached the foot of the stage and stood there, looking up at the singers. Slowly she raised one hand above her head, just as Reed had seen adults do in a Pentecostal church he'd once visited with a high school buddy in north Alabama.

"If you don't believe I've been redeemed . . . God's gonna trouble the water . . . Just follow me down to Jordan's stream . . . God's gonna trouble the water . . ."

"Forgimme, sir, but is that yo' baby girl down front?"

Reed and Daisy turned to see an elderly colored man with white hair and a bright yellow tie standing behind them with his hat in his hands.

"No, sir, we don't know her," Reed answered. "She came from somewhere outside. We watched her walk all the way down the aisle."

"Well, would you and Mrs. mind goin' down there and fetchin' her?"

"But we don't know who she is," Daisy said.

"Yes'm, I understand. But whoever she be, if her folks was to catch her in here with us or see one o' us carryin' her out, well . . ."

"We'll see if we can find her parents," Reed said.

The old man smiled. "You kind, sir, ma'am." With that, he left them and disappeared into the crowd.

"Want me to do it?" Reed asked Daisy.

She shook her head. "I'll go with you."

Reed held Daisy's hand as the two of them walked down the aisle together, passing row after row of curious faces turning to see what the only white people in the tent were about to do. They knelt down on either side of the child, who still had her hand outstretched. Her face was upturned, her eyes closed. She calmly opened them—eyes the color of aquamarines—when Daisy put an arm around her.

"Honey, are you lost?"

The little girl turned her back to the stage and looked from Reed to Daisy. Then she raised her arms and laid a hand on each of their foreheads. Reed felt a wave of warmth all through his body and thought he might faint. He saw Daisy sway slightly on her knees and sit back on the grass as a shout went up from the crowd. Then the child retraced her steps in an unhurried walk back up the aisle and out of the tent as the singers carried on.

"Every time I feel the Spirit movin' in my heart, I will pray. Every time I feel the Spirit . . ."

Reed helped Daisy stand and get her balance. The two of them held on to each other as they walked up the aisle and out into the sunlight, then stopped to breathe in the fresh air just beyond the tent.

Daisy was feverishly flapping the Liberty National fan she had held on to. "There she is."

She pointed to the child, now holding the hand of a woman who looked to be about forty. The woman was wearing a faded purple gingham dress with a white collar. Her salt-and-pepper hair was pinned into a bun at the nape of her neck.

"Ma'am, is that your little girl?" Reed asked as he and Daisy approached them.

The woman put a protective arm around the child. "Yessir. She done something wrong?"

"Oh, no, ma'am. It's just that we saw her come into the tent by herself and wanted to make sure she got back with her family."

The woman smiled. "Yessir, she did. My Susanna loves her a camp meetin'. Never could keep her away from them tents."

Susanna and her mother turned to walk away, but after a few steps they both stopped, looking first at each other, then back at Reed and Daisy. Susanna tugged at her mother's hand. "Go on and tell 'em, Mama. That's how come I brung 'em to you."

259

The woman let go of Susanna's hand and returned to Reed and Daisy. Staring at them, she frowned and said, "Well, ain't that peculiar."

"What?" Daisy asked.

"It's the same," Susanna's mother said.

Reed and Daisy looked at each other. "What's the same, ma'am?" he asked.

"The message. You're both s'posed to get the same one: 'Turn a-loose.' I ain't never seen that happen before."

With that, she returned to her daughter, and the two of them crossed the park to a sidewalk, where they stepped onto a street-car and disappeared into the city.

"Let's find some shade," Reed said, showing Daisy to a park bench under a sprawling oak. She flapped the Liberty National fan near his face to help him cool off.

They sat together, taking more deep breaths and fanning, before he said, "Did you feel a warm—I don't know—wave, maybe, come over you when Susanna touched you?"

"Uh-huh."

"And it was kinda peaceful?"

"That was strange, Reed. That was *real* strange. But it was movin' too."

He nodded.

"And it was comfortin'."

"What do you make of it, Daisy—what her mama said: 'Turn loose'?"

Daisy thought it over. "I think the Lord's done sent my dead husband to talk to us, and now we've seen a country prophet in downtown Birmingham. I hope there ain't no cast iron in heaven, 'cause if there is, I reckon the Almighty's 'bout ready to whack us upside the head with a skillet. He's tellin' us we gotta turn loose of our old hurts, Reed. I see it now. They ain't holdin' on to us. We're holdin' on to them."

"But we've been tryin'."

"I know, but we owe it to Charlie and Deacon to try harder. I see that now too. No matter what troubles you and me have got, we're alive. We're here on this earth, and we're meant to make the most of it. Charlie and Deacon are fine. They're happy where they are. And no matter how bad we feel about their time here gettin' cut short, their dyin' wasn't our doin'. We've been throwin' time away, Reed. And time's a gift. We oughta be usin' every minute we've got." Daisy reached down and picked a dandelion from the grass. "Count o' three?"

Reed nodded and smiled. "Count o' three."

"One. Two. Three."

They blew on the dandelion, sending its feathery shower into the breeze and leaving only the bare stem, which Daisy threw over her shoulder. Reed leaned over and kissed her.

"Do you consider this our first date?" she asked.

"I reckon. Why?"

"Well, from what I understand, most fellas take a girl to the movies or out to dinner on their first date. You, on the other hand, went with a fancy lunch, a new dress, and a Pentecostal religious experience."

They both broke into laughter.

"I'll try to tone it down next time," Reed said.

"I don't know what just happened," Daisy said. "But the weird thing is . . . I feel better. I feel like everything's gonna be okay—maybe not right away, but somewhere down the road."

"Me too."

"Now, take me home before the angel Gabriel steps offa the next streetcar."

thirty-eight

Once again Reed was staring at the ceiling, a million thoughts racing through his head. He had stretched out on the twin bed on his porch, hoping the night air would put him to sleep. But his mind was a whirligig.

He was in love with Daisy. No. He was crazy in love with Daisy. If things kept going the way he hoped, he owed it to her to decide, once and for all, how he would provide for her. The truth was that Reed had come to believe life was far too short and precious to waste it working a job just for money. What he wanted was a purpose, a life's work that meant something.

That wasn't the only puzzle he was struggling to sort out. He kept hearing noises in the dark hours and could never be sure if they were real or the shadows of a nightmare, but he had finally swallowed his pride and confided in Si, just in case whoever dropped that gas can was still up to no good.

He lay perfectly still and listened. There it was again. Something off. Something outside that didn't belong there, like a copperhead in the green beans. And this time there was the smell—far too familiar—of something burning.

Reed got up, stepped into the backyard, and stared in disbelief at the skating rink, oddly glowing from the inside. Was it real? Of course it was real.

"Fire!" He grabbed the quickest thing he could find to put on—the old Army fatigues he had worn earlier to help Dolly in her garden—then ran shirtless and barefoot through the house, waking everybody up. Dolly, in her housecoat and slippers, began ringing the dinner bell on her front lawn to try to rouse the neighbors. Reed threw on his sneakers and sprinted to Si's toolshed.

Soon a crowd—most of them still wearing their nightgowns and pajamas—had formed two human chains, buckets in hand, from the lake to each end of the skating rink. If they could've rigged up some hoses, Si's pump in the creek would've been far more effective in extinguishing the fire, but there was no time for that. So everybody passed bucket after bucket of water as fast as they could from the lake to the rink. Again Reed smelled gasoline and could only hope that whoever did this only used it to start the fire. If they had covered the rink with fuel, no amount of water would put it out.

He had grabbed a couple of shovels and now handed one to Jesse. "We need to dig a fire line to protect the house!" he shouted over the crowd. "The creek'll stop it if it heads west."

The two of them began deepening the shallow trench that ran parallel to the road between Dolly's house and the blazing skating rink. Spotting a couple of teenagers who also had brought shovels, Reed got them started digging on the south side of the rink. Between the lake, the creek, and the trenches, they should be able to keep the fire contained so that none of the families on the loop lost their homes.

Jesse and Reed were both coughing from the smoke, their faces darkening with soot as the fire burned on. With every shovel of dirt he lifted, Reed saw flashes of foxholes and explosions and charred arms and legs, yet he kept digging, as if each time he pierced the ground with that metal blade, he might slay another war demon.

Daisy came running up the road and joined Anna on the boardwalk. The two of them took up spots at the far end of the lake and helped pass buckets of water to the flaming rink. On and on the community battled the flames, until they heard a loud pop and then a crash as the roof of the skating rink started caving in, and the few men inside came running out. A collective cry went up from the crowd as the building folded into a heap.

"Si!" Dolly was calling. "Si, where are you?" Reed could hear the panic in her voice.

"Dolly!" Si came staggering out of the smoke and found his wife standing on the boardwalk. Reed looked up to see them collapse into each other, holding on for dear life as their hope for future prosperity turned to cinders.

thirty-nine

It was almost four in the morning before Dolly and Si, with their boarders and neighbors, reduced the raging fire to smoldering embers. They had managed to get enough water on the board-walk and the flooring of the rink's side porch to save them so the lake could reopen, but the rink and everything in it were gone.

As the crowd slowly dispersed, Reed and Jesse tossed their shovels to the ground and lay down on Dolly's lawn to catch their breath. They were covered with soot, both of them coughing from all the smoke.

"Man," Jesse said as he rubbed his eyes. "How do you ever get over something like this?"

"Don't know," Reed said. "Never owned anything."

"Me and Anna lost a lot, but we've still got a home and a farm. I don't know how the two of us could get back up if we had to watch our house and barn go up in flames."

"You'd work together just like Si and Dolly. You two would make it somehow."

"Hope I never have to find out. Want to grab some clean clothes and head for the slough?"

"I'll be along in a little bit. Thanks for your help."

Reed sat up and looked around as Anna followed Jesse to the

house. Daisy came and sat down next to him, and the two of them watched in silence as neighbors stumbled out of the smoke and solemnly made their way home. The loop girls, all with curlers in their hair, were wearing raincoats over their night-gowns. An elderly man, no doubt frightened beyond thinking when he heard the alarm bell, had put on his Sunday hat with his pajamas and slippers.

After everyone was gone, Reed said, "I don't feel like bein' around everybody just now. Wanna walk with me over to the lake?"

He helped Daisy up and held her hand as they crossed the road to the lake. Daisy sat down on the steps that led into the water as Reed took off his shoes and went in. Standing chest high in the lake, he washed away all the soot and smoke that covered him from the waist up.

Once he had cleaned away all the grit from the fire, he started wading back to Daisy. He was in knee-deep water when he real-ized that she was looking at him the same way she had when they first met on the creek bank—studying him as if she were trying to figure something out.

"What?" he said.

She pointed to his fatigues. "You look like a soldier. Is that how you looked in the Army?"

He wasn't sure what to say. "I was . . . never this clean in the Army."

Daisy waded into the water with him. She slowly ran her hand over a scar just above his collarbone and another on his shoulder. "I saw these before . . . that first time we went swim-min' at the slough. I was afraid to ask you then . . . Who did this to you, Reed?"

She looked like she was about to cry, as if she could feel the painful wounds that had left their mark.

"They're just scars, Daisy. They can't hurt me anymore."

He pulled her hand away from his shoulder and kissed her palm, then put his arms around her and held her close. They were standing there together in the moonlit lake when he said, "I wanna marry you."

And she answered softly, "Okay."

forty

Anna and Jesse came into the kitchen, where everyone had gathered, just in time to hear Evelyn declare it "beyond imaginable" for Dolly to prepare a full breakfast and serve everyone in the dining room, especially since it was Saturday and none of the men had to go to work.

"But I know ever'body's hungry," Dolly objected as she slid a pan of biscuits into the oven, "and I think I need somethin' to do with my hands."

"Well then, we can serve ourselves off the stove and eat in here," Evelyn said, "rather than have you bothered with all those serving pieces."

"Y'all sure that would be alright?"

"Absolutely," Joe said as the others agreed.

"If you trust me with the bacon and eggs, I can do that while you work your magic on the sausage gravy," Anna said.

"Thank you, honey."

Dolly and her boarders tried to calm themselves with their usual morning chatter, but Si remained silent, staring into his coffee cup at the end of the table.

Reed came into the kitchen and sat down at the table.

"Where's Daisy?" Anna asked him.

"She went home to clean up."

"Joe, I don't know where you came by this bandage to brace my arthritic wrist, but it has worked wonders," Harry said.

"The infirmary nurse at the plant is sweet on him," Jesse said.

"Watch and learn, Jesse, watch and learn," Joe said, which made everybody laugh, except for Si, who kept staring into his cup.

Jesse winked at Joe. "Hey, Joe, did you notice anything peculiar at the lake when we came back from the slough?"

"No, nothin' in particular," Joe said. "Just your typical lovebirds, standin' in the middle o' the lake and smoochin' like there was no tomorrow.'

Reed threw a napkin at Jesse.

The boarders laughed as Jesse kept on. "Can I be the best man?"

Reed smiled and shook his head. "I'm fixin' to make you a dead man."

Dolly came over and kissed Reed on the cheek. "We couldn't be happier for you, honey."

Evelyn helped Dolly and Anna carry loaded plates to the table. The room got quiet as everybody ate, and the quiet brought a sobering reminder of what had just happened and why they were all gathered in the kitchen instead of Dolly's dining room.

Finally, Si spoke. "I know who did this."

"What, Si?" Dolly asked.

"It was them Clanahans that burned us out. I'd bet my life on it."

"But how do you know they're anywhere around here?" Dolly asked.

"I just know it was them. There was gas on that fire. We ain't got no other enemies would wanna put us out o' business. And there ain't no kids around here mean enough to do something like that for a prank—they all enjoy the rink too much. I guarantee you them sorry Reno people did this. I'm gonna make 'em pay for it too."

Dolly sat down next to him. "Si, you know what can happen when you lose your temper. You've worked real hard on that, and I'm so proud o' you. Please promise me you won't do anything till you've cooled off and thought it through."

"I don't know about that, Dolly."

She reached out and laid her hand over his. "Please, Si. Bad things come in clusters, remember? We got to be careful."

Dolly was obviously frightened. No doubt Si could see it. He sighed and kissed his wife's hand. "You sit right there and let me get you some coffee for a change."

Dolly's boarders resumed their morning conversation as Si brought the coffeepot from the stove and began filling his wife's cup.

"That's enough, honey . . . That's plenty . . . Si, honey, you're gonna spill it . . . Si?"

Everybody stopped talking and watched in shock as Si kept on pouring even as the coffee overflowed from Dolly's cup and spilled onto the table. The coffeepot fell from his hand as he frowned, clutched his chest, and collapsed onto the kitchen floor.

PART 3

The Goodbyes

August 14, 1944

Dear Violet,

My precious sister. Please forgive me. I got your letter at the first of the month, and I've been too overwhelmed to answer. How is Wiley doing after his accident? I was so happy to hear that he's out of the hospital and back home in your loving care. Can't any doctor look after you the way family can. Please give him our love.

Si's doing about as well as could be expected. The doctor says his heart's probably always been weak. Can you imagine that—Si, who's never been scared to take on anything, no matter how hard it was? If you'd asked me about his heart all these years, I would've told you it's the strongest one in the county. But it's not, Violet. It's sure not.

I look at Daisy and how she's managed to pull herself up after losing her husband. Reed and her will end up getting married, I just know it. And I'm going to do my best to talk them into marrying at Little Mama's so we can have just one more happy time here before we have to let the house go.

I'm sorry I couldn't hold on to it, sweet Vi. It took everything Si and me had. I can't make it by myself, and I won't take a single ounce of Si's strength away to save it. Never again. Because I'm not like Daisy, Vi. She's young and strong and got a future ahead of her. I'm not young anymore. And I can't even think about any future that don't include Si. So we'll have to let the house go. You be thinking what all you want out of it, and I'll save it back for you.

Tell Wiley I'm praying for him and give all the young'uns a kiss for me.

Your loving sister,
Dolly

forty-one

Reed, Anna, and Jesse stood on Dolly's front porch with Joe Dolphus and the Hastings.

"I just can't believe y'all are leaving," Anna said.

"We think it's for the best," Evelyn said. "Dolly seems committed to selling the house. And if our rent money can't change that, we feel we would be contributing to her stress by staying. Since the university called, we should probably go—so many soldiers are beginning to come home and enroll that there's work again for stodgy academics like us."

"My daughter's been after me to come back now that the grandkids are gettin' big enough to take fishin'," Joe said. "And I think the less Dolly has to worry about right now, the better. But I want y'all to promise me that if things change, and there's anything at all I can do to help save this house, you'll get on that phone and call me collect. Day or night. It don't matter. I'll do anything in the world for her and Si."

"The same goes for us," Harry said.

Anna looked as if she were barely holding herself together as she hugged them all. Reed and Jesse helped carry their luggage and load it. Everybody waved goodbye one last time before

Joe and the Hastings drove away. As Reed and Jesse came back on the porch, Anna burst into tears and ran inside the house.

"You better go see to that," Reed said. "I'll check on Dolly." He went inside to Si and Dolly's bedroom and quietly tapped on the door.

Dolly opened it and smiled. "Come on in, honey."

He kissed her on the cheek before they sat down in two rockers next to the bed. "How is he this mornin'?"

"Pretty good. He's restin' mostly. Stirs around a little bit but not too much. I'm just so thankful you're here, Reed. I don't think I could give him those shots."

"Glad I can help. When's Dr. Sesser comin' back?"

"Tomorrow. I don't know how he finds the time with ever'body else he's tendin' to, but I'm mighty glad to see him when he walks through that door."

They sat quietly together before she said, "Reed, don't you never put nothin' material ahead o' the people you love."

"Is that what you think you did, Miss Dolly?"

"I know it's what I did—lettin' Si work hisself to death 'cause I thought I couldn't live without this ol' house. And now look at him a-layin' there with his heart so weak. What good is this house without him in it?"

"But you didn't want the house for any material reason—not for a possession. You wanted it because it's part o' your family. It's how you remember 'em. You ain't got a selfish bone in your body, Miss Dolly."

She patted his hand and dabbed at her eyes with her embroidered handkerchief. "I sure hope you're right, honey."

"He's absolutely right."

They were startled to see Si awake and smiling at them.

"Oh, Si, how do you feel?" Dolly jumped up to lay her hand on his forehead.

His breathing was slow and labored. "Fine . . . And you?"

She shook her head. "Si Chandler, don't you dare die on me."

He reached for her hand and held it. "Doin' my best, Dolly, m'dear." He closed his eyes and went back to sleep.

Dolly sat back down next to Reed. "It's strange how we get attached to places like they were people," she said. "I guess they take on part o' us, and we take on part o' them, and before you know it, ain't neither one of us quite whole without the other. That's how come Little Mama's house has always been so dear to me. I just breathe a little different in these big ol' rooms. You got a place like that, Reed—a place where you breathe a little different?"

He smiled and nodded. "The Tanyard. And Hick'ry Mountain. I guess my special places are all outside. But if there's ever been a house that meant anything to me, it was this one. I understand why you love it so much, Miss Dolly."

"You were a little bitty thing—prob'ly not more'n five years old—when we lost our Samuel. Nothin's more heartbreakin' than rockin' a sick child no medicine can help. This house is my last connection to my boy, Reed. It's the last place he ever was, before the cemetery, and to tell you the truth, sometimes I can't find the strength to follow that path to his little grave. But every now and again, I can feel him in these ol' walls—maybe in the flutterin' of a curtain or the echo o' footsteps on old wood. Don't get me wrong—I don't believe my sweet boy's hauntin' this house. I believe he's with the Lord. But maybe he got to leave behind just enough o' his little self to comfort his mama. You reckon that's possible?" Dolly dabbed at her eyes again.

"When it comes to you, Miss Dolly, I believe the Lord makes all kinda special allowances."

"Oh, honey, I'm just plain ol' me."

"Miss Dolly . . . I know how upset you are right now, and I know you're blamin' yourself and the house for what happened to Si . . . but it's not your fault. And it's not the house's fault.

It just happened. I sure wish you'd think it over before you give up on payin' those property taxes. Me and Jesse—we'll help however we can. So will Joe and the Hastings."

"I 'preciate that, honey, but no. You and Jesse are young men. I know you've been through a lot, and it's made you both older'n your years, but you're still just gettin' started in life. You got to be thinkin' about your future. It's a mighty special house, Reed. But it's not my life. That's my life layin' there in that bed."

They rocked silently together for a moment before she said, "I'll tell you somethin' you *can* do for me."

"Anything."

Dolly winked at him. "Go on and give Daisy a ring so Little Mama's house can see one more weddin' before we have to let her go."

forty-two

Reed needed to occupy his mind. He grabbed a pick, sledge-hammer, shovel, and work gloves from Si's toolshed and headed for the ruins of the skating rink.

Most of the big timbers that once held up the roof had been consumed by the fire, but there were charred chunks of them scattered all over the place. He picked a corner and set to work, first pulling out any good tin left from the roof and stacking it in a clearing behind the rink. Then he cleared the remains of the timbers and studs, putting them in a big pile near the front of the rink so they could be hauled away or burned.

With the roof out of the way, he could see that Si had built the rink by gutting the horse barn of its stalls and corncribs, building a frame with floor joists to completely fill the space, and laying a wood floor for the skating rink on top. The fire had destroyed the floor but not all the joists, which created an obstacle course as they stuck up and out every which way. Reed took the sledgehammer and started slamming at one after another, finally breaking the floor frame apart. That would have to be enough for one day. He was hot, sweaty, and exhausted.

Wading into the lake to cool off, he splashed water on his

face, chest, and back and then sat down in one of the Adirondacks on the porch to dry off. He thought about his conversation with Dolly and how long it had been since he'd had any contact with his own family. He would take a walk in the woods and pay his respects to a marble lamb. And then he would go back to Dolly's and call his mother.

After supper, Reed, Daisy, Anna, and Jesse walked across the loop road to the porch of the skating rink and circled four chairs together. They enjoyed looking out over the water in the moonlight, and distance from the house gave them a place to talk without disturbing Dolly.

"There's got to be a way to save the house," Anna said.

"None of us has that kind of money or we'd give it to her," Jesse said. "And it's way too late to get a crop in the ground to make any more."

"I tried to give her what's left o' my Army pay, but she wouldn't take it," Reed said. "I even tried to go down to the courthouse and give it to them, but it wouldn'a come close to payin' those taxes."

"Well, what about the journal?" Jesse asked. "Catherine said they were about to make an escape out of here—maybe there's something useful in figuring out how they got away."

Reed and Daisy stared at him.

"He's been reading it at night to catch up with the rest of us," Anna explained.

"I mean, I know it's far-fetched, but what have we got to lose?"

"A whole lotta people have tried to find Andre's stash—if there ever was one," Reed said.

"Yeah, but they didn't have the journal," Jesse countered.

"Got a point," Daisy agreed.

"I'll be right back." Jesse left the group for a few minutes and came back with Catherine's second journal and a lantern. "Anna, think you're up to it now?"

She took the journal while Jesse used a couple of old crates to rig up a table for the light. They all settled in as Anna began to read.

July 20, 1844

Dear Self,

Where do I begin? So much has happened. I suppose I should start with this: I know my husband's real name. And now that we are beyond harm, I can say it. My beloved is Andre Chauvin.

"Oh my gosh!" Anna said. "Dolly will be thrilled! Well—at least, she would've been." She continued reading.

I should also tell you that he might well read every word of this, as I no longer hide my journal from him. I no longer hide anything from him. Still, I have become accustomed to writing in my little book and find it helps me sort out my thoughts. Andre says I should do whatever I like whenever I like, so when he is out working on his boat, which he loves, I sometimes sit on a high rock overlooking the water and scribble on my pages, with Andre glancing up to wave and smile at me now and again. But I should back up to our wedding night.

It was a far cry from what Sister had led me to anticipate. I expected to spend it in fear and dread in a marriage bed with a stranger. Instead, I spent it swiftly sailing downriver under an Easter moon, with a man who completely fascinates me.

Jesse elbowed Reed. "Do we completely fascinate you ladies?" he said with a grin.

"We're so dang fascinated we can't stand ourselves," Daisy said as the four of them had a laugh. "Go on, Anna. I'll send Jesse to his room if he acts up again."

Even though we are far away from Blackberry Springs, I do not think it wise to put in writing all the details of what drove us away. I'll say only that an evil phantom was relentlessly chasing Andre, but it chases us no more. Ending its pursuit endangered someone dear. And so we had to leave.

Our escape was like a scene from the Coleridge poem that Andre and I love, "where Alph, the sacred river, ran through caverns measureless to man down to a sacred sea." An underground tributary of the Coosa River runs beneath the rolling green pastures that Andre purchased on the Tanyard. Can you believe it? A river flowing beneath the ground?

Long ago, during his "vagabond life," he met a fisherman who traveled the Coosa and had spotted a strangely large opening in a high bluff. The fisherman couldn't resist rowing in to investigate and found what turned out to be a cavern, which held an underground waterway. Andre was excited by its possibilities—for somewhat nefarious purposes at the time, he confessed—and he never forgot about it. Then, when he set about trying to find me, it turned out that his river cave and I were in the same place—little unassuming Blackberry Springs.

"Good night!" Daisy said. "Reckon we're sittin' on top of a river right now? Sorry, Anna. Keep goin'."

The night we fled, we left on foot. Andre had released all of his fine horses into their pasturelands, with a pond for drinking water. He said he would send someone for them as soon as we were a safe distance away. He carried the small grip Appolline had packed for me. Neither of them brought anything from the house, which puzzled me.

Through a trapdoor covered with hay, we made our way down a dark flight of stone steps, with Andre holding my hand and Appolline carrying a torch to light the way. I couldn't imagine where we could be going, when suddenly, I caught the distinctive smell of river water—the dank muddiness of it, the humid air. And there it was, right before us. A river, or at least a canal—a flowing stream of water underground.

I stood in amazement, not just at the river itself but at the equipage I saw—a fine skiff moored at a small dock, jugs of water and other provisions, a large grip, and even an iron bench like the one by the Tanyard.

Andre loaded all of our supplies into a small boat tied to the skiff and covered them with a heavy canvas, which he tied down. Then he grabbed the iron bench and pushed it backward. When the bench tilted back, I could see that it covered yet another trapdoor, from which Andre drew as many bags as the large grip would hold before lowering the bench back down.

"If that ain't money in them bags, I'm Scarlett O'Hara," Daisy said. "Go on, Anna. Let's see what they do with it."

After placing the grip in the center of the skiff, he climbed in and held his arms out to me. "Come, Catherine," he said. "We should hurry."

I stepped off the dock and into his arms as Appolline

climbed into the back of the skiff and untied it from the dock. Then we were off.

Andre seated me in the center of the boat, then lit a lantern, hung it on the bow, and took the oars in front. He and Appolline began rowing together, moving us steadily along in a channel that grew darker and darker as we moved away from the torchlight at the dock. The lantern cast just enough light for Andre to keep us centered between the banks.

On and on we went, through caverns that grew at times very close—I could reach up and touch the roof of them—only to open wide again. At last we rounded a bend, and I couldn't stifle a gasp. Through an arched opening ahead, I saw the light of a full moon. How can I even describe it? A dark channel of water, hidden beneath the earth, flowing into a moonlit archway that opened onto the Coosa River. Imagine—river below and night sky above, all bathed in silver-white moonlight.

As the skiff floated onto the Coosa and under the moon, Andre stopped rowing for just a moment and turned to look at me. "Moonlight suits you, Catherine," he said with a smile.

He and Appolline resumed their rowing, the spring river current so strong that they needed to do little more than guide the boat with their oars. I asked Appolline if I might rest her, but she refused.

At last the two of them rowed us into a narrow canal off the river. It opened into a small harbor, where a much larger boat than our skiff was moored, anchored there alone, its white sails gleaming through the night shadows.

As Andre tied the skiff to the dock and helped me out, Appolline began uncovering the supplies towed behind us. I hadn't noticed the handful of fishing shacks built on high *pilings, scattered around the dock, but as Andre started unloading, four or five men came out of the shacks and began shouting hellos to him. The men all shook hands and clapped shoulders, clearly happy to see each other, though I couldn't understand what they were saying. They all spoke the same strange way as Andre and Appolline when they were talking with one another.*

"Come." Appolline motioned for me to follow her to one of the fishing shacks as Andre and the men began transferring our supplies onto the boat with the tall white sails.

Inside the shack, a woman who looked about the same age as Appolline poured us cups of strong, hot tea and then left us alone.

"Bébé thinks I will come with you on your journey, but I will not," Appolline said.

I told her I didn't understand.

"Bébé got the woman now," she said. "He need to make a home, make the babies, make a life. He wander too long for the sake of others. He be still now for his own sake."

I couldn't understand where she would go if she didn't come with us. But she said the people in the fishing shacks were also from Louisiana—like family—and would take her to safety.

We stared at each other across the table, and I just had to ask her, "Who are you?"

But she just smiled at me and said, "You trust Bébé. You love Bébé. He make you a happy woman."

"Back up a minute, Anna," Jesse said. "The journal said he took as many bags as his grip would hold. Sounded to me like he might've left some behind."

"And they left on foot," Anna said, "through a door that was covered with hay."

"So the money's not in the house," Reed said. "And if they could walk to it, then it couldn'a been all that far away."

"It had to be here," Daisy said. "Andre built the horse barn that Si turned into a skatin' rink, right? If they could walk to it from the house and it connected to the river, and hay was coverin' up the door—sure makes sense for it to be here."

"We'll just have to keep clearin' what's left o' the rink and see if anything turns up," Reed said. "Maybe we'll get lucky. Dolly sure could use some luck right now."

forty-three

Daisy poured Reed some ice water from a thermos and handed him a dry T-shirt Dolly had sent over. He had been working at the rink since breakfast, clearing away scrap lumber and nails and sweeping the dirt floor that was now exposed. He changed his shirt and sat down with Daisy on the porch, where they unwrapped sandwiches Dolly had made.

"I figured Anna would be over here by daylight," Reed said.

"She would have, but she felt like Dolly really needed her at the house."

"How's Miss Dolly doin'?"

Daisy shook her head. "I think part of her's prayin' we find somethin' and part of her wishes we'd quit lookin'."

"Can't say I blame her."

They ate their lunch and looked out at the water. "So what you thinkin' about?" he finally asked her.

"I thought you said women are the ones always askin' that."

"It's contagious."

Daisy looked at him and frowned. "Does it bother you that we're talkin' about gettin' married and we've never done much of anything normal together?"

"What do you mean?"

"Well, think about it. I stepped on a snake, you operated on my foot, my dead husband came to me in a vision, I had a come-apart in the middle of a funeral, you kissed me in the middle of a department store, we met a prophet in downtown Birmingham, the skatin' rink caught on fire . . ."

"I see your point. Maybe we should get some life insurance."

They both had to laugh at the thought of everything that had happened in just a few months.

"But *seriously*, Reed—"

"I know what you're sayin'. As a matter o' fact, Dolly gave me an idea for somethin' completely normal we can do together—go ring shoppin'."

Now Daisy was beaming. "You mean it?"

"I do. No pun intended." He leaned over and kissed her. "But right now, we gotta search a burned-down horse barn for an underground river and a sack o' hundred-year-old pirate money that prob'ly don't exist and never did."

~∞~

Dolly awoke in her rocking chair to see Si looking at her and smiling. She sat down on the edge of his bed and held his hand.

"Where's all the young'uns?" he asked her.

"Here and there. Every night after supper, Anna tells me they're goin' over to the rink to sit on the porch and look at the lake. But they're lookin' for that pirate's gold."

"Well, let 'em believe in hidden treasure while they're young. We did."

Dolly shook her head. "Si, I'm so sorry I held on tight to this ol' house. You've had to work like a dog to keep it all these years, and I'd gladly give it to the county just to have you well again."

"Now, Dolly," he said, resting to catch his breath before he talked again. "This ol' house gave me an excuse . . . to chase after all o' my . . . my money-makin' schemes. I tried but . . . just never did take to the plow."

She kissed his hand and held it against her cheek for a moment. "I know, honey. I know. You've done just fine. I'm so proud of all the wonderful ideas you've had and everything you've built."

Si's expression turned very serious. "I don't want you . . . to pile no blame on yourself, Dolly . . . I never talked about . . . my family too much . . . Lotta scalawags in that bunch. I was worried . . . you'd think I was one . . . But my daddy and both my brothers . . . they had weak hearts too . . . Just runs in my family . . . don't have nothin' to do with the house."

"You never told me that, Si."

"Didn't wanna worry you."

Dolly bent down and kissed her husband. "You can worry me anytime."

Si smiled at her and then turned to look out the window beside his bed. Something outside made him struggle to sit up.

"Si! What are you doin'? You know you can't exert yourself."

"Where's Reed, Dolly?"

"He's in the kitchen makin' a sandwich."

"Go get him. And go get the key to my gun cabinet."

"Si, what on earth—" As she leaned across the bed to see what he was looking at, her hand flew to her mouth. "Oh no!"

"Go, Dolly. Go get Reed and go get my shotgun."

~◦~

"I'd be willin' to bet you're missin' a gas can," Reed said to the man sauntering down the porch at the skating rink, looking as if he were tallying up the value of the place.

The man spun around, grinning, and walked toward Reed. "Now, that would be mighty hard to prove. What business is it of yours anyway?"

"What are you doin' here?"

"Again I'll say it—what business is it of yours?"

"Friend of the family. You're Clanahan?"

The man broke into a satisfied smile and nodded. "Say, what you reckon this old place is worth, now that it's not worth anything? Nobody around this two-bit town can afford to buy that big old house. Bet they're too stupid to know all they gotta do is pay off the taxes when it hits the auction block—which it will."

"Get outta here."

Clanahan stepped a little closer to where Reed was standing, near what used to be the entrance to the rink. "Last time it took a shotgun to get me out of here." He stepped closer and closer to Reed, then stopped just inches away. "I don't see a gun on you."

"Don't need one."

Clanahan lunged at Reed, who threw his fist into his opponent's throat and sent him sailing to the ground, clutching his windpipe, coughing, and gasping for air.

"Get up."

Writhing on the porch floor, Clanahan managed to get up on all fours and crawl aimlessly into the charred remains of the skating rink, with Reed following close behind him.

"Get up," Reed repeated.

Clanahan slowly got to his feet, staggering as he backed away from Reed.

"How did you get here?"

The man coughed, wheezed, and pointed in the general direction of the cemetery road.

"So you hid your vehicle in Dolly's family cemetery to come and admire your handiwork while you made plans to take her house?"

Clanahan said nothing but kept backing toward the far corner of the skating rink.

"That's about as low as anything I ever saw a German do, and I saw Germans do some mighty low stuff." Reed kept slowly walking toward Clanahan. "I don't think I'm gonna let you leave here."

"Reed! Reed, stop!"

"Daisy?"

Clanahan used the temporary distraction to make a run for it, stumbling his way toward the back of the rink, next to the woods.

As Reed turned to chase after him, he heard a loud pop and watched in disbelief as Clanahan's legs disappeared into the dirt floor of the rink. The trapped man began screaming for help.

Reed and Daisy looked at each other, speechless, and cautiously approached the strange sight: Clanahan screaming his head off, visible only from the waist up, his legs somewhere beneath the floor.

"Dang," Daisy said.

"'Dang' don't begin to cover it," Reed said.

"Mr. Clanahan," Daisy said, "I'd say you got yourself a situation." She giggled, and her giggle turned into laughter she couldn't control. Soon Reed was laughing too.

"He's not goin' anywhere," Reed said. "Let's go to the house and call the sheriff."

As Reed and Daisy walked back to Dolly's, Clanahan kept up his cries for help, flailing his arms and likely kicking his legs, wherever they were.

"Hey, when you said you weren't gonna let him leave, I was scared you were gonna . . . you know." Daisy pantomimed slitting her throat with a knife.

"'Course not."

"Well, that's a relief."

Reed grinned at her. "I had somethin' slower in mind."

forty-four

By the time the sheriff got there, collected the gas can Reed had retrieved from behind the rink, and arrested the man who likely left it there, Jesse was home from work. After supper, he and Reed gathered shovels and lanterns from Si's shed and met Daisy and Anna at the rink.

As Reed shone a light into the opening Clanahan had fallen through, they could see a flight of stone steps leading into darkness.

"Man alive!" Jesse said.

"I smell river," Daisy said.

"How can you smell a river?" Anna wanted to know.

"Trust me. If you grew up on the Mississippi, you can smell a river."

"So now what?" Jesse asked Reed. "Maybe Anna and Daisy should stay up here while we check it out?"

"No! I want to go!" Anna insisted.

"Daisy?" Reed asked.

"I'm goin'."

"Well then, I guess we'll all go," Reed said.

He and Jesse used their shovels to tear apart what remained of a trapdoor, leaving a large opening above the steps. The four of them made their way slowly down and into the darkness below. They could hear the water before they could see it, lapping against something in the pitch black.

As their eyes adjusted to the eerie glow of their lanterns in the darkness, they could finally see what Catherine had seen—an underground tributary that had been cutting caverns beneath the pasturelands above for hundreds of years.

"I feel like we all just fell into one o' those dang Hardy Boys books," Daisy said. "Somebody write somethin' in invisible ink so we'll fit in. Hey, y'all shine your lanterns over there. What's that?"

Reed and Jesse moved in the direction Daisy was pointing until their lights struck what must have been the dock described in Catherine's journal. Most of it had long since rotted away, but a couple of the pilings were still there.

"So if the dock's there," Jesse said, "then the iron bench should be right about . . . here." His lantern struck the remains of an iron bench. Its wooden slats were long gone, but the iron frame remained—rusty but still whole.

The foursome gathered around the bench. Jesse pushed against it, and it tilted, just as Catherine had described. He and Reed held their lanterns over an iron box below and saw two dingy white bags about the size of ten-pound flour sacks. Jesse jumped in and picked up one of the sacks. He handed it out to Reed, who set it down, opened it up, and poured out very small coins that looked like they were made of gold.

"Dang!" Daisy said.

"They've got a five-dollar mark on the back," Reed said. "Looks like they came outta the plain ol' US Treasury instead of a treasure chest."

Jesse lifted the other bag from the iron box before climbing out.

"Looks like the same kinda coins in here," Reed said.

"We need to figure out exactly what this is before we tell Dolly," Anna said. "She couldn't take another disappointment."

Daisy nodded. "Anna's right."

"Well then, tomorrow mornin' Daisy and me can take it to the bank and see what's what," Reed said. "Anna should prob'ly come too. This looks to be a lotta money, and I want everybody to feel sure we handled it fair."

"Nobody here thinks you're a thief, Reed," Anna said. "You and Daisy go to the bank, and I'll stay with Dolly. Right now, I think I need to go back up, Jesse. I don't feel so good."

"What's the matter?"

"Maybe it's the dampness down here and the smell of the water—it's making me queasy."

"Let's get you some fresh air, then."

"I'll go up with Anna so y'all can take care o' the loot," Daisy said. "How 'bout that, y'all—we've got actual loot."

Daisy took one of the lanterns and helped Anna up the stairs, leaving Jesse and Reed behind to carry up one last hope for Dolly's house.

CHAPTER

forty-five

Reed brought Dolly into the parlor, where Daisy, Anna, and Jesse were waiting. "Honey, what's this all about?" she said.

"You should prob'ly sit down," Reed said, joining Dolly on her velvet settee. "We didn't wanna tell you in front o' Si because we know he's not s'posed to have any excitement. But, well . . . we found it, Miss Dolly. We found the money Catherine and Andre left behind."

Dolly blinked at Reed, as if she couldn't comprehend what he was saying. "You found *what*, honey?"

"The money, Miss Dolly—Andre's stash. We found it. A lot of it."

Anna got up from her chair and knelt on the floor by Dolly. "Isn't it just too wonderful? Now you and Si won't ever have to worry again!"

Dolly blotted her forehead with her hand, but Reed couldn't tell if she was about to shout hallelujah or faint dead away.

"I just can't believe this."

"It's true, Dolly," Anna said. "We found their passage to the river. And you don't ever have to give a thought to property taxes again. Reed and Daisy took care of that this morning."

Dolly grabbed a cardboard fan from the table by her settee

and started flapping it as fast as she could in front of her face. "I'm just—I mean, I can't—could y'all back up a little bit and take me through this real slow?"

"Jesse started readin' the journals," Reed explained. "And he thought we oughta use 'em to try one last time to find the money. So that's what we did. Funny thing is, if the skatin' rink hadn't burned to the ground, that good-for-nothin' Clanahan couldn't have fallen through the trapdoor and opened the way to the money, because the passage leadin' to the river was under the rink floor. It was buried under hay in one o' the original horse stalls. Losin' your business saved your house, Miss Dolly."

"We found an underground canal running beneath your property, Dolly," Jesse added. "And it connects to the Coosa River. The remains of a dock are still down there."

"And y'all think Andre left behind enough money to pay my property taxes this year?"

Daisy joined Anna on the floor at Dolly's feet. "Andre left behind enough money for you to buy Alabama if you want to. You can prob'ly swing Georgia too."

"It was all gold coins, Miss Dolly, and they've increased in value over the years," Reed said.

"How much money are we talkin' about, honey?"

"Well . . . give or take a little . . . 'bout four million dollars."

Dolly turned as white as cake flour, and little beads of perspiration appeared all over her face.

"I'll get her some water," Anna said. She hurried to the kitchen and returned with water for Dolly.

"Four *million* dollars?" Dolly said between sips of water. "That's more money than anybody could ever spend."

"Give it your best shot, Dolly." Daisy took the cardboard fan from Dolly, who couldn't seem to gather her wits enough to flap it, and waved it in front of her.

"You sweet children, I just can't imagine how you did this."

"Daisy and me paid a little visit to the tax assessor's office today," Reed said. "You oughta be free and clear through about 1994, so take good care o' yourself. You're gonna need to live a real long time to get your money's worth."

The curtains fluttered away from the windows, but there was no sign of a breeze.

Dolly laughed out loud. "I'm right there with you, Little Mama."

forty-six

Reed watched as Daisy tried to take it all in—the sky-high ceiling, the elegant gilded balconies and stately sweep of stairs, the rich burgundy fabrics everywhere. The Tutwiler was Birmingham's finest hotel, and it was a sight to behold.

"Listen to the echo in here," she said.

Reed smiled at her. "I know. You feel like you could whisper down here and they could hear it upstairs. You like it?"

"It's gorgeous."

"Good enough for our wedding night?"

"What?"

"Well, I figure since we're gettin' married in the afternoon, we'll wanna stay someplace close to home. So we could spend the night here and then catch the mornin' train to New Orleans."

"*New Orleans?* We're goin' to New Orleans?"

"You said you wanted to see it. So let's go see it."

"Dang!" Daisy threw her arms around Reed's neck, and he kissed her as he twirled her around the lobby.

"People are starin'," she said with a big smile.

"Let 'em stare. How 'bout an early lunch?"

"You mean here?"

"There's the main restaurant, and then there's a little café and bar—don't tell Dolly—called the Jewel Box. Either way, we need to go ahead and get a table. We've still gotta get to Loveman's to buy rings, and then we've got a 2:00 date with Rhoda."

forty-seven

On a warm September morning, Dolly, Anna, and Daisy had gathered in Jesse and Anna's room. They were sitting on the bed, circled around a wooden jewelry chest with several velvet pouches scattered around it.

"Dolly, are you sure you don't mind me wearin' your jewelry for the weddin'?" Daisy asked.

"Oh, heavens no, honey! It's just sittin' here in this box. I tried to get Violet to take all of it, but she wouldn't. See, our mother and Little Mama were very social women—always throwin' big parties or goin' to dances. The family had plenty o' money back then. But things are different for me and Vi. She's too busy with young'uns, and I'm too busy helpin' Si to be the belle o' the ball. Let's take your dress outta the bag so we can see what we're workin' with."

Dolly unzipped the Loveman's dress bag hanging from a hook on the door. She and Anna both gasped.

"Oh, Daisy, it's the prettiest thing I've ever seen!" Anna exclaimed. "Let me look at your ring one more time."

Daisy held out her hand to show her friend the engagement ring Reed had bought for her at Loveman's—a marquise-cut solitaire.

Anna sighed. "It's amazing, Daisy."

"Never had a diamond before," Daisy said. "I can't quit starin' at it. You sure Jesse don't mind me leavin' all my stuff in here?"

"I've already told him that from here on out, it's a boy-girl arrangement. All of his clothes for tonight and tomorrow are in Reed's room."

"And Jesse's gonna pick up Ella on his way home from work and bring her over here so she can eat supper with us and stay in Joe's old room tonight," Dolly explained. "I thought that'd be easier on her since she's havin' trouble gettin' around these days. And just so you don't worry about her, Si's hired R.W. to take care o' things and look in on her. It'll do the boy good to have some responsibility, and he can earn a little money to help his mama."

Daisy gave Dolly a hug. "You think of everything, don't you?"

"Well, I try, but my mind ain't what it used to be. I just can't get over this dress." Dolly ran her hand over the flowy skirt, which hit Daisy just below her knees. The dress was made of ivory French lace over champagne silk satin, with a fitted bodice, V-neck, and elbow-length sleeves.

"Are you wearing a veil?" Anna wanted to know.

Daisy shook her head. "I think I'd feel silly, as old as I am."

"Honey, wait till you're on the backside o' fifty," Dolly said. "You girls are young! I tell you what, though—you don't need much with that dress. I'd say it speaks for itself. Here, what about this?" She reached into the jewelry chest and pulled out the simple pearl tiara that Anna had worn when Daisy drew her portrait for Jesse. She slipped it over Daisy's hair and passed her a hand mirror.

"It's perfect, Daisy!" Anna said.

Daisy giggled. "Y'all are gonna mess around and have me lookin' like a girl on my weddin' day."

"I know you wanna wear Reed's pearls—can we call that

301

your something old and the dress your something new?" Anna asked. "Dolly's headband is borrowed, so you just need something blue . . . I know!" She pulled a blue lace handkerchief from her Bible on the bed stand. "You can tuck this into your bouquet. It belonged to my grandmother, so it covers old *and* blue—just in case Reed's necklace is too new to qualify."

"What about you, Miss Anna?" Dolly said. "What are you wearin'?"

"The first new dress I've had in two years, hallelujah!" Anna said. "Jesse took me shopping." She went to the wardrobe and pulled out a pale lilac dress made of silk.

"That's mighty pretty, Anna," Daisy said.

"I think I could wear it plain to church and dress it up for anything special—like a wedding."

"Lemme fish around in this ol' pouch right here—I've got something o' Little Mama's that oughta do the trick." Dolly handed Anna a necklace and earrings made of amethyst stones set in gold.

"Oh, Dolly! I can't borrow these!"

"It's just a bunch o' baubles, honey. Wear 'em and enjoy 'em. Matter o' fact, keep 'em."

"I couldn't take these, Dolly."

"What good are they doin' in that bag? Keep 'em and wear 'em. Don't hide 'em away like I did."

"This is the most beautiful gift in the world," Anna said as she put on the necklace and gave Dolly a hug.

"No, honey—you girls are. I've got to go see about Si, but y'all can rummage through Little Mama's jewelry till the cows come home and wear whatever you want."

"We'll be down to help, Dolly," Daisy said. "I can't believe Reed's folks are gonna be here tonight. Sure hope they like me."

"They'll like you just fine," Dolly assured her. "You girls have fun."

Anna and Daisy went through the jewelry boxes, showing each other brooches, bracelets, earrings, and necklaces that had been in Dolly's family for generations.

"I'm sorry your folks can't come," Anna said.

"It's okay." Daisy shrugged. "Can't say I blame 'em. Just worked out that Mack came home from the Navy the same weekend I'm gettin' married. They haven't seen him since he shipped out."

"Well, don't you worry. We'll be here for you."

Daisy smiled at her. "You always are."

"Can you keep a secret?"

"Kept plenty o' yours."

"Well, this is a big one," Anna said. "I'm bringing a guest to your wedding."

"Who?"

Anna smiled and patted her belly.

"Oh my gosh, Anna!" Daisy hugged her and bounced them both up and down on the bed. "Sorry! Guess I shouldn't jostle little Jesse Junior like that."

They erupted into giggles.

"How long have you known?" Daisy asked.

"Remember how I got queasy when we found the money? Well, I've been queasy ever since. I went to see Dr. Sesser last week. We want to wait till after the wedding to tell everybody. This ought to be your time—yours and Reed's."

"You know I don't care about that stuff."

"You think you don't, but just wait. You'll be glad you had this little moment in the sunshine. And I want it for you."

Daisy fingered an antique ruby brooch on the bedspread. "I ain't never gonna have another friend like you, Anna."

"And I'll never have one like you."

Daisy grinned. "I'm bequeathin' you my overalls when I leave on my honeymoon."

Anna rolled her eyes. "Not those *dang* overalls!"

The two friends giggled like twelve-year-olds at a slumber party.

"It's weird, ain't it?" Daisy said when they were quiet again. "You and Jesse were livin' your life in Illinois, and Reed was in Alabama, and I was in Mississippi, and wouldn't none of us have even met if it wasn't for the war. We woulda just lived our lives without each other. But now I can't imagine life without y'all—just like a coupla years ago, I couldn't imagine life without Charlie."

"I know what you mean. It broke my heart to leave Illinois, but now . . . I'll cry just as hard when we leave Alabama."

"I think it's a good thing that we can't see what's comin'," Daisy said. "If we could, it'd scare us so bad we might run from it, and then we'd never get to see how good it could be. Got any idea when y'all are goin' back?"

"Soon, I think. The 'little nest egg' Dolly gave each of us was plenty to get the farm going again. And now that we know Dolly and Si can afford any help they need, I don't think we'll stay much longer. What about y'all?"

"Reed starts school at Tulane in two weeks. So we're gonna look for a place to live while we're on our honeymoon. Can you believe he kept that a secret? Had me thinkin' we were just takin' a trip to New Orleans, and the whole time he had decided to go to school there."

"New Orleans, Daisy! Are you excited?"

"'Bout to bust. I woulda been happy just to see it, but to live there while Reed's in college—never thought this ol' Delta girl would end up in the big city. Hang on just a second." Daisy climbed off the bed and opened her suitcase, which was sitting on the stool in front of Dolly's dressing table. "I got somethin' for you."

Daisy pulled out a drawing, meticulously done with her colored pencils. It was Anna, standing in Dolly's garden, her face turned to the sky, her eyes closed, and a serene smile on her face. Her long auburn hair and green-and-white gingham skirt looked blown by a breeze. She had one hand on her straw hat, the other holding a basket overflowing with green beans.

Anna stared at the drawing. "I think you drew me a lot more special than I am."

"We see each other true, Anna. That's what makes us sister-friends. "

Anna reached over and hugged Daisy tight. "I love you dearly. And before you even say it, I know I'm getting mushy. You'll just have to deal with it."

❧

"You sure it's okay for me to steal you away for a little while?" Reed asked Daisy. They had left their shoes on the bank and were wading the shallows of the Tanyard.

"The house is clean, the table's set, the food's warmin' on the stove, and Dolly said the bride shouldn't have to strain herself on the day before her weddin', so she threw me out while I was tryin' to dust the parlor. My meet-the-family clothes are over at Dolly's, so it won't take me long to get ready."

"In that case, I'm gonna be selfish and hide out with you till my family gets here."

Reed took her hand as they waded along, the sunlight filtering through tall pines that softened its shades of gold before they lit up the water. He could see that Daisy was as captivated by the light as he was.

"It's pretty perfect, right?" he said.

"I keep tryin' to draw that light, but I can't quite get it."

"You will. Just keep tryin'."

"You sound mighty sure."

"I am mighty sure. You're talented, Daisy."

She smiled at him. "Thanks for that." They took their time wading a long, winding, shallow stretch of the creek.

"You nervous about me meetin' your folks?" she asked him.

"You mean am I worried they'll scare you away?"

"No, *I'm* worried they'll tell you to head for the hills and get as far away from this crazy woman as you can."

"They're gonna love you just like I do. Hey, look." He pointed to a flat rock in the creek, where four baby turtles were resting with their mother.

"Were you a turtle catcher when you were a kid?" she asked.

"Not really. I caught a couple one time and put 'em in the bathtub when Mama wasn't lookin'. But they didn't seem happy there, so I felt bad and took 'em back to the creek."

"That's so *weird*."

"What—feelin' sorry for a turtle?"

"No, I mean it's weird that I did the exact same thing. My brothers used to catch 'em all the time, and I thought I had to do everything they did, so I caught one and put it in a box with a bowl o' water in my room. But it just sat in a corner of the box, hidin' under its shell. I couldn't stand to see anything that miserable, so I took it to our creek and turned it loose. Ain't never liked to see anything hemmed up. Never cared for zoos or dog pens or birdcages."

"Always knew you were a softie."

"Now, see, that worries me."

"What—that I think you're a softie?"

"I'm worried you're seein' all kinda good things in me that'll turn out not to be there, Reed."

"You're worried I'm seein' things that aren't there, and I can't sleep at night thinkin' about all the things I haven't even found yet."

Mourning doves were calling in the woods as the space between Reed and Daisy dissolved, and the thought of being anywhere but here, together, flowed away with the light-dappled creek water.

"I'm sorry you're gonna be late gettin' ready for supper."

Daisy laughed. "No, you're not."

"No, I'm really not," Reed said as he kissed her again. They were sitting under a cottonwood tree on the creek bank. Her head was resting on his shoulder, and he had his arms around her.

"If we don't turn up at the house soon, Dolly's gonna miss us and think we're up to no good."

"I wouldn't be entirely opposed to that . . ."

Daisy gave him a nudge. "C'mon, while Dolly still thinks you're an angel."

Reed reluctantly helped her up, taking the opportunity to kiss her one last time.

She was looking up at him, holding his face in her hands, when she broke into a big smile.

"What?" he said.

"Next time you kiss me, I'll be your wife."

"I don't know about that. Pretty sure we can squeeze in a few more before tomorrow."

Daisy shook her head. "Nope. I want the next one to be *the* one. Now come on to the house before I change my mind."

forty-eight

"Reed, buddy, I sure could use your military expertise right about now." Jesse was standing in front of the mirror over Reed's chest of drawers, struggling with his tie.

Reed came over and began working a Windsor knot. "Got any advice for me since you're the ol' married man?"

"Lemme think . . . Don't leave your clothes on the floor. They hate that. No matter what her cooking tastes like, tell her it's better than your mother's. They take it real hard when you don't like their food. And flowers will get you through a lot."

Reed stepped back and examined his work. "That cover it?"

"Not even a start, but it'll keep you alive those first few months," Jesse said with a grin. "Just love her, my friend. Take good care of her. Enjoy being surprised by her. And never, ever let your stupid pride come between you. Anytime you got doubts about what to do, just picture Si and Dolly, and you'll be fine."

"I'll remember that."

Jesse shook Reed's hand. "Now, let's go get you married."

At two o'clock in the afternoon, Si escorted Daisy into Dolly's parlor. He walked with a cane, and the stairs were too much for him now, but Daisy said she'd rather have Si at her side than make a grand entrance. So they had waited in the kitchen together and then walked down the hallway into the parlor, where the Baptist preacher was standing in front of the fireplace. With their friends and Reed's family looking on, and Little Mama's curtains dancing in the breeze, Reed and Daisy got married.

Dolly made a chocolate cake for the reception. Reed only ate the icing.

Epilogue

"What you got there?" Reed sat down in the porch swing next to Daisy.

When they first moved to New Orleans, they had rented this Creole cottage overlooking Audubon Park, near Tulane. The minute they wrote Dolly with their new address, she had promptly called her banker—a man who couldn't do enough for his millionaire customer—and asked him if it would be too much trouble to track down the owner of that house and buy it for Reed and Daisy. The banker said it would be no trouble at all.

"I'm readin' the latest news from Dolly—and she's passin' along Catherine's journal for Anna. Wanna hear it?"

"Wouldn't miss it."

October 1, 1945

Dear Daisy, Anna, and Evelyn,
I'm hoping y'all won't mind passing my letter along to one another since I want to tell you all the very same news. I'm enclosing some extra stamps so it won't be a burden on anybody.

"Is that not just like her?" Daisy said.

Anna, honey, I was honored beyond words to hear that y'all named your little girl Dolly. Give Jesse a big hug for me, and tell him I think he'll make a real fine daddy. You keep those pictures coming, okay? And be sure to send me some of your farm now that you're all settled in.

Evelyn, how are you and Harry? I bet all the boys that are coming home and enrolling at the college are thrilled to pieces to be learning from the two of you instead of fighting that awful war. I give thanks every day that it's finally over. Tell Harry to look for a package that ought to get there soon. I asked Daisy to pick him out some records in New Orleans, and she's sending them your way.

"Are those the records we bought in the Quarter a coupla weeks ago?" Reed asked.

Daisy nodded. "Yeah. Harry oughta be set for a while."

I know Reed's just getting started at Tulane, Daisy, but when he's all done, he'll be a doctor. Doesn't that just thrill your soul?

"Sure does," she said, giving Reed a kiss.

Be sure and tell him that Dr. Sesser was over the moon when I said Reed had heard about young doctors going in together and starting clinics where they take turns looking after us country folks and still keep up their learning in big-city hospitals. If Reed ends up doing that in Blackberry Springs, he won't even need to advertise. Why, there will be a line the minute he opens the doors.

"Miss Dolly will see to that," Reed said.

I hope y'all won't think bad of me for saying this, but I just love having money! I've spent it like it's going out of style, which I've never been able to do before. Whoever said money can't make you happy probably didn't know what to buy.

Reed and Daisy laughed at the vision of Dolly and her money. "Well, I'm glad she's havin' some fun with it," Daisy said.

First off, we bought a new organ for the church. That old one was practically wheezing. Then we hired sweet R.W. to do any yard work that needs doing—plowing the garden and keeping the grass cut—so Si can just do the things he enjoys without any worry. We don't pay R.W. by the hour—we pay him by the quality of his work, which is always very good. So I put however much I imagine his mama needs into that envelope, plus some spending money for R.W., because Si says a boy that age likes to feel a little folding money in his pocket. It makes me so happy to see the look on that young'un's face when he collects his salary. It's changing him, knowing he can provide for his family. I see character building by the day. I've got him a college fund all set up when the time comes. I want to see him make something of himself after all these years of doing without.

"Selfish as always, Miss Dolly," Reed said.

R.W.'s put me up what I call a Needs Box over at the lake. It's just a wooden box with a slot—sits on a post like a mailbox—and we painted "I Need" on the side of it.

At first we had a sign dangling beneath it that read, "All Needs Confidential," but then we figured out that some of the folks on the loop didn't know what "confidential" meant. So we took that down and put up another sign that reads, "Won't Nobody Know but Dolly." Everybody on the loop that needs something leaves a little note in there, and then once a week, I empty out the box and meet their needs.

Sometimes, of course, children leave me notes that have more to do with wants, but they think they're needs: "I need a new pair of roller skates." I evaluate those on a case-by-case basis. But what a joy it is to meet the real needs in our community. Some of those notes will break your heart: "I need money to take my children to the doctor." "I need any food you can spare." "I need shoes for my little girl so she won't have to go to school barefoot." I go to my Needs Box with the same excitement I used to go to the mailbox, looking for letters from Violet.

And as a little tribute to Catherine and Andre, I have R.W. slip and leave the food and money we provide in little burlap bags on families' front porches. Violet (more on her in a minute) embroiders a tiny red robin on each of my burlap bags—our way of saying thank you to Andre the River Robin.

"Dang!" Daisy said. "That is just too bloomin' perfect."

We got so many requests for food—and always from the same five or six families—that Si hit on another one of his wonderful ideas. He said it was likely embarrassing for those mothers to ask for food again and again. So we had a pretty little store with a big front porch built on the front end of the old skating rink, and we keep it stocked with all the essentials. Everything in it's free to whoever needs it. Si just loves running it—he named it The Backup Store because it's your backup when you run out of money. But everybody's done shortened the name—they just call it The Backup. And it has become quite the gathering spot. Si invites some of the boys with their fiddles and guitars to come and play on the weekend. We don't charge to swim in the lake anymore—we just let everybody come and enjoy it.

One weekend, Si hit on the idea of bringing a couple of ponies to The Backup so him and R.W. could give the children rides while the adults enjoy the music. Now he's thinking about opening a circus, and that has put such a spring in his step!

"Well, if anybody can start a circus in Blackberry Springs, I reckon it's Si," Reed said.

But here's my big news. Violet and her family have moved into the house with us! Wiley was out so long after his accident that he lost his job, and his back is too bad now to do anything that requires physical strength. He knew how bad Violet wanted to come home, so we talked it over and they took the second floor of Little Mama's house for now. With Violet's share of Catherine and Andre's money, they can do anything they want, so they're building them a house on the Coosa River, and Wiley's going to open a little marina for all the fishermen. For now, I get to have three young'uns darting in and out of my kitchen, pestering their Aunt Dolly for chocolate cake.

Reed kissed Daisy on the cheek. "I'd like to thank my lovely wife for masterin' that recipe."

"Lucky for you, I like the cake part."

Back to the money. Little Mama would say it's tacky to talk about it the way I am—I know you all said you didn't want no more of it. But that's not right. I wouldn't even have it without you. Of course, I don't understand how all this works, so I had to let the banker in Childersburg set it up for me. (Y'all, it's amazing how nice he is. I never knew a man so eager to help a customer.) Anyhow, he's set up an account for each of you—one at the bank in Red Bud, one at the Whitney Bank in New Orleans, and one at First Chicago. No need to fret over it—just know you've got a financial cushion in there if you need it. And in case you're feeling bad for Joe, I sent him a little something too, just to thank him for his kindness when things were so hard.

"What you reckon she means by 'financial cushion'?" Daisy asked.

Reed shook his head. "Knowin' Miss Dolly, it's the size of a mattress. I hope it's not possible to give away four million dollars, but if she can find a way, she will."

"She sounds happier than she's ever been—spendin' all her money helpin' other people."

Well, that's about all I have to report. As Anna requested, I'm enclosing Catherine's second journal so you can all finish reading it. I hate we couldn't finish it together, but everything just fell apart after the rink burned. Never seemed to be any time to circle us up again. Violet and me read it together last night, and Anna was right—there's a surprise in there, ladies. Just pass the journal along to one another, and make sure it gets back to Red

Bud. (Anna, honey, thank you so much for letting us keep
our little reading circle going all these miles apart. Me
and Violet opened your package yesterday and got started
on journal number three. That one's coming soon, Daisy
and Evelyn!)

Give the men (and little Dolly) my love!

> *Your friend always,*
> *Dolly*

"There ain't never gonna be another Dolly," Daisy said.

"You wanna go see her and Si on my next break?"

"Yeah, I do. Maybe we could—"

"Stop over in Gulfport and eat at Vrazel's?"

Daisy laughed. "I guess I'm a creature o' habit. How'd it go today?"

"Fine. I just get frustrated with some o' the younger ones comin' in. They spend way too much time worryin' about what'll be on the exam when they need to be learnin' everything they can so they can save somebody's life one day."

Daisy smiled. "Well, listen at you—the senior statesman of the class."

Reed laughed. "Do I sound preachy?"

"I was gonna say wise, but if that's the way you wanna go . . ."

"Did you make it to Royal Street today?"

"Reed, I just can't quit lookin' at it. The light and the wrought iron and the old plaster—I've been drawin' so much my hand's gonna fall off. Do you have any idea how old some o' those buildings are? I checked out some books at the lib'ry. There's Spanish stuff and French stuff and it's been here for hundreds of years. And all the courtyards and fountains . . ."

"I believe my wife is in love."

Daisy smiled at him. "With you *and* New Orleans."

"I have a confession to make. I stole some o' your drawin's and took 'em to a professor in the art department last week."

Daisy rolled her eyes. "He prob'ly thinks my sketches are—"

"Some o' the best he's ever seen, as a matter o' fact. He says you've got some things to learn about technique, but the talent is absolutely there. So, Mrs. Ingram, the brilliant artist—what you gonna do about that?"

"Well . . . there's somethin' I've been meanin' to talk to you about. I do wanna go to school . . . but not for my art. That's somethin' I love doin' and always will, but it's not what I wanna go to school for."

"What you got in mind?"

"Nursin'."

"What? I had no idea you were even interested in medicine."

"I'm interested in you—and watchin' you heal people the way you healed me. You're not gonna be in school forever, and I know you wanna start a clinic in Blackberry Springs. You're gonna need a nurse at your side. And the thought o' somebody else bein' right there with you when you're helpin' all those people—that makes me sad. I wanna be the one. You think I'm smart enough to be a nurse?"

Reed smiled and put his arms around her. "I think you're smart enough to be a brain surgeon. Daisy, I don't know what to say. I think it would be amazin' for us to work side by side. I just want you to be sure nursin' would make you as happy as medicine makes me."

"It will. It absolutely will."

"Why don't we take some o' the rent money we saved up and go out to dinner tonight? We could even gussy up and go to Galatoire's since it's still early enough to get a spot in line."

Daisy smiled. "It'll be a sacrifice on my part not to cook, but okay."

"I'll go clean up and we'll catch a streetcar."

"Right behind you. I just need to put this stuff away." As she slipped Dolly's letter back into the envelope, Daisy noticed a narrow ribbon marking a spot in Catherine's journal. She couldn't resist taking just a quick look before getting ready for dinner.

March 1, 1845

Dear Self,

   This is the last time I'll be writing to you. From now on, I'll address my little jottings to another—one who makes my heart overflow. My time is near. I am going to have a child—Andre's child—and I am filled with so much happiness that I cannot contain it. I've heard about the terrible pains of childbirth. But I welcome them, as they will bring our baby into this world. I don't care if it's a boy or a girl. I just hope our child has its father's beautiful smile. And his courage and strength.

March 12, 1845

My Precious Angel,

   You are so perfect that I can hardly bear all the joy I feel inside! I fear my heart will burst every time I look at you. I see your father—and, I'll confess, just a little bit of myself—in you. My baby girl, you are a wonder, a miracle. Your father and I will love you forever. We have named you for his beautiful mother, sweet Lillian . . .

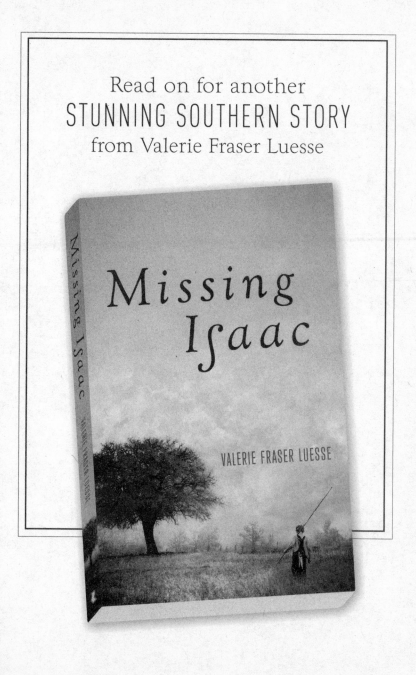

CHAPTER

one

OCTOBER 10, 1962

A sleepy purple twilight wrapped around the farmhouse, its tall windows glowing with warmth from somewhere inside. It was suppertime, and the cool October air smelled of cotton lint and field dust. Inside was an eleven-year-old boy playing checkers with his grandfather. As was his custom lately, he wore a flannel shirt many sizes too big for him.

"Pete, honey, you've got a closetful of clothes—why do you insist on wearing that old hand-me-down of your daddy's?" his mother asked.

"I don't know," he said with a shrug. "'Cause he gave it to me, I guess."

There was more to it than that, of course. The truth was that Pete's father was both his hero and his best friend. There was no one he admired more than Jack McLean, no one he so longed to emulate. Not only that, but he thoroughly enjoyed his father's company—and Pete could tell the feeling was mutual.

So there he sat at his mother's kitchen table, wearing his

daddy's shirt and holding a tentative finger on one of two red checkers still remaining on the board. "Okay, Daddy Ballard," he said to his grandfather as he lifted his finger and leaned back in his chair. "Your move." Their checkers game had become a weeknight ritual.

"You sure, son?" his grandfather said with a grin.

"Yes, sir."

Pete's mother peeled a colander of potatoes at the sink as a radio played in the windowsill.

Mrs. Kennedy attended a charity luncheon in Washington this afternoon. The First Lady wore an autumnal suit of red wool crepe . . .

Daddy Ballard made the only remaining move left to him. Pete's face lit up when he saw his opportunity—the long-awaited winning jump.

"I won! I finally won!" he cried as his grandfather laughed. "Wanna play again?"

His mother shook her head. "Now, Pete, you know your daddy'll be home before too much long—"

She was interrupted by the blaring of a truck horn. It blew and blew all the way from the county blacktop, and you could hear the tires slinging gravel as they sped up the driveway and into the backyard. Pete looked at his mother, whose face had frozen in fear and dread.

All three of them had heard it—the split-second transformation of ordinary sounds into a cry of alarm. Truck horns, tires churning gravel, men yelling to be heard over machinery—these were everyday background noises on the farm. But when something went wrong, when someone got hurt, those very same sounds took on an urgent tenor. You could hear it. You could feel it in your bones.

"Y'all in there? Come quick!" It was Isaac, one of Daddy Ballard's field hands, who helped Pete's father work the cotton.

The adults bolted for Isaac's truck, with Pete leaping over the tailgate and crouching in back before they had time to tell him not to. Cold wind blasted his face as they raced down the narrow strip of pavement to a dirt road that divided two sprawling cotton fields. He had to hold on tight as Isaac drove straight through the cotton, bouncing over furrows and tearing through tall, brittle stalks to get to a giant ball of light glowing in the distance.

So many trucks were beaming headlights onto the accident that it looked like a football stadium on Friday night. Chains rattled and clouds of red dust swirled everywhere as the field hands and Pete's uncles—summoned from their own family farm—made a frantic attempt at a rescue.

"Shut that engine off!"

"Get the slack out! I said get the slack out!"

"Back up, back up, back up!"

"Can you see him? I said can you *see* him!"

Daddy Ballard held Pete's mother back.

"Jack!" She screamed his name over and over and over.

At the center of it all was a massive red machine, his father's cotton picker, turned upside down in a sinkhole like a cork in a bottle. One of its back wheels was still spinning against the night sky, like it was trying to run over the moon. Pete could hear—or maybe he just imagined—clods of red clay splashing into the watery sinkhole far below the snowy clouds of cotton. And he knew, without anybody telling him, that his father was lost.

Spotting him standing beside the truck, wide-eyed and horrified, Isaac came to pick him up. But with nowhere to take him, Isaac just walked around and around the truck, Pete's legs dangling like a rag doll.

"You gonna be alright. You gonna be alright. We gonna make it alright." Isaac was shaking.

Pete heard a loud, booming crash as the trucks pulled the picker over onto its side to clear the hole.

"There he is! Lower me down! Hurry!" That was Uncle Danny, his father's oldest brother. Isaac had stopped in a spot that kept Pete's back to the accident. "Pull! Ever'body pull harder!"

There was a momentary silence before Pete heard the sound of water dripping off of something heavy. It reminded him of the sound his father's Sunday shirts made when his mother hand-washed them, plunging the saturated cloth up and down in the sink.

Soon the field hands began to moan. "Sweet Jesus. Mister Jack . . ."

Only then did Pete realize it—Isaac was soaking wet.

Acknowledgments

Writing makes me grateful—and not just because it brings me joy. Every time I sit down to write a new story, I'm aware of all the friends and family whose support makes it possible for me to do this thing that I love. I'm especially thankful for all the family members who have told me stories of our shared past, stories that have been sparking my imagination since I was a child. Thank you especially to "Grandme," Uncle Bud, Uncle Chick, cousin Jimmy, and sweet Aunt Patsy, who gave me one of the funniest lines in the book.

As always, love and gratitude to my husband, Dave, who took over the house, the laundry, the grocery shopping, the cooking, and everything else while I finished the manuscript for *Almost Home*—and still found time to let me read chapters to him so he could reassure me that they weren't terrible.

Last year, while I was promoting my first novel, *Missing Isaac*, I discovered that there's no end to the number of book signings my parents will attend, or the number of copies my aunts, uncles, cousins, and friends will buy. (Thank you, Jenny, for single-handedly boosting sales.) Blessed. That's all I can say.

Special thanks to the very talented Mark Sandlin, whose photography has amazed me for years now. It's not easy getting an appealing portrait from a camera-shy subject, but somehow he managed.

Many thanks to my agent and friend, Leslie Stoker of Stoker Literary in New York. One day I hope to persuade her to move south so we can garden together. I also owe a great debt to an amazing team at Revell: two terrific editors, Kelsey Bowen, whose insightful guidance transformed the first draft of this book, and Jessica English, whose refined sensibilities elevate every manuscript she works with; creative director Cheryl Van Andel and her group, who produced a front porch I want to sit on for the cover; senior publicist Karen Steele, who never stops looking for new channels for promoting my work; and Hannah Brinks Korns, Michele Misiak, and the marketing and sales teams at Revell, whose time, talent, and creativity have been a gift.

Much gratitude to Sid Evans, Krissy Tiglias, Nellah McGough, Lil Petrusnek, Carole Cain, and the *Southern Living* staff for your support, friendship, and encouragement.

For sharing their valuable time and reading advance copies of the book, I sincerely thank Sid and Krissy at *Southern Living*; authors J. I. Baker, Michael Morris, and Nancy Dorman-Hickson; *Leland Progress* editor and publisher Stephanie Patton; *Birmingham Home & Garden* editor Cathy Still McGowin; and *HGTV Magazine* editor in chief Sara Peterson.

Special thanks to my church family at First Baptist Church of Harpersville, Alabama, and to my oldest and dearest circle of friends back home. (Sarah Slaughter, thank you for being our trail boss and keeping us together! I love all of you.) And much love to my Ging, who was there for so much.

Finally, I owe a great debt to a fellow Alabamian I never had the pleasure of meeting, the late Eugene B. Sledge, whose memoirs of his World War II experience are nothing short of phenomenal. I stumbled onto his books—and the miniseries *The Pacific*, based on one of them—not because I was researching a novel but because I wanted to understand my Uncle Ferrell's wartime experience on Okinawa. He never talked about it, and many years after he died, I felt I owed it to him somehow to learn what I could. Eugene Sledge was the son of a physician in Mobile, Alabama, and later became a professor at the University of Montevallo. He would later write one of the most gripping and harrowing books I've ever read—*With the Old Breed: At Peleliu and Okinawa*. Mercifully, I'll never know what combat is like. But Dr. Sledge brought me as close as I'll ever come. I wish I could've met him. I wish I could thank him for bearing and sharing his wartime experience.

The following sources were used for research or inspiration:

Cronenberg, Allen. *Forth to the Mighty Conflict: Alabama and World War II*. Tuscaloosa, AL: The University of Alabama Press, 1995.

Hollis, Tim. *Birmingham's Theater and Retail District*. Charleston, SC: Arcadia Publishing, 2005.

Sandlin, Lee. *Wicked River: The Mississippi When It Last Ran Wild*. New York: Vintage Books/Random House, 2011.

Sledge, E. B. *China Marine: An Infantryman's Life after World War II*. New York: Oxford University Press, 2002.

Sledge, E. B. *With the Old Breed: At Peleliu and Okinawa*. Novato, CA: Presidio Press, 1981.

ww2today.com

warhistoryonline.com

Valerie Fraser Luesse is the bestselling author of *Missing Isaac* and is an award-winning magazine writer best known for her feature stories and essays in *Southern Living*, where she is currently a senior travel editor. Specializing in stories about unique pockets of Southern culture, Luesse has published major pieces on the Gulf Coast, the Mississippi Delta, Louisiana's Acadian Prairie, and the Outer Banks of North Carolina. Her editorial section on Hurricane Katrina recovery in Mississippi and Louisiana won the 2009 Writer of the Year award from the Southeast Tourism Society. She lives in Birmingham, Alabama.

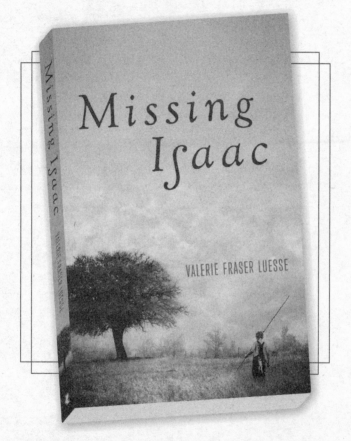